TALES FROM

'TERRY NOT ONLY TELLS A GREAT STORY BUT ALSO TAKES THE READER INTO THE HEART OF AN EXPERIENCE'

FOUNDER OF CINNAMON PRESS

'UNPRETENTIOUSLY ROOTED IN THE 1970S, MELIA USES THAT IMMERSIVE AND RICH BACKDROP TO EXPLORE REDEMPTION, MATURITY, AND MASCULINITY WITH WIT AND SUBTLETY'

DR ROWAN B. FORTUNE

'LIVERPOOL'S ANSWER TO TRAINSPOTTING'

MATT ADCOCK, AUTHOR OF COMPLETE DARKNESS

'AUTHENTIC DOWN TO THE LAST OPAL FRUIT AND SCRATCHED VINYL RECORD'

CARLY RHEILAN, AUTHOR OF ASYLUM

Hello Reader,
Hope you enjoy the book
Maybe leave a few words
of a review on Good-Reads
Terry Melia

TERRY MELIA held various occupations before working as an IT specialist for 30 years, including serving as a reservist in the Liverpool Scottish Territorial Army, driving a warehouse forklift truck, serving as an engineer in the Merchant Navy, and teaching English Literature in adult education.

Terry has a BA (Hons) degree in librarianship and is a postgraduate at John Moore University Screenwriting School. He has written hundreds of short stories, film scripts, and BBC Radio drama scripts. Currently, he is working on books two and three of the Greenhills trilogy.

When Terry isn't writing, he enjoys spending time with his five grandchildren, weekends in Llangollen, North Wales, watching old movies, creating podcasts for his YouTube channel, and reading as many books as possible.

Although *Tales from Greenhills* is fictional, three deep scars on the back of his head may tell a different story...

X - Terry - Writer & Podcaster @GreenhillsChats
https://www.youtube.com/@GreenhillsChats

TALES FROM THE GREEN HILLS

TWO WEEKS IN THE SUMMER OF '76

TERRY MELIA

HORTUS
IN ASSOCIATION WITH
Lex Lunae
Luna Eden Publishing

LUNA EDEN PUBLISHING
Staffordshire, United Kingdom

First published in Great Britain in 2024
by Luna Eden Publishing.

This edition published in November 2024

Credit for book cover image - Tom Keane of Northodox Press

ISBN 978-1-917519-00-7
Amazon Edition

To find more books from Luna Eden Publishing,
Visit Lunaedenpublishing.co.uk.

For my wife, Julie.

My wonderful children,
Lisa, Terry, and Alex,

My beautiful grandchildren, Jon, Lily, Tom, Sophia, Isabella, and the late Charlie and Honey

Michelle, Darren, and Lisha. For all my past and present friends, near and far—you know who you are...

Broadgreen Hospital Accident and Emergency Casualty Ward, Liverpool, in the heatwave summer of 1976.

Linda searches the cubicles, dreading a familiar face and praying he is not among them. She stops and glances at the corridor to the Emergency Operating Theatre. She passes young men, blood splattered, burnt, stabbed and clubbed, and her heartbeat intensifies.

A public address system breaks into a staccato, and the student nurse, Linda, recalls a childhood wish for invisibility. Her clipboard is shaking. The coppery stink of fresh blood is invasive. Rubber shoes squeak past her across the tiled floors as more nurses attend to agonised cries.

A young man lies on the operating table. Intravenous drips are fed into him. The fresh bandages that cover his head and face only expose his eyes and lips. Turning slowly, her heart races as she glances at the whiteboard:

Tommy Dwyer—Comatose.

1
HOT LOVE

At seventeen, a master of the universe, Tommy knew everything; he could handle every situation and had the hairy arse to prove it. Morality was opinion. That's the way it was for many kids in Liverpool. It was the summer of 1976, the hottest on record.

With the curtains closed, silver darts of sunlight broke through gaps to highlight dancing dust motes. Marc Bolan and T. Rex performed 'Hot Love' on the record player.

Perhaps this was the night. Birthdays, Christmases, break-ups, reconciliations, and even an anniversary had all passed without any physical intimacy between them. They had yet to be intimate with each other. For Tommy, who had just returned to the city after five weeks, this situation felt strange and unnatural.

Lying next to Linda, they had their eyes closed as they kissed. Tommy slid a hand up her skirt. Opening her eyes, Linda slapped Tommy hard across the face.

'I said no!'

Tommy glided off the bed and scratched the needle across the T. Rex album. He shook his head. 'Linda, it's been what, over a year? We're not kids. I mean, we are not really fucking kids.'

Linda sat up and straightened her clothes. She stood and waved a hand at Tommy.

'I knew I shouldn't have come. 'Our last night together, music and cuddles.' That's what you said. I knew you'd do this.'

'Well, you are going away for a fortnight.'

'And you've been away for over a month. What's that got to do with anything? We haven't yet, and we won't be when I get back.'

'Well, what's the point of seeing each other?'

'That's what I keep trying to tell you!'

Tommy opened the curtains. Colours entered the room. It was late, yet the bright sunlight was dazzling. He glanced at a half-smoked cigarette on the windowsill. Shaking his head, he pulled the curtains back closed. He was dying for a smoke.

Linda took a deep pantomime sniff. 'You've been smoking. Smelt it as soon as I walked in. I knew you hadn't packed in. Who are you lying to, Tommy, me or yourself?'

Tommy opened the window—thinking he should have left it open before Linda got there. Much too hot anyway… He had hoped the heat would make Linda hot.

'I have packed in. I don't use ciggies anymore. The smokes are not from me. Me-al fella's been kipping here while I was away.'

'In this pokey little room? Still sleeping here with you, is he? Or does he come in for a sly smoke?'

Tommy shook his head.

'When did he get out?' asked Linda.

'What's that supposed to mean?'

'Oh, come on, I knew from day one your dad was inside.'

'He's not in fucking nick.'

'No need to fucking swear!'

'Well, don't act so stupid. Who gets locked up for two weeks, then out for two frigging weeks? What kind of jail is that? I've told you, he's in the Merchant Navy. You've never said anything like this before… What's got into you? because I know… I haven't…'

Linda didn't reply. She raised both hands and said, 'I'm going home. Smoke whatever you like. I'm sick and tired of the same arguments every time we come here. And for some stupid bloody reason, I thought you might have changed.'

'Be different if I had a decent job though.'

'You had a job. You've had two jobs. I thought your dad had got that job after a few weeks, especially now that your nan…'

'Say it, Linda, with my grandma out the way.'

Shaking her head, Linda sat back on the bed. 'I didn't mean it to sound like that… You were gone for so long.'

'I told you why I had to stay.'

'A letter after two weeks?' Linda stood and opened her arms wide. 'Tommy, your mother looks fine to me. Apart from last night, not a single phone call.'

'I told you, they're not on the phone.'

'Oh, so they don't have phone boxes in Walsall? I would have gone with you, Tommy. It would have been nice to have been asked.'

'Well…'

'Was she peaceful at the end?'

'I had the last words with her… Held her hand.'

'That's sad. What did she say?'

'Told me to look after me mam and Patricia. Made me make a promise…'

'Of what?'

'To well… make something of myself.'

'That's what I keep telling you, Tommy; your nan was right.'

'Why does everyone tell me what to do?'

'She was right. You go to college, get the qualifications.'

'I can get a job, earn some money, take more driving lessons.'

'Tommy, you always want everything right now; can't wait, can you?'

‘Well, if I did have a decent job and a car, right now, and a snotty mam and dad like your ex, whatsit? Danny frigging Clarke.’

‘Here we go; no chip on your shoulder, is there? Snotty mam and dad, like my mam and dad, what are you trying to say?’ Tommy ignored this. Although, it was what he’d meant.

‘Danny Clarke… Did you tell him to wait? Give him the prick-teasing treatment, hey?’

Linda lashed out, and Tommy snatched her hand an inch from his face. They stared at each other before they were jolted by an argument downstairs. Tommy’s dad was shouting, and a dog was barking. Dishes were smashed. Tommy’s dad was back home from the boozer.

‘His dinner will be in the dogs’ belly again,’ said Tommy quietly.

His mother was screaming, ‘Shut up—shut up—just shut up!’

Tommy opened the curtains. The night was darkening. He put David Bowie’s *Diamond Dogs* album on the record player, turning up the speaker to full blast.

Linda placed her hands over her ears. As well as the commotion from downstairs, she’d heard Tommy’s younger sister Patricia crying in the next-door bedroom. What was going on downstairs was what had been going on in this room. Patricia had been getting it in stereo.

‘Tommy, turn it down. Too much noise, it’s like… violence. I get scared when he shouts like that. Listen to your poor sister… She’s heard every word. I’m sorry for your family, but I don’t want to be here. I don’t want to be with you, Tommy.’

Muttering curses, Tommy switched the light on. An eerie illumination bathed the room from the blue-shaded light bulb.

Tommy snatched at the three wooden wedges he used as a doorstopper and headed downstairs.

Linda lifted the needle off the still-spinning record player. Dull harmonic feedback resounded through the speakers. She heard more shouting and made out Tommy pleading with his mom and dad for less screaming. *Come on! Linda is upstairs...* The dog stopped barking.

Linda sat back on the bed and rummaged through her handbag. She took out her lipstick and pouted into a small pocket mirror as Butch, an enormous Alsatian, burst into the room, greeting her nose to nose, his tongue lapping around her face. The lipstick smeared across her lips and cheeks. Butch's tail sent the needle scratching across the vinyl, distorting the Bowie *Diamond Dogs* song... Trying to push him off, the dog was winning and had her pinned on the mattress. Tommy eyed the scene from the doorway.

'You want me to wait outside while you put the wedges back in? Have you seen his lipstick? He's got it out for you.' Linda looked down under the dog's belly.

'That's disgusting!'

They both laughed.

Later, Barry White took over from David Bowie, and the blue light was turned off again. Tommy and Linda sat on the pillows on the floor. Wedges were firmly in the door. Butch was snoring on the bed.

'This is what I mean. You know that, Tommy? Why do you keep trying to force me into it? What's wrong with waiting? When it does happen, it'll be much better.' Linda spoke softly. They sat close, peaceful, with no commotion downstairs, listening to Barry White's 'Don't Go Changing'.

Tommy ran his fingers through her hair, thinking, *you go away for a whole fortnight, and I've got a big packet of Johnnies...* he was about to speak as the electricity went off and the music slurred to a halt. Tommy stood and pulled the wedges from the door. He mumbled, 'I thought it was still on the fix.'

'What?' asked Linda.

Butch followed him downstairs, where Tommy opened the small cupboard to put a fifty-pence piece into the electricity meter. He heard his dad snoring on the couch. The house came back to life, and he saw his mother, cigarette in hand, idly staring out of the kitchen window into the dark, empty garden.

Back upstairs, the needle scratched across the Barry White album. All of Tommy's records were scratched anyway, and he saw Linda had her coat on. *Let's forget it again...*

2
THE GREENHILLS

Tommy paused at the front door. He picked up a collar and lead and whistled for Butch. The dog looked thrilled.

'I thought we were getting the bus?' asked Linda.

'Come on, look him in the eye and tell him. He probably hasn't been further than the garden in weeks. He can taste the cats and hedgehogs in his gob already—he's ready to eat or chase anything that walks.'

'That's not funny. He fights with other dogs, Tommy.'

'…Besides, I was talking to Joey Finn today. We might need a big dog. There's been pitched battles on the Greenhills the past few weeks—been murder. Mad-Mick's crew fighting with Chris Lawler's mob. I think the heat's turned everyone mad.'

'The Greenhills have been on the news. A pensioner got mugged there last week… Look, I'll call for a taxi. Just walk me to the phone box.' Linda watched as Tommy searched his empty pockets before saying in a huff, 'I've got money, Tommy.'

'But look at his face.' Staring at Butch's eyes, Linda reached over and scratched his head. 'At least agree on this with me, please Linda. I won't see you for a while. Let me walk you home?'

Linda paused, about to speak, before looking beyond Tommy, seeing his mother in the dark kitchen, cigarette in hand, staring right back. Linda looked away. 'Okay, but his lead stays on. I don't like seeing dogs fighting. And Tommy, if we bump into any of your old mates, we keep walking, okay?'

Outside, on Score Lane, Tommy stopped Linda from crossing the road as a convoy of a dozen mopeds and scooters screamed past, making too much noise as the young riders over-revved their bikes. One performed a wheelie.

'Frigging hair dryers in a biscuit tin,' said Tommy over the engine noise.

Linda covered her ears.

As they approached the shops at the beginning of the Greenhills, Tommy spotted Joey Finn and his mates outside the launderette and off-licence on Bentham Drive. This was the youngest of the three Childwall gangs: twelve to fifteen-year-olds with acne spots, some with voices barely broken. Joey was the oldest and loudest. He was cheeky and had the most spots, his face an eruption that called to be squeezed with tweezers. Seeing Tommy and Linda in linked arms, Joey called out, 'This the bird you were telling me about, Tommy? Any chance of sloppy seconds?'

'Lovely,' said Linda, staring at Tommy.

Blushing, Tommy repressed the urge to say sloppy seconds would have to have involved a first. Instead, he said, 'Watch it, Joey, you little bastard. Butch, fetch!' Butch snarled, and most of the kids dashed off to hide behind the shops; Joey effortlessly jumped over the nearby wall.

On the wall next to the launderette, someone had newly sprayed 'Chris Lawler's mam is a gozzy-eyed drug dealer. Don't buy from her Mobies.'

'The mobile shops, one of them tried to park up by ours. The neighbours rang the police to make it move on. It wouldn't surprise me if they were selling drugs,' said Linda.

'Yep, and these are all hard-faced little bastards. It'll be Joey who sprayed the wall.'

'He's a cousin of Mad-Micks, isn't he?'

'Yeah, Joey, Mad-Mick and Chris Lawler—the Kid, the Big and the Ugly…'

They walked to the rise, up the hill, and despite Linda's protests, Tommy let Butch off the leash. The dog bounded ahead, searching, sniffing intently at the grass. Arms linked, Tommy and Linda started singing 'One Man Band' by Leo Sayer.

Approaching the top of the hill, Tommy continued singing as he saw the second Childwall gang, Chris Lawler and his crew. It was a mixture of posh and scally Childwall teenagers, between sixteen and eighteen—maybe ten lads and ten girls.

Downwind, the aromatic waft of marijuana was inescapable. Getting closer, Tommy could see several members of the gang with a distinct redness around the whites of their eyes. Some were on the path. Tommy could hear more on the other side of the slope.

No threat to Tommy.

The last time he was here, he'd watched two teenage girls beat up a housewife walking her dog. He'd intervened and helped the woman home with an earful of abuse from the girls.

Breaking off the link with Linda, Tommy put the leash back onto Butch's collar. Linda whispered, 'Who's this?' as she saw a teenager jump from the overhanging branch of a tree and head towards them.

'Tommy kidder, where've you been hiding?'

Tommy nodded.

'We're going pegging. You two fancy it?' His speech was a high-pitched slur.

'Begging?' asked Linda.

'Pegging,' Tommy corrected, 'Robbing clotheslines. No thanks, Sean. I'm just walking me bird home. Linda, this is my old mate Sean Duncan; remember him from the Cadwa disco, when we first met? Went to school with me.'

'Before they kicked me out, posh bastards. This is my new bird, Rita.' A tall girl, knowingly ripe, stepped forward. Tommy recalled the image of the housewife, a dog straining on the leash, getting her head kicked by Rita as she lay on this path.

'Bet your bird hasn't got one of these.' Sean held up Rita's hand. Tattooed in crude ink were the initials SD next to a heart symbol. *Damaged goods*, thought Tommy.

'Could get her some decent knickers,' offered Rita in a thick nasal drawl.

'Who says she wears any? She is with Tommy Dwyer,' cackled a shorter, skinny girl. The girls erupted in laughter.

Chris Lawler was a skinhead. He was fatter than most of the lads Tommy knew. There was a deep scar above his forehead, and his eyes crossed, so Tommy never knew who he was looking at. He emerged onto the path with his mouth hanging agape like a trap door, displaying his awful dentistry. Tommy remembered the phrase teeth like a witch doctor's necklace.

He was wearing painter-style white bib-and-brace overalls with a tartan stripe sewn onto the bottom of each leg, a red T-shirt, and cherry-red glossed Dr Martens AirWair boots. Tommy glanced at the unremarkable dull sheen on his own AirWair boots.

Chris Lawler pointed at Tommy. The girls had stopped laughing. 'Here's the shit-kicking stranger.'

The hairs on Butch's neck hackled. Tommy pulled him closer. He could really do with a ciggie. Sean slapped Tommy gently on the shoulder as Chris asked, 'Have you got a match?' He was holding a badly rolled joint. Tommy thought *my arse and your face* as he reached for his pocket, stopping short.

'Packed them in for Lent, Chris; don't use them anymore.'

'You want to buy some weed for you and your bird?'

'I've got asthma,' Linda lied, coughing.

Chris nodded. 'I have as well. I thought it'd be bad for you, but it does help.'

Linda shook her head.

Chris asked, 'We're looking for Joey Finn and his dickhead mates. Have you seen them tonight?'

'Haven't seen him… As I said to Sean, just taking me bird home,' Tommy said as Linda squeezed his arm, nudging him on their way.

'Yeah, well, we're going to get them,' said Rita. Tommy started walking and nodded back to Chris. The Lawlers' drug trade was common knowledge. 'I thought you lot were going pegging?'

'We're going to do 'em first, then hang the little bastards on the line,' said Rita as all the girls laughed again.

Tommy realised that walking Linda home was not a good idea after all.

'I can't believe I've been talking to drug dealers and addicts. What's wrong with his teeth?' asked Linda quietly. 'Looked like a Mr Ed that needs a vet.'

'Of course, of course, the talking horse,' said Tommy, without smiling.

Nearing the bottom of the hill, Tommy stopped. He'd seen the third Childwall gang. Mad-Mick and his crew, the *baddest*, were gathering at the crossroads below, staring up at the hill.

Welcome back to sunny Liverpool, Tommy thought; they walked on, holding hands. No more singing.

'Tommy, when I say get the bus or a taxi, we get the bus or a taxi. There's going to be murder here… It scares me. Shit, there's Mad Mick Finn with them lads. Tommy, only say hello, please. I don't want any trouble.'

'I can't just nod to him. Oh, hello, Davey Crocket's with them. Not his style. Used to go to junior school with him.'

'I know him, Davey Jones. Why does he get called Crocket? My mum and dad know his from the tennis club.'

'Well, he's with the wild frontier now…'

They walked on, approaching Mad-Mick's crew: ten lads, no girls. Tommy saw two of them sitting high on a tree branch, scanning the Greenhills through binoculars. He looked again at the gang, lined up as for a military parade. They were mostly bigger and older than Tommy, in khaki army camouflage trousers and jackets, except Davey, who stood out in a black T-shirt and flared jeans. Tommy thought he looked scared, and rightly so.

The over-revving of another biker convoy could be heard from Childwall Valley Road, half a mile away. Tommy let go of Linda's hand and stepped closer to Mad Mick. Standing over six feet four, Mad-Mick had dark curly hair, bushy sideburns, a short frizzy beard and a moustache. He reminded Tommy of Bluto, Popeye the sailor man's archenemy.

Butch's neck was hackling again.

'All right, Mick? Just seen your Joey and his mates by the shops.' Tommy nodded to Davey and got one back. Davey stole a glance that said to Tommy, 'Walk on eggs… There's going to be murder tonight.'

'Been watching you coming down the hill,' said Mad-Mick. 'That gozzy-eyed gob-shite up there. Lawler. What did he want you for?' Tommy stared up at him meekly.

'He asked us to go pegging with him,' said Linda hurriedly.

'They're going pegging. They're supposed to be the main drug dealers. Out robbing knickers off clotheslines.' Mad-Mick laughed, and the rest of the crew joined in. Linda gave Tommy a subtle nudge and nodded ta-ra at the boys. Looking back, Tommy saw Davey forcing laughter, staring at them.

They skirted around Court Hey Park. Cutting through the park would have been a decent shortcut to Linda's house, but it was local knowledge that Court Hey Park was to be avoided.

Tommy would hesitate to enter it in daylight. Someone had daubed 'there be monsters here' on the entrance sign.

At the corner of the shops next to Linda's house, they stopped, and Tommy opened his arms, beckoning for their usual parting cuddle. Linda pulled away. Tommy slipped Butch off the lead. The dog was being strangely obedient. 'So, in the morrow, you're off for a fortnight's holiday…'

'It's not a holiday, I keep telling you. And it's not a fortnight, it's thirteen days.'

'Thirteen, that's unlucky for someone.'

Linda stared back coldly. 'Well, actually, Tommy, that's what I…'

'Sounds like a holiday to me. July in Gay Paree! Not exactly hard work, is it?'

'Tommy, will you let me speak? It's an end-of-sixth-form school exchange trip. I knew you'd go on about it. You know the difference between us?' Tommy glanced her up and down. Linda shook her head.

'No, Tommy, you know exactly what I mean. You leave school as soon as you can. Get a decent job in a shipping office, then pack that in to work as a labourer.'

'Yeah, and twice the money.'

'Okay, great, fantastic money for a sixteen-year-old in Liverpool. What did you do with the wages, use them to buy a *bloody* sword!'

'It's not any old *bloody* sword, it's a genuine antique samurai sword.'

'What are you going to do with it—chop someone's head off?'

'Well, I could, I suppose.'

'Tommy, you need to grow up!' Tommy had heard it before; Christ, he was dying for a smoke.

‘Tommy, look at me. I want you to get the bus home. This late, it’ll be all right with the dog. I want you to promise—look at me, Tommy—when I’m away, promise me you won’t start hanging around with them gangs again: the Lawlers, Mad-Mick or Sean, whatever his name is with the slutty girlfriend. Any of them?’

Tommy put his hand in his pocket. The money he’d put in the electricity meter had skint him. Linda reached into her purse and passed him a one-pound note.

‘Davey Jones, Crocket, he’s okay. I’ve just thought, he looks like you. Why don’t you start hanging around with him? You know you’re better than any of the other lot. You’ll be seeing him in September when you get in at the Sixth Form College.’

Tommy shuffled, looking at the ground. ‘Tommy, you haven’t lied to me, have you? They have accepted you?’ She grabbed him by his jacket lapels. ‘Tommy, I’m a year older than you. I’ve stayed on in school to get qualifications so I can have a career in nursing. I won’t earn as much as you did as a labourer—but in two years, as I qualify, well, I’m prepared to wait. Get rid of your ‘give it to me now’ attitude. Do you understand me?’

‘Yes…’

‘And Tommy, maybe I should have said this last night on the phone…’

‘Said what?’ A familiar dread roiled in the pit of Tommy’s stomach.

‘I want to stop seeing you… For a while at least.’

‘What? You already have, I’ve been away for a month.’

‘I know, and it gave me a long time to think about things. To think about us.’

‘Don’t say this, Linda. Please…’

'It needs to be said. When I get back, I start my career. It's what I've always wanted—you know this. I want to spend my full time learning the job, learning about me being a nurse, a good nurse. We'll keep in touch—still be friends.'

'You want to finish with me…'

'Let's see what happens over the next few weeks, the next month or so, hey? When are you going to sign back on at the dole? They can help get you a job until September, at least you'd have some regular money coming in.'

Tommy didn't answer; Linda had not given him a chance to. Again, he opened his arms for a cuddle. Linda pecked a kiss on his cheek and headed off the short distance to her house. She did not look back.

Her scent hung in the air as Tommy and Butch stood on the corner, watching as she opened her front porch door. They saw the porch light flick on and off twice.

She was gone.

Tommy fought back tears that had not been wept at his grandmother's funeral. He looked about to see if anyone was watching and breathed deeply.

'It's not the first time,' he said out loud. 'She didn't say she'd finished with me…'

Butch barked.

'I'll treat it as a break. I need a break…' The previous five weeks had weighed on his emotions. Maybe it was time to do whatever the hell he felt like. Linda would be back, and after she'd settled into her new lifestyle, well—who knows?

Time to put the Clint Eastwood head on and take the leash off…

The match was struck and applied to the cigarette at lightning speed. He waited at the bus stop long enough to draw the ciggie to the filter. Flicking the butt into the road, he decided to walk home with a short detour into the nearest off licence.

Yep, a bottle of that there, cider, please, Missus. Tommy was going to live the next few weeks as though they were his last on Earth, and if that involved joining a battle that night, *let's go look em in the eye and kick some arses...*

3

SCHOOLS OUT

There was no sign of Mad-Mick and his crew at the bottom of the Greenhills. Tommy expected to see blood and hair, maybe a few teeth. All was silent. After he and Butch squeezed through a gap in the fencing, Tommy sat on the slopes overlooking Childwall High School for Girls playing fields, taking in the darkness, supping on the cider and drawing on a Players No. 6 tipped. Tommy looked towards the school and spotted two lads viewing through binoculars held to their necks with leather straps, like the Titanic's watchmen on the lookout for icebergs. They were keeping an eye on both sides of the school. One was the ginger-haired Nobby.

Mad-Mick and the boys were no doubt robbing the school, going for the chemistry labs again. In Tommy's mind, he heard the heavy drum and bass from Gary Glitter and the Glitter Band, 'Rock and Roll Part Two'.

He stashed the cider amongst the roots of a huge tree Butch had taken a shine to.

'Stop pissing on me cider, you giant walking rat.' He dragged Butch from the tree and headed towards the school and Nobby in stealth mode.

Nobby was taken by surprise. 'P-piss off Tommy; put the shites right up me, you did.'

'And nice it is to see you again too, Nobby, you tit. They all inside?'

'Told you to p-p-piss off, mind that.' Nobby pointed to his nose. *He's taking this a bit too seriously,* thought Tommy. The school was broken into at least once a week; why the secrecy? The police would arrive within (what time was it—about half ten? Tommy's watch had stopped) the half hour, for the regular routine check. Tommy whistled Butch over. The big dog started a frantic sniff at Nobby's groin.

'Hey, that's some sweet plums you got, Nobby; my dog Butch eats them two at a time whenever he can—and he can!' Nobby backed off, shooing at Butch with the expensive binoculars. Butch snapped at the leather strap, which Nobby let go before racing towards the tennis courts.

Taking the binoculars, Tommy ran back to the tree where he'd stashed the cider. Climbing a few branches, he used the lens to scan the school windows.

Yep, the chemistry lab again. Smashed windows. How many times had Tommy been there? He'd even been legitimately once with an ex-girlfriend who attended the school. No sign of bizzies yet. Tommy undid the leather strap from the binoculars and tied this to the dog lead to secure Butch to the base of the tree.

'Who's a clever Butch for getting me these bins?' He stashed the binoculars along with the cider in knee-high grass. 'Stay here, mate, and guard; I won't be long. Bark to me if you see the bizzies before I do. Better still, whistle Dixie through your arse.' Butch's head bounced up and down as if nodding.

Tommy approached the smashed window. No sign of Mad-Mick's crew. He climbed inside. Shattered test tubes were strewn across the floor. A smell of rotten eggs infused the classroom. In the far corner, a metal cabinet had been forced open. Its door was labelled 'WARNING—EXTREME CAUTION' followed by a skull and cross bones sign. *Uh-oh—they got acid*, Tommy warned himself.

He heard laughter from a distant room along the corridor.

My Spidey senses are tingling, thought Tommy. Following the sounds, shoes scrunching glass, he headed along the corridor to the sports hall changing rooms. He heard running water. The boys were in the shower room. Tommy knew there was no way into the gym (and expensive sports equipment) from the changing rooms—the doors were too solid to force.

Popping his head around the corner, he spotted Davey Crocket standing aside from the others near the door. He was looking close to panic. Lads were prising open the flimsy metallic changing room lockers. One lad, Lil, had found a sports bag inside a busted locker. He unzipped it and found a pair of white shorts and socks. Putting them to his nose, he shouted, 'Let's head for the showers!' Shaking his head in disgust, Tommy thought about his young sister who had friends attending the school. He fought an urge to run in and punch Lil, but there were far too many for him to take on.

He saw that enthusiasm was spreading. He watched Mad-Mick snatch the clothing from Lil, 'Shit in the showers is right.' Mad-Mick pointed the way.

Appalled, Davey backed off towards the door. Tommy tapped him gently on the shoulder and mouthed, 'Shush, follow me.'

Back down the corridor, Davey whispered, 'They're all perverts. How could they? Mad-Mick, he's a… he's insane. He's mad!'

Tommy nodded. He twirled a finger around his ear. 'The clue is in the name... How come you've teamed up with his crew?'

'I haven't teamed up with anyone. I was on my way home from my mate Jack's when I sort of bumped into them. Because I didn't leg it, they must have thought I was a friend of a friend. That Mad-Mick, he said something like 'alright, our cuz?' and the rest accepted I was one, because he knew me.'

'The Finn family are renowned for having so many cousins. You were lucky he didn't knock you out.'

'Yeah, well I can tell you I was bricking myself. Still am. They were talking about going after Chris Lawler and his mob but decided to raid the school. I was waiting for a chance to skulk off. Shall we go now, please?'

Tommy pondered. 'What time is it? My watch has stopped.'

'Er, just gone twenty past ten. Why?'

'We haven't got long but seeing as we are here.' He nudged Davey to follow. 'Come ed, Mr. Bruce Lee doesn't pay to see himself.'

'What?' asked Davey.

They headed through a series of dark corridors, the sounds from the changing rooms becoming distant. There was a back entrance to the gym if you could climb a high window frame and jump from a height. Tommy lit a match. They saw two double doors (firmly locked) above which were two separate windows. Tommy knew one of them opened.

'Give us a leg up.' Tommy put a foot into Davey's cupped hands and hoisted himself high on the top of the double doors, getting a purchase on the window frame. With his head touching the ceiling, he edged along the glass, feeling for the hidden latch. Nipping through the open window, Tommy was inside.

Holding onto the window frame, Tommy dangled ten feet above the gym. On a count of three, he let go and rolled with the impact as he hit the wooden floor. He heard tapping at the door.

'Tommy. Are you okay?'

He opened a bolt from the top and bottom of the door, opening it slowly as though addressing a door-to-door salesman: 'Not today, thanks.'

Inside, the door half-locked again, they heard Mad-Mick and his crew trying to batter their way through the doors at the far end of the gym. Tommy lit another match and looked around. Near the climbing ropes was a rack chock-a-block with brand-spanking, easily sellable tennis racquets. Nearby were several cartons of tennis balls.

Working together, they shifted armfuls of racquets towards the huge door.

'Why don't we let them in? We're not going to manage this lot ourselves,' suggested Davey.

Tommy paused. 'Nah, I mean, well, I don't know… Just bollocks to them, the dirty bastards…'

Tommy had spotted a couple of large sports bags, so they loaded up what they could carry. Back through the wooden doors, along the corridor, opening a window that led onto the sports field, they saw the watchmen. Nobby, sharing binoculars with the other guard, was keeping Dixie on the roads. Tommy climbed out, and Davey passed over the two heavy bags.

Butch lolloped to them a fair distance from the school. 'How did you get away, clever boy!'

Sitting by the roots of the huge tree. Tommy passed the bottle of cider to Davey and lit up a ciggie.

Through the binoculars, Tommy saw a plume of smoke from the chemistry lab windows. In the distance, a police siren approached. 'Nobby and that other guard are going to get collared first. If the sirens are going now, it means there's already a crew of bizzies on the scene. The siren car's been called in for backup.'

From the safety of the trees, they saw Nobby realising he was about to be collared. He hurled the second pair of binoculars into a bush near the tennis courts. A huge police dog raced across the field, sticking its snout deep into his crotch.

'Yep, told him they were sweet,' said Tommy, noting Nobby's location.

'Where are we going to stash this lot?' asked Davey.

'Back to your place?'

'Are you kidding?'

‘Yep. Looks like back to mine.’

‘But what will your mum and dad say when we bring it in?’

‘Davey—that’s not a problem, mate.’

4
THE EARLY BIRD

At five a.m. the next morning, Tommy walked a delighted Butch through the early morning mists. They passed the block of high-rise flats near Childwall Valley Road and onto the Childwall High School playing fields. With binoculars raised, Tommy appeared to the world as the quintessential man and dog out bird watching. For a moment, he spied what looked like a fox dashing to the disused railway line.

'Didn't sniff that, did you?' he asked Butch. Whatever it had been was short-legged and swift.

Some five miles from the river Mersey, seagulls honked at smaller birds. Tommy saw a huge seabird pull a worm free from a fresh dog turd... Tommy made a mental note to get worming tablets.

The mist was rising from the grass and yep—bingo. The early bird gets the binoculars in the bush.

Tommy put the second set of binoculars into his bag. 'Nice one, Nobby!'

As he zipped the bag, Tommy sensed something approaching… Coming in swiftly, panting, he turned as a brindled Staffordshire bull terrier leapt onto Butch's back, jaws snapping around Butch's neck. Butch was dragged to one side on the grass, yelping.

What the hell! The brutality and speed rendered Tommy dumbstruck, but only briefly. His dog's life was at stake—*don't let it lockjaw onto Butch's neck*. He swung the bag at the staff's head, catching it with the force of the binoculars. Releasing its hold on Butch, it turned, foaming and growling, displaying a nightmarish set of shark-like teeth. Tommy stepped back as the staff moved away from Butch and crouched by Tommy. Butch recovered, regained his footing, and snapped a bite at the attacker's back legs as Tommy aimed a kick into its chest.

The staff twisted and snarled deliberatively at Butch and back at Tommy. Butch took a bite again at the staff's haunches. With a high-pitched yap, the staff backed off, darting away.

Tommy bent to examine Butch's neck and head: sticky white froth but no obvious puncture wounds.

'Really, what the fuck?'

Butch was sniffing furiously at blood droplets leading in the direction the staff had run. Unsure what to do, Tommy allowed Butch to follow the trail.

Tommy could not keep pace and found himself on the disused railway line heading to the high bridge, which overlooked the busy Childwall Valley Road. Butch had stopped and was growling, staring into overgrown, head-high bushes and brambles. His hackles were raised. One of the bushes was shaking, as a man, a walking scarecrow, stepped out. The injured staff was crawling timidly behind.

'Him hurt my dog,' said the man, in a dialect Tommy had never heard. At first, the man appeared black, but when Tommy got closer, it was clear it was ingrained grime. Dried grass jutted from his dirty woollen jumper and under his dark hat, confirming a resemblance to the Scarecrow Man from the *Wizard of Oz.*

Although he was taller than Tommy, the man was extremely thin, with hardly any width to his shoulders. Tommy caught a whiff and almost gagged.

'Him hurt my dog,' repeated the scarecrow man, nodding at Butch, before producing a sharp fifteen-inch machete. He waved it at Butch and Tommy in turn.

'Give me the bag. Bag and money.'

Tommy resisted the growing urge to run. The machete could have inflicted massive damage to him, let alone the threat to Butch. He looked about for a weapon—a branch or sharp stick. The samurai sword hidden under his bed would have been useful. He picked up a handful of loose stones from the railway line. He kept his hand low to show he was not about to throw them at the man's head.

Breathing deeply, slowly, he attempted to reason. 'Your dog attacked us. We were walking in the field and your dog just ran at us.' Tommy backed away as he spoke.

The scarecrow man was edging around Tommy, again pointing the machete at him and Butch. The staff, no longer whimpering, emboldened by its master, made guttural growls. The machete was swapped from hand to hand—the right of which Tommy saw was bright red. Tommy was poised to flee, a rush of adrenalin surging through him. He dropped a few stones.

Forget reason. 'Look, Mister Scarecrow or Mack the Knife, whoever you are, your dog attacked us. We were out for a walk and that pet of yours—that walking jaw—attacked my dog. Butch just fought back…'

The scarecrow man continued circling. Tommy had backed up against the metal bridge. Below, early morning traffic sped along the road. A realisation dawned on Tommy. This was no payback over a dogfight. What had Linda said? 'Pensioners getting mugged…'

Butch was crouched, about to leap at the man. Tommy slipped the lead onto his collar and pulled him back. He took deeper breaths. Calmly working up his rage… He closed his eyes and reopened them as if seeing the situation for the first time. An otherworldly emotion had surfaced, and time appeared to stand still. Tommy felt a heightened sense of awareness. He saw the torn cloth patches on the man's ragged knees.

'Mugging, is it? Mugging little old ladies for their handbags—you dirty smelling bastard—come on, try it with me, you stinking shit bag, come on!'

Doubt entered the man's eyes. He held the blade in his red right hand, holding its point end between his fingers and thumb, raising his right arm high over his shoulder. Tommy ducked to waist level and charged, hitting the man hard in the stomach, grabbing the knife hand and bending his knees, pulling the man easily over his shoulders before jerking back upright and heaving him clean over the bridge.

In what seemed like slow motion, the man's body lifted and flailed onto the busy road twenty feet below. Tommy closed his eyes, hoping to avoid hearing the impact as the man landed. He then heard a lorry braking before skidding to a halt. Looking down, there was no sign of a body, only the lorry swerved across the road, blocking both directions. Looking closer, Tommy saw the machete in the middle of the roadway. A dark puddle of blood ran from under the front wheels, covering the blade.

Sitting on the track, Tommy lit a cigarette. Both of his hands were shaking. He dropped the burning match onto his trousers, scorching a black patch over his knee. There was no sign of the staff. Butch whimpered and licked at Tommy's face. Minutes passed. Police sirens approached from two directions. Tommy took another peek over the bridge and saw a distant blue flashing siren coming from the valley below. On instinct, he turned and gazed at the high-rise flats a hundred yards from the railway line. Something had caught his eye. Taking out the binoculars, he trained them at the bottom of the flats, traced upwards—and there it was again—a brief flash of light halfway up. Someone on the sixth-floor balcony was watching through binoculars.

‘Time to go,’ he said quietly, putting the binoculars away and dismissing the ramifications of any eyewitnesses. ‘No need for any quick ambulance… What the fuck…’ Keeping below the level of the bridge, Tommy and Butch headed off the railway track, moving into the dense brambles, taking a long detour as he made for home.

Tommy wiped his brow, attempting to push the events of the previous ten minutes into the darkest recess of his mind, hoping they would only resurface during nightmares. He’d seen and smelt death before. But Tommy knew that in the act of committing a mortal sin, taking someone’s life—even a scumbag cowardly mugger, even in justifiable self-defence—he had reached a turning point, and a silent witness had seen.

5
THE YOUNG YANK

July 1976 was turning into a scorcher. Hosepipe bans were causing neighbours to fall out or to grass on each other. The spacecraft Viking was about to land on Mars. Two days ago, the U.S. of A. was officially two hundred years old.

Tommy was lying on his bed reading Alastair Maclean's *Guns of Navarone*. The sequel, *Force 10 to Navarone*, sat on the bookshelf on the windowsill, next to a hardback library copy of Mario Puzo's *The Godfather*, which he'd read several times. Seeing the film *The Godfather* was high on Tommy's agenda. He'd immerse himself in reading, robbing and selling while Linda was away. He'd spent the previous two days with his nose in the book, shutting out images of Linda and the encounter with the scarecrow man.

He'd had to reassure himself it wasn't his fault. Even so, he kept the volume low on his record player, ready to bolt over the back gardens if the police knocked. The silent witness, from their high vantage, must have seen Tommy had been acting in self-defence. Besides, he'd had a growing inkling of who it may have been. Chris Lawler's family lived in a flat on the sixth floor, and Tommy knew they were not the type to report to the police. What would they gain?

Tommy had thought of seeing a priest for confession, but he hadn't done that since leaving junior school and had little inclination since. Davey Crocket had knocked twice, but Tommy had his sister tell Davey he wasn't in. Davey had left his phone number with Patricia, scrawled on the back of a medical prescription note.

Tommy pondered the Beatles song 'Can't Buy Me Love'. There was stuff under his bed that he needed to sell. Bruce Lee was coming to town that day, Saturday 6 July; *Enter the Dragon* was opening in the Abbey cinema. In Tommy's eyes, the only thing money could not buy was poverty. The scarecrow man was in poverty; he silenced the thought.

Whenever he could, he read sequences of an author's work. Amongst the current collection were six Sven Hassel novels, several reference books (overdue from the Childwall library) and Edward De Bono's *Lateral Thinking, Creativity, Step by Step.*

Tommy was soaked in sweat. Opening the window as wide as possible made no difference, there was no breeze. Tommy noted that the room needed a fan. Butch lay stretched, panting on the floor. Tommy picked up Davey's prescription note and decided to rejoin the world. Searching for the loose change stashed in his pillowcase, he dug out two pence coins and went out to the phone box around the corner. He invited Davey round.

In his bedroom, Tommy stared at Butch. The Alsatian's tongue drooled out like a piece of ham in search of slices of bread. Intermittently, his lipstick would pop out. Too hot to read, Tommy stood and warned, 'You can put that away you dirty bastard. I've got a packet of Johnnies. If I see it again, I'll stick it right up your…' he stopped, as his young sister Patricia walked in, holding a tennis racquet.

'You're still alive?'

He'd forgotten to put the wedges in the door. 'What do you want?'

From downstairs, he heard an old record playing, 'Sea of Love' by Phil Phillips

'Mum's been crying again.' They listened. From somewhere in the house, they heard their father singing along sadly. Patricia's bottom lip wobbled. Tommy looked out the window and saw his mother, sitting, smoking in the garden, head in her hands.

'Come here,' he said, giving his sister a gentle cuddle. 'She'll be alright soon. She'll get over it.'

'What's happened, Tommy, that's made you lock yourself away?'

'Nothing.'

'Where did you get these?' Patricia picked up one of the binoculars. 'These look expensive! Can I have a go?'

'Go on, you can play with that one for a while, but make sure you don't scratch the lenses, or drop them, okay? And the racquet, that's yours to keep.'

Patricia happily rushed from the room, adding, 'I'm not a kid, Tommy. I'm fourteen.'

Tommy examined the other set of binoculars. Steiner of Germany. He'd been testing the magnification, aiming them into the bedroom windows at houses overlooking his back garden, hoping for a glimpse of freshly bathed female flesh. He'd had no luck. The only image worthy of interest had been an overweight middle-aged man sparring himself in a mirror. The binoculars were hefty. Got to be worth a good few quid, he thought.

Setting them aside, Tommy stared at the room from the soon-to-arrive Davey Crocket's perspective. Davey lived in a bigger house, in an even posher street than Linda's, and damn! Why did he have to think of her again? He had managed to avoid this for ten whole minutes, but somehow her image always crept in.

'Stop it,' he said out loud. Butch sat and cocked his head at Tommy. 'Not you, good boy. I'll bet Davey's mam and dad wouldn't allow him a dog like you.'

He mused on Davey's mam and dad. Both probably worked decent jobs. Probably had accounts with the gas and electricity companies rather than a hungry frigging slot meter. Even if they had meters, Tommy knew Davey's dad would be clueless about how to use the metal clip from wooden clothes pegs to dip into the lock and pocket the coins inside. Tommy was certain they had never put their meters on the fix.

Another mental note—put the electricity back on the fix now that they were back home. Tommy could never imagine Davey's mam and dad roaring at each other. From nowhere, he felt jealous as he recalled Linda's comments about Davey. 'Davey Jones is all right…' Maybe Davey had given her one? She did mention they looked alike. He felt determined to find this out. He checked his watch; *useless piece of shit*, the watch had stopped again. He decided to get the vacuum cleaner to spruce up the room. He sprinkled a few droplets of Brut lotion here and there, and Butch took the hint and left.

'Stinks of dog farts in here.'

Tommy switched on the immersion heater, and the electricity shut off. 'Fuck, should have put it on the fix first.'

Downstairs, in the hall, he opened the electricity cupboard. Remembering his Uncle Darren's instructions from two years ago, he turned the mains off and lit a candle. Then, using a small screwdriver from a kitchen drawer, he slipped the contact point from the spinning dial of the meter. The mains supply came back on. Checking the dial was no longer spinning… Bingo, electricity on the fix.

Back in bed, he half-read, flicking past narrative description, homing in on the action in *The Guns of Navarone.*

On the windowsill were the many tins and bottles of Brut aftershave, hairspray, splash-on lotion, and deodorant. Posters adorned the walls. Bruce Lee dominated in a classic fighting pose, his chest raked with three deep scratches. Next to this was a poster showing a teenage Kwai Chang Caine—the Shaolin monk—along with his blind Master from the TV series *Kung Fu*.

Forty minutes, thirty pages on, his Spidey senses told him the immersion heater had cooked the water. Taking his wedges to the bathroom, he turned on the hot water, smoking two ciggies as he waited for the bath to fill.

Bored of multitasking—watching and listening as the bath filled while skim-reading—Tommy took off his clothes and slid the wedges under the door. Do not disturb. He took stock as he posed in the mirror and began to talk to himself.

'Okay, Grasshopper. Your bird, who won't let you shag her, has gone for a fortnight—or thirteen days. And when she gets back, she'll be putting on a nurse's outfit... Hmm...

'No, stop it!

'Your Grandmother has died and you are lying and cheating wherever you can. But you have to...

'Chris Lawler and his crew, you can take anyone on their own. Mad-Mick—avoid him.

'He can kill you.

'My mam is messed up; she always got us on a train to Grandma's when my al-fella screwed up...

'I am never going to die, I haven't even lived yet, and I am going to fight you all! Don't try and start with me—because I am a master of the universe, and why am I getting angry?

'I wasted some stinking bastard scarecrow tramp, and I feel no guilt, so why am I getting sad?'

The bath was full. The steam in the air vaporised the image in the mirror. The water was scalding. He inched in, lobster-like. Painfully, luxuriously, he placed a small flannel over his face. Take it day by day.

Davey arrived on time at noon. Patricia shouted upstairs, 'Tommy, you're wanted.'

'Who is it?'

'Same posh boy who's knocked for the past two days; looks a bit like you. Better dressed. Think he went to Christ the King school.'

'Send him up.'

'Is that you, Patricia? I'm Davey. I didn't recognise you when I knocked the other day. I remember you when you were only this big.' Davey held his hand to his thigh, 'How old are you now?'

'Fourteen. Can you give this to him from the postman?' She passed Davey a long cardboard tube.

Butch followed Davey upstairs. Davey passed the tube to Tommy and shooed the dog, whose snout was wedged between Davy's bum cheeks.

'Oh, great, wonder who this is?' said Tommy tearing at the 'Sellotape' around the lid. He explained, pointing at the various posters on the walls. 'Me mam's brother, Uncle Brian. He's a printer down in Walsall; well, he works for one. Just been staying with them. *Me* mam's mam lived with him. Keeps sending me all the original posters and stuff his company makes. He's sound.'

Rolling out the latest poster on the bed, they saw an enlarged photograph print copy of Roy Wood and Wizard in concert.

'Excellent,' said Tommy, eyeing the walls for space to hang it. He gestured to Davey to drag out the two large sports bags from under the bed. Davey was fascinated. Alongside dozens of cardboard tubes, he saw a wide and dusty tennis court net and an ornate long wooden box. He pulled the box towards him and looked at Tommy for permission. Tommy nodded. Davey opened the box. Inside was an antique samurai sword.

'I never saw that,' he said, pointing at the sword. 'But I don't remember taking a net.' He scratched his head. 'Just the two bags with the tennis sticks and balls.'

‘I’ve had the net since last summer, you tit. Along with these.’ Tommy fished under the net and dragged out two smaller bags. One was full of felt tip pens, the other of musical woodwind recorders.

‘What have you got these for?’ Davey asked.

‘Name a tune, anything you like so long as I know it.’

Davey thought, watching Tommy flex his fingers and blow dust through one of the recorders. ‘You’ll never walk alone?’

Tommy nodded, tuned up, and closed his fingers around the frets. After a false start, he performed a recognisable rendition of the Rodgers and Hammerstein classic, known to Tommy as the Liverpool football club anthem. Davey looked impressed. ‘I could never get my head around those things. It was an option in school, but I didn’t have any talent. Are you going for the music class in sixth form?’

‘What makes you think that?’

‘Well, a little bird told me that you applied to go back to school for the sixth form?’

‘A little bird, hey? And who would that be, maybe my bird Linda?’

Davey reddened, ‘I can’t remember, just heard it in passing. That’s all. I’d heard you’ve maybe been inside, locked up for a few weeks or something…’ Davey was crimson-faced, nervously scratching his head. ‘But you’ve told me now, been with the family in Walsall.’

Tommy stood, looking at the Master and Bruce Lee posters; he shook his head as if dismissing a line of thought. Had Davey shagged Linda? He blew a note through the recorder and deftly passed into the High Noon ballad—'Do not forsake me oh my Darling’. There was an awkward silence. Butch broke it by singing his tune, a fine high-pitched doggy yodel.

'Tommy, you'd walk that music exam mate, honestly, you and your dog.' Clearly, Davey was searching for the right thing to say.

Both laughed.

'Shall I tell you why I've got these?' Tommy indicated the recorders. Davey nodded and sat on the bed. 'When I was at the Collegiate, in the first year,'

'That's a Comprehensive now?'

'Yeah. Anyway, in first year, music was compulsory. *Me* mam couldn't afford to buy me one, a decent one anyway. Only the six bob crappie plastic frigging toy jobbie. I pretended to lose it. I sagged off most of the music classes. Anyway, on the last day of term, I couldn't sag off for some reason, so there I was in the class for the music exam. The teacher, a big, horrible bastard with a beard, was going around the desk-to-desk, giving everyone a separate piece of music to play. I'm sitting right at the back, listening to all the snotty bastards playing the bastard things like they were in the Gary Glitter Band or something.'

'This was a Grammar school at that time?'

'Yeah, right. So anyway, I'm sitting there shitting myself, as he's getting closer. At last, the bastard was there in my face. 'I'm waiting Dwyer,' he tells me. I had this brainwave, top-notch get-out clause. 'Sorry, Sir, my recorder has been stolen.' I sit back and think, yep, stick that in your beard and smoke it, you big, horrible bastard. He looks at me, turns to the class, 'Can anyone be kind enough to loan a recorder to Mister Dwyer please?' I tried to look him in the eye and at the same time give out daggers to anyone that moved, never mind, loan me their stinking recorders.'

'And did they?'

'Only the whole frigging class! Thirty-odd recorders were shoved in my face. There was no way around it. He gave me a sheet of music. He may as well have given me a phrasebook and asked me to translate Russian into Chinese. I blew into that thing like Cat Baloo riding pissed on a donkey.'

'So, because you couldn't play it in school, you robbed a load of them from a school and taught yourself to play?'

'Yep, I suppose so.'

'But why?'

'Uh, how the hell do I know!'

'And why the felt tip pens?'

'Think about it.'

'Ah… your mother couldn't afford felt tip pens?'

Tommy nodded and mimicked the Master from *Kung Fu*. 'You learn quickly, grasshopper. Soon may be time for you to leave.' Both laughed. 'Come ed,' said Tommy, 'Let's go and make some money.'

Outside, it had become hotter. Finding Joey Finn was easy. It was a short walk to the shops, and he was sitting on a bollard outside the launderette, giving cheek to anyone walking by. The message 'Chris Lawler's mam is a gozzy-eyed drug dealing slag …' had been painted over but was still legible.

As young Joey didn't have any bruising on his face, Tommy surmised Chris Lawler and his team hadn't paid a visit. Yet.

Butch growled as they approached. Joey stood from the bollard and leapt onto the five-foot wall. Pacing, he began a monologue:

Tommy Dwyer peed on the fire,
The fire was too hot so he peed on the pot,
The pot was too round so peed on the ground,
The ground was too flat,
So he peed on his hat

He bowed gracefully. 'How's it going, Tommy?' asked Joey.

Davey couldn't keep it in, laughter snorted down his nose.

‘I haven’t heard that since junior school.’ Tommy shook his head ruefully. A couple of old ladies had stopped to listen in on the performance. Joey bowed, ‘Today’s matinee was for your pleasure only, Missus…’

‘Joey, you little tit. He’s one hard-faced little bastard him,’ said Tommy. The old ladies nodded.

‘No, I’m not,’ said Joey, caressing his acned face. ‘I always use Cream of Camay soap, keeps my skin so soft and gentle.’ The old ladies walked on.

‘Get down, Joey, we got money business.’ Joey jumped off the wall, following Tommy and Davey to the bottom of the Greenhills.

‘We need to shift a load of tennis racquets.’

‘From over there a few nights ago?’ Joey pointed towards the High School. ‘Our Mick and loads of his mates got collared there.’ Tommy stretched a finger across his mouth, zipping his lips.

‘We’ve got twenty-six of them, plus three cartons of balls.’

‘All in good nick?’

‘Mint.’

Davey said, ‘I thought we had nearer thirty?’

‘Yeah, but one each for us, my sister’s got one, and I’m giving my bird one.’ Too late, Tommy regretted saying this.

‘I’d give your bird one,’ said Joey.

‘Do you know what, Davey, I’m tempted to go home and fetch my secret sword and come back here and chop this little bastard into slices for Butch?’ Butch licked his lips.

‘Hang on…’ Joey was serious again, worrying at a pimple on his chin. He squeezed out a tiny droplet of blood. Butch looked at this. ‘I can get rid of the whole lot in one go. Take ages getting rid in dribs and drabs, get you the dosh straight away, minus my little cut.’

‘Sell them to who?’

'New kid round here, Suggoski, Jewish Yank family, moved into the Valley Road. His al fella's taken over Scully's Emporium in Wavertree. Told me to keep my eye out for stuff. He works there himself every Wednesday, even when he's supposed to be at school.'

'Suggoski, sounds more Russian than Yank,' said Tommy.

'He really is a proper American,' said Joey.

'Why did they move to Liverpool?' asked Davey. 'Was that the Scully bloke who got murdered in his shop?'

'Who gives a shit, so long as he's got money,' said Tommy, but thinking, *Yep, that was the Scully who had been in the news, the one I saw getting strangled.* He shivered involuntarily.

Tommy, Davey and Butch waited on the grass verge of the road outside the Suggoski house. They'd brought heavy sports bags. A brand-new top-of-the-range Mercedes was parked in the driveway. They saw Suggoski open the door solemnly. Fifteen or so. Unmistakably Jewish from his olive features and, if nothing else, the small cap on his head. After a few minutes of discussion, Joey came back.

'He's offering ten.'

Tommy said, 'Tell him to piss off.' Joey nodded and re-entered negotiations. Moments later, he was back down the path.

'Fifteen?'

Tommy repeated, 'Tell him to piss off.'

Joey set off again. Tommy had a full smoke. Davey nervously glanced at the cars passing on the busy road. Tommy took a second smoke. Butch started to get restless, pulling on his leash. He needed feeding.

'Hang on,' said Tommy. 'I can't be arsed with this all-frigging day.' He headed up the path. 'Suggoski, nice to meet you, mate. Looks like you've done business with Joey before. If you've got the dosh, I can bring you more stuff. I'm okay—

ask around about me. Name's Tommy Dwyer and this is Davey Crocket. Now, I'd take a guess and say you went to King David High School. I'm sure you could knock them out to your mates there for a decent profit. But they are worth more than fifteen squid.'

With dignity, Suggoski nodded and blinked several times. 'Buddy, who said fifteen squids? I told your intermediary here, twenty squids the first time. What he says to you, I don't know, but still, I'd prefer it if you sent him to me rather than coming to my door. Nothing personal. We all want a profit, hey? And, again, nothing personal, buddy, but your pet wolf scares me.'

Heading back towards the shops, money in pocket, striding ahead, Tommy and Davey ignored as Joey protested innocence and pleaded for his share. Back outside the launderette, Tommy made an 'up and over' gesture to Davey. Grabbing an arm and leg each, they swung Joey high until they got a rhythm going and Joey was screaming. At the highest point, Tommy signalled a stop—and they dropped Joey hard.

As they walked away, Joey shouted, 'I'm getting our Mad-Mick onto you two!'

Heading past Jake's newsagents, they saw a banner on the Liverpool Echo newspaper billboard outside the shop. 'LOCAL TEARAWAYS PLEAD GUILTY TO SCHOOL RAMPAGE.' Both stopped to consider.

'We made the news,' said Tommy. They each bought a copy. 'You got plans for this afternoon?' Tommy asked.

Davey looked up from the newspaper, 'Not really.'

'Fancy heading into town? Some shoplifting, maybe go to my al fella's mam's?'

'Okay'

'Train or bus?'

'The seventy-nine is nearer than Broadgreen Station, but we wouldn't have to pay on the train. The conductor doesn't bother checking after Huyton station.'

'Who says we pay for either?'

6

DOWNTOWN

Tommy and Davey jumped the number seventy-nine bus into town. Upstairs, Tommy had no need to spark up a ciggie; the fuggy air was laden with a breath-taking arsenal of pipe, cigarette and cigar smoke. Tommy detected a whiff of marijuana. Wafting at the smoke, they took a seat at the back.

'Bloody hell, Tommy, did we have to come upstairs?' coughed Davey.

'Nah, sniff it in, Davey lad, put hairs on your chest, mate.' Tommy took in deep breaths. 'That weed aroma, sniffing it more and more these days.' Davey cocked his head in an effort to single out the particular odour.

'Someone's on it,' he agreed, looking around. Tommy nodded towards two hippies sitting at the front, sharing a joint.

'It's the hippy-dippy weedy twins, frigging state of them.' Davey nodded. Tommy had seen them lurking near the flats where Chris Lawler lived on Hartsbourne Avenue, near the mobies the Lawler family ran.

Both wore long Afghan coats. Their hair was so long that it could have easily been mistaken for women from behind.

'It's not a bad smell,' said Davey, 'Bit like dry hay burning. Better than pipe smoke. That smells like shit.' A man with a curly Sherlock Holmes pipe in his gob turned and stared malevolently at Davey. Tommy gave him the wanker sign, outstaring him for a full five minutes until the man got off the bus at Childwall Fiveways.

As the bus pulled away, the man waved two fingers in the *V* sign up at Tommy—screw you! Tommy repeated the wanker gesture but stopped when Davey nudged him. The bus conductor was patrolling the upper deck. He was a tall and handsome Black man.

'Fares, please,' he called out cheerfully. He stopped and took a pantomime sniff near the two hippies. 'You can put that right out the window; I'm not having it on my bus.'

'They've been at it since Hartsbourne Avenue,' said an elderly woman. Another passenger piped up, 'Ring the police, I say.'

'Pass it round, don't be tight—let's all get high,' suggested a gummy ancient man who was wearing a blue Benny Hill-style beret. There was a general murmur of disapproval. The conductor held up a hand for silence. This was his bus.

'Out or off,' he ordered. The hippies both took huge hits before the joint was slung out of the window. The conductor nodded in satisfaction and moved along towards the back of the bus. 'Now, any more fares, please?' Tommy and Davey adopted a posture and body language suggesting, 'do not disturb us; we had previously paid in good faith for our bus tickets.'

It worked, the conductor barely passing a glance over them, before heading back downstairs. Tommy and Davey passed silent thumbs up to each other.

'You fancy bunking on the ferry?' asked Tommy.

'Yeah, sounds good,' agreed Davey.

'Ferry, back into town, Woollies pick and nick, then to my al fella's mam's?'

'Why don't you call her your Nan, or Grandma?'

'I do, but… with me other Grandma just dying like, I don't feel right saying the word. Not yet…' The bus had pulled up at the Pier Head terminus.

Getting off the bus, heading down the steep runway to the ferry berth. Tommy experienced a familiar invigoration. The sight, smell and sound of the river Mersey, seagulls laughing as they honked at each other, the salt sea taste on the wind, the gentle rise and fall of the tides and the sunlight on the black waters. He closed his eyes so that he could hear, feel and sense it all. The brand-new floating landing stage rocked gently below.

Davey nudged him. 'Tommy? Tommy, are you okay mate?' Tommy opened his eyes and nodded—regained focus.

'It always relaxes me. Sorry Davey, got a bit lost in meself for a minute.'

'I thought the weed on the bus had gotten to you.'

'The weed on the bus goes round and round, up and down, round and round…'

They laughed. The Royal Daffodil ferry was approaching, turning slowly to berth against the huge tyres chained to the landing stage. A crowd had gathered, queuing to board. Tommy and Davey walked over the lowered drawbridge and headed downstairs to the subsea café for cans of coke. Back on deck, Tommy clocked the direction of the conductor, milling about the passengers to take their fares.

'Upstairs, we'll keep ahead of him,' said Tommy.

On the upper deck, the sight of the three graces—the pollution-blackened Royal Liver, the Cunard, and the domed Port of Liverpool buildings—was breathtaking. A mile above and beyond these buildings, overlooking the Mersey, the Anglican Cathedral added the grandeur of sheer monumental scale to the Liverpool skyline. Tourists were clicking away, posing with the buildings in the background.

Tommy had read the ferries had been in operation since the twelfth century when monks from a priory in Birkenhead provided a cross-river service for a small fee.

The conductor was on his last rounds on the top deck as the ferry turned to berth against the Birkenhead landing stage. Tommy and Davey headed back downstairs where they hid in the toilets until the ferry set off again for the ten-minute return voyage to the Pier Head.

'It's much better when you don't pay,' said Tommy, as they headed back up the landing stage towards the bus terminus. 'Gives you that little thrill, hey?' Tommy tickled at his stomach and Davey nodded.

Heading to Church Street, Tommy and Davey kept a sharp lookout for attractive women in the busy Saturday crowds. The heatwave had brought out the best-looking women, dressed in summer clothes, into the city centre.

'Frigging hell,' said Tommy, eyeing an attractive young woman in a miniskirt and low top.

'Where—where?' asked Davey.

'Over there, in front of the one with the pram, they're heading inside the Tattler now.'

'Wow! Shall we follow her in?'

'What film's on?' Davey eyed the cinema's billboard.

'*The Sound of Music.*'

'Sod that, You'd have to pay me to watch that shit. There's plenty more around, don't panic.' Davey nodded. This was true.

'*Enter the Dragon* is on at the Abbey tonight you know,' said Davey.

'That's why I robbed the tennis bats,' said Tommy.

'How do you mean?'

'To get the dosh to go and see it.'

'Well, wouldn't your parents have given you the money?'

'No. We're not all as rich as your family,' said Tommy sharply. He knew Davey had witnessed meaner, bigger kids bullying Tommy in junior school over this issue.

'Are you signing on?' asked Davey.

'Nah, dole fucked me off when I missed two signings.'

'How do you mean?'

‘Supposed to sign on every two weeks. I missed them with being in Walsall. I rang them and they said I was on ‘benefit suspension’ for three months. That plus with packing my job in at the pallet-making yard.’

‘Didn’t you explain you were staying with your nan because she was so ill?’

‘Nah, besides missing signing on, I’d packed in two other jobs in the past year. The dole was only giving me peanuts anyway. I hated reporting to them; made out as if they owned me or something. Have you ever signed on?’

‘No, my mother gets the family allowance for me with me being in full-time education.’

‘That’s probably more than I got from the dole.’

Davey nodded. ‘Well, you’ve got money now. Do you fancy going to the pictures tonight?’ Tommy perked up.

‘Sounds good to me, mate.’

Inside the Woolworth store, Tommy had pinched a tin of cherry red tile floor polish from the second-floor hardware section. It took an effort to squeeze it into his trouser pocket.

‘What have you got that for?’ asked Davey, covertly. Tommy, without moving his lips, replied, ‘To paint me toenails.’ Davey scratched his head.

On the ground floor, Davey was flicking through the record albums. He selected David Bowie’s *Hunky Dory* LP.

‘Great stuff… have you heard this one, ‘Changes’ and ‘Oh You Pretty Things.’ Feel like bunking in the Tattler and singing to that bird.’

‘I think she prefers 'The Hills Are Alive.' Maybe she’s a nun and it’s her day off?’ said Tommy. ‘I’d love to get into her dirty habit...’ They paid for the album and then headed to the pick-and-mix counter. ‘Pick and nick, pick and nick,’ Tommy chanted.

Both stood with their backs to the kiosk. Tommy sneaked a backhand into the mix and grabbed a handful of Roses chocolates.

'These grow on me,' he said. Davey swiped two handfuls of Smarties.

'Just thought,' said Davey, 'I need to go the Army and Navy store.'

'What for, a General's uniform?'

'Got to get a new small campfire heater.'

'What for?'

'Well, to use for camping like…'

'Oh, okay.' They took the long route around the town centre to browse in the clothing stores. Outside one store, Tommy stopped to feel the lapels of a leather jacket. He could smell the luxurious scent of fine leather.

'Can I help you, lads?' asked a keen, pimpled sales assistant.

'Nah, only looking, mate,' said Tommy. He lit a ciggie, which caused the sales assistant to stare sharply. Tommy moved from the shop doorway and looked at the magnificent St Georges Hall across the road. Several kids had climbed onto the lion statues in front of the building and mimed a racing game, whacking at the haunches and bouncing.

Inside the Army and Navy store, Davey had selected a small butane-burning camp stove. Tommy was rifling through the army surplus supply of haversacks. He picked a decent, medium-sized bag.

'Should hold me books and the sports kit,' he said. Davey was gazing at the vast selection of army boots. They walked over to take a closer look. Davey picked up a pair of black AirWair boots.

'What do you reckon to these, Tommy? My mother's always refused to get me a pair. 'Bovver boots,' she calls them.' Tommy hefted the boots in both hands.

'Nice and light,' he said, 'but these are a better colour.' He picked a pair of Dr. Martens AirWair boots that matched his own dull brown shade. With effort, he fished out the stolen tin of floor polish from his pocket. 'I'll lend you some of this.'

'But that's not meant for leather. It's floor polish Tommy.'

'Frigging hell, Davey, look at the shade mate. Cherry red gloss! Chris Lawler has got them on his boots; they look great. There's not much else to admire about him.'

'Er, it is bright…'

'Davey, you don't look at the fireplace when you poke the fire…' Davey scratched his head, undecided.

'Err… if I buy these, could I keep them in yours?'

'No problem, but you're doing the polishing.'

'Okay. Hey, this will be my first pair of boots!'

'Let it rip, Davey lad, we'll arrange for the Christening next Sunday.' They laughed. Davey took off his shoes and tried on the boots. Pacing the shop, he looked delighted.

'These are more comfortable than they look. Really light! It's like I'm walking on, er…' Davey clicked his fingers, seeking an elusive phrase.

'Like walking on air?'

'That's it, like walking on air!'

'Hence the name on the label—'AirWair'—you tit.' Davey decided to leave them on and took the label over to a cashier.

Their payments were placed inside a small Bakelite container and sent inside a long pneumatic steel tube, the whole store housed a maze of these things. He could hear the cash flying down the tube to wherever it ended below the shop.

Outside, Tommy suggested Davey put the small camp stove and his old shoes into the haversack. 'That's good of you,' said Davey.

'You're carrying it, your shoes stink,' said Tommy, handing the bag over. 'We'll have to jump the twenty-six to me al fella's mam's,' said Tommy. 'And we'll have to pay.'

'How come?'

'They haven't got bus conductors like all the other buses.'

'Well, who do you pay?'

'The driver.'

'What?'

'I know. Sounds mad. My Uncle Darren was telling me that all the buses in the future would have one driver who takes the money as you get on.'

'But that would take forever, stopping and paying and getting your change. And what if there was murder on the bus? What if everyone's upstairs smoking the weed like them hippies on the seventy-nine?'

'He reckons the twenty-six drivers are all the hard cases from the MPTE. All the Blakey bus Inspector types. Any shit and they knock you out.'

'They'd have to be hard on that bus route. It takes you to the match doesn't it, the twenty-six?'

'Match specials, they call them. I think they still have the conductors on. They're not that hard to knock out a whole crew of Kopites who've had a tank full before the match.'

'And Evertonians,' said Davey.

'Whoa, you're not a blue, are you, Davey?'

'To be honest, I like to see them both win it, red and blue.' They were both at the twenty-six-bus stop. A bus appeared in the distance. 'Whereabouts does your nan live Tommy?'

'Just off Scotty—Bevington Bush area. Nice place called Eldon Grove. You can see the new Mersey tunnel from their maisonette.'

'Bevington Bush…' Davey stroked his chin. 'Where've I heard that from?'

'My Uncle Darren told me it's where the word 'bevvy' comes from. Years ago, it was a really nice place for sailors to get off the ships, head down Vauxhall Road—away from the dirty docks for a quiet pint—a bevvy in Bevington Bush.'

'Okay… But I've heard it in an old song?'

'The 'Ballad of Seth Davy'—ha, sounds like your song, Davey lad!'

Eldon Grove was one of the first council labourer villages built before the First World War. It was the first building of its kind to have balcony-access flats or maisonettes: the Tudor style of dark timbers stretched across the white paint on the three blocks. To Tommy, it was like stepping back into a previous generation. At the corner of the first block, Tommy pointed out a pattern of deep holes in the stone.

'Have a guess what that is?'

'Dunno…' Davey stuck a finger an inch deep into one of the holes.

'Bullets,' said Tommy.

'Get away!'

'Honest. The Second World War. The Germans were bombing the shit out of the docks. Bastards flew in low down here shooting at the people in the street.'

'Why would they shoot them here?'

'These were built for dock workers, honest, these are real bullet holes…'

'I suppose your Uncle Darren told you about this?' said Davey, doubtful.

'Don't believe me, ask him yourself.' Tommy was waving at a man in overalls working on the engine of a small van. Darren waved a spanner at Tommy, before wiping his hands on an oily rag.

'Hiya Tommy, how you doing?'

'Darren, this is me mate Davey.'

'I won't shake hands,' said Darren, smiling. 'Bet you've been into town, eyeing up all the birds in the short dresses, hey?' He winked. 'How long are you around for?'

'Thought we'd pop in for five minutes.'

'And how's your mam and our Robert?'

'Okay.'

'I was sorry to hear about the funeral. Tell your mam I was asking about her. I might call into yours, actually; I need to give this old van a good run around, and charge the battery up. You going home from here?'

'We're going to the pictures.'

'Drop you off if you want? Reminds me. Take this bit of paper out of the top pocket, my hands are caked in oil.' Tommy happily suspected where this was leading. He fished a hand inside the overall breast pocket and took out a crisp five-pound note. 'Early birthday present,' said Darren.

'All of it!'

'Unless you want to rip it in half?'

'Aw, thanks Uncle Darren…'

'Go on in, Michelle's in there, tell her to put the kettle on. Parched here.'

'Darren, tell Davey about the bullet holes,' said Tommy, pointing at the wall. Darren's smile faded. He saw the disbelief on Davey's face.

'It's true. Liverpool was the most heavily bombed outside of London. Because of the docks, the largest port from here to America. About four thousand people were killed here by the

Luftwaffe.' Darren spat at the name. He wasn't smiling anymore. Davey shifted from one leg to the other.

'Told you,' said Tommy, pulling Davey to the door of his al fellas' mam's flat. Inside, a tiny, elderly woman was chuckling as she watched *Rowan and Martin's Laugh-In* show on an ancient black and white television.

'Tommy! Give us a kiss, lad.' She opened her arms to get a hug from Tommy. 'Who's this, one of your cousins from your mam's side?' she asked, eyeing Davey. 'He looks like you.'

Tommy's Auntie Michelle emerged from the kitchen, heavily pregnant.

'He's even better looking than you. I see a new pair of Bovver boots,' she said, giving Tommy a hug.

'This is my mate Davey,' said Tommy, as Davey blushed.

'How was the funeral?' Michelle asked.

Tommy sighed. 'Sad…' Michelle gave Tommy another hug in sympathy. 'Darren said, 'Can you put the kettle on?''

'Did he now! You can go and tell him to put it on himself, the lazy get. Pretending to work on that old van. He's just blimping the girls going by.'

'Don't let him near the sink, with his dirty great hands.'

'All right, mother….' Michelle straightened and headed back to the kitchen, saying, 'I'm sorry about your other Grandma. Is your mam okay?'

'She's getting better, thanks,' replied Tommy. He felt awkward displaying his sadness in front of Davey. Darren entered the flat, the smile back on his face.

'Brew's up, then drop you at the pictures lads.'

Tommy nodded. This was one of the few places he felt at ease with family. The unexpected fiver, plus the haul from the tennis racquets, was burning a soothing hole deep in his pocket.

7
THE BACK ROW

The Abbey cinema, Wavertree, was on a junction which contained, on one side, the infamous historic High St 'lock up' and, on the other, the high standing Picton clock, with public toilets below. It opened in 1936 with *The Joy of Living*, the first film to be screened. It was named 'Abbey' cinema to ensure top billing in advertising, ahead of the Aintree Palace, the Astoria and the Atlas cinemas. Tommy's Uncle Darren had given the history lesson as he drove. Darren had agreed to drop off the haversack at Tommy's house.

To any casual observer inside the palatial theatre, Tommy and Davey were the Kings of the Abbey. Sat in the best location—the Top Circle—legs draped over the seat in front. Tommy smoked a huge stinking cigar, dipping into an expensive box of chocolates. Davey was tucking into his third tub of ice cream. As the National Anthem started, Davey rushed from his seat and accosted the retreating usherette. He was shushed several times as he ordered another tub of ice cream.

As the opening 'B' movie began, Davey had grown a vanilla moustache. The audience soon laughed throughout the spoof Western *Blazing Saddles*.

After the curtains closed, there was a cinema announcement on the Tannoy, 'Ladies and Gentlemen, there will be a twenty-minute interval before the start of the main feature. The bar is now open on the Circle level, twenty minutes…'

In the bar, Tommy and Davey waited to get served. 'What you having, Davey, a cider?'

'No, best if we both get brown mix.'

Tommy caught the barmaid's eye. 'Okay, err… two pints of brown Micks please, love.'

'You mean brown mix, bottle of brown over bitter? Do you mind if I ask how old you are, Sir?' Tommy blushed.

Davey intervened, 'He's kidding you love, two bottles of brown over draught bitter, please. And take your own as well.' The barmaid beamed at Davey, who was patting at his pockets, before digging in and fishing out a slip of paper. It was a medical prescription note from a GP. 'This has got my date of birth on it love. Should have gone to the chemist earlier today.' The barmaid glanced at the prescription, still smiling.

'Quite the smoothie on the side, aren't you?' Davey paid the twenty pence plus an extra shilling tip for the barmaid. 'Would never have thought of using a prescription. But, hang on, how come the doctor got your age wrong?'

'Robbed a whole blank pad of them. I change them every now and then. Sometimes on antibiotics or cough medicine or whatever. I've even signed myself as a twenty-year-old. I'll sort one out for you tomorrow.' Tommy was even more impressed. Supping the brown mixed, Tommy nodded approval; it was sweet.

'Apart from the taste, you always get more for your money with this pint.' Davey explained, 'best get a refill with about a third left in your glass. More often than not, the barmaid will fill it back to a pint with the draught bitter.' In Tommy's eyes, Davey was getting better and better.

Back in the theatre, the house was filling up for the main feature. Tommy and Davey mooched around for the best seats.

'Tommy, I can't see a single bird in here!' It was true. Apart from the obvious housewives, there wasn't a single decent woman around their age in there.

'Mr Bruce Lee is a man's man,' said Tommy. 'Let's sit here.' Tommy selected a seat with three empty aisles around them. Comfortable, Tommy rubbed his hands together. Mr Bruce Lee—the King of Kung Fu—bar none, was about to kick arse in Enter The Dragon.

Also entering was a heavy crew from Wavertree. The leader, 'Blueface' Maloney, was rumoured to have chopped someone's leg off with an axe. He was over six feet two, six feet six if you included his afro. His skin had a bluish sheen.

Blueface had a good shifty at the available seats and the two lads in front, sitting like they owned the place. There were enough seats at the back of them for him and his crew. He nodded in that direction.

Five minutes into the movie, Tommy felt something slight land on his head. He flicked it away, irritated. He was trying to watch the Master! A great waft of smoke billowed from behind Tommy, and a definitive something landed on his head. He wiped at it. Sniffed his fingers… ciggie ash. Turning in fury, he got an eyeful of a grinning Blueface Maloney and his crew. The big guy was smoking a cigar and casually flicking the ash onto Davey's head. Still grinning, he took a long pull and blew a smoke ring into Tommy's face. He nodded and pointed the cigar at Tommy, cocked a forefinger and thumb like a pistol, which he aimed at Tommy's head. Having fired the gun, he blew an exaggerated kiss down the barrel.

Tommy turned back to the screen. Davey was blissfully scratching away at his head. As discreetly as possible, Tommy slid down smaller into the seat. He gently elbowed Davey. Mimed 'slide down.' Leaning into Davey's ear, he whispered the bad news. Davey's eyes went wider as he fought the urge to look. They needed an action sequence to mask their escape. Mr Bruce Lee obliged, making bird noises as he kicked someone's arse. On hands and knees, Tommy and Davey crawled to the end of the aisles. After a quick check, they moved off, still crawling, dog-like, to the neon exit sign.

Fire door kicked open, they sprinted a full half mile from the Abbey. There was no pursuit.

'Fuck me, that was close! Blueface Maloney and his crew, fucking hell!' said Tommy.

'Is he the fella who's supposed to have chopped someone's arm off?'

'Nah, it was some bastard's leg.'

'Bloody hell!' said Davey. Both breathed heavily after the exertion. Tommy lit a ciggie. They'd missed the film but caught the gist, Bruce Lee kicked arse. Selecting a flimsy wooden fence panel, Tommy made a high-pitched Bruce Lee noise and wellied the panel away from the fence. Davey joined in, and they kicked along a street of garden fences without, remarkably, a single householder coming out to chase them off.

They had to knock it off as they reached the King David High School near the Childwall Fiveways simply because the fence was metal.

'Suggoski, his gaffe,' said Tommy, pointing to the school sign and checking for anyone nearby. 'Fancy making more headlines, do another school?' asked Tommy. Davey nodded.

They sloped over the gates and into the schoolyard. 'The music rooms in the far corner.' They headed into the school grounds, checking for unlocked ground-floor windows.

'Do you know, before robbing the girls' high school, I'd never done anything like this before,' admitted Davey.

'Do you want to do one?'

'We're here now!' They smiled. Tommy scanned the first-floor windows. Bingo—one was slightly ajar.

'Give us a bunk up,' he told Davey, who was backing away, taking in the height of the climb and shaking his head. Tommy put his foot into Davey's reluctant cupped hands and hoisted himself onto the top of the ground floor window frames next to the cast iron drainpipe.

Gripping tightly with hands and feet, Tommy climbed the pipe to the first floor, which was tricky. A slip and he'd fall twenty feet onto concrete. Gripping tighter, Tommy shuffled along the window frame until he reached the open window. Davey was looking up at him, holding his cigarettes and matches. He pulled his collar closer to his neck. It was getting chilly. He walked to both ends of the schoolyard to check they were clear. Below the window, there was still no sign of Tommy. Davey sparked up a ciggie. He inhaled and almost choked in a coughing fit. He heard a muffled warning, 'Get inside, soft lad, and keep the frigging noise down, hey!'

Inside the music room, Tommy smiled at the irony—they were creeping silently through a music room. Davey headed towards a collection of acoustic guitars, whilst Tommy focussed on a huge bass drum, and after picking up a sixteen-inch drumstick, marked as 'American Hickory', he raised his arm *boom, boom, boom*. Davey cried out, 'For god's sake, Tommy! I'm out of here, mate; I am doing one…'

'Uno memento,' said Tommy and pointed to a glass cabinet housing expensive-looking brass and woodwind instruments. Using the drumstick, he smashed through the glass. Gingerly avoiding shards, he selected an ornate Soprano saxophone. Davey snatched at a brass bugle, cutting his hand on the jagged glass.

'Let's go,' said Tommy. He passed Davey a hankie to stem the blood flow. 'Snatch softly, grasshopper,' he said with his Kung Fu Master head on.

In Tommy's bedroom, listening to Bowie's *Hunky Dory* album, Tommy poured out a glass of cider for Davey. Two sets of Dr. Martens boots, polished to a bright cherry red, sat on the windowsill. They looked impressive. Butch was sat on the floor. Tommy decided to blow the dust through his new toy and fingered the keys open and closed on the sax. Davey picked up the trumpet. 'So, we flog this to that Suggoski kid?'

'Yep, how much do you reckon?'

'Dunno, fiver?' Tommy nodded at the sax. 'I'm keeping this. I'll have it sussed in no time. You'll see me on Top of The Pops, Jimmy wiggy-head Saville saying 'now then, now then, guys and gals, what have we got for you tonight? At number one, it's Tommy Dwyer and Stranger's Shagging on the Sea Shore!" Tommy blew an almost recognisable Acker Bilk solo. Both laughed. Even Butch appeared impressed.

Davey had his palm cleaned and wrapped in a large strip of plaster tape.

'Do you want to know why I robbed the recorders?'

'You never had a chance to learn on a decent one?'

'Nah, not that. I robbed them because I wanted to learn how to play them. I wanted to, not because someone told me I had to do it.'

Davey nodded. 'You fancy a game of tennis in the morrow? School courts?'

Tommy considered. 'Sound. What time?'

'Twelve bells?'

'It's a deal. Best bring a spare arse, I'll run you ragged grasshopper.' Davey smiled quietly. 'We'll see…'

That night, Tommy dreamt in Technicolor of Linda in Gay Paree. She was sitting on a French bidet. Outside the door, the sly old French Monsieur Le Fox was standing on hind legs, wearing a smoking jacket and pince-nez. He adjusted the pince-nez and tapped the door. From inside, he heard Linda whisper hoarsely, 'You know it's open.'

From somewhere outside of the dream, there was a booming unnatural noise from above. This hovered over the periphery. A shadow entered the room and connected with the noise. Butch whimpered, before getting on the bed with the sleeping Tommy. Tommy opened his eyes in half sleep and shoved Butch off.

Slowly, back to the dream… The sly fox entered the bathroom and watched her, still peeing. Linda's eyes glazed. She slid a finger deep into her mouth. The fox's pince-nez had almost steamed up.

Tommy was drenched in sweat and looked down to see the sheet at his waist. He was aroused, and Butch was back on the bed sniffing at his balls. Slapping Butch on the head, he said, 'Move, I'm dying for a piss.' Christ, he was missing Linda so much it hurt.

In the pitch-black darkness, tottering into the bathroom, he aimed into the toilet from muscle memory, with only one eye focused. He caught a glimpse of himself in the mirror; his skin had darkened into blackness, and long shoots of grass were sticking out of his hair. He darted out of the bathroom and back into bed, pulling the blankets over his head.

8

ANYONE FOR TENNIS

Unable to sustain more than snatches of sleep, Tommy headed downstairs to the electricity cupboard. Torch in hand, he squeezed into the tight space under the stairs. The lock was off the electricity meter. Sliding the coin box out, he didn't need to check, the box was empty.

'Nice one, Dad,' he said, wondering what the hell his al fella had spent his wages on.

Tommy decided to take another well-earned bath. The radio news confirmed that the UK was experiencing record-breaking heat. Heathrow had twelve consecutive days with temperatures over 98°F from June 23 to July 5, marking its longest spell on record.

Ironing his T-Shirt, listening to Elton John and Kiki Dee on Radio 1—'Don't go breaking my heart', Tommy felt an ache to be back with Linda and at the enormity of the week before she was back.

'Got to get on with it,' he told himself out loud before advising Butch that he was barred from sleeping in his bedroom. The dirty bastard dog was grounded for at least a week.

Squirts of Brut deodorant, plus a dab of the Brut splash on lotion, and Tommy smelt good. Looking in the mirror, he decided that acquiring Mr Bruce Lee's physique meant a muscleman routine. He reached under the bed and fetched his samurai sword. Carefully exposing the blade from the dragon-decorated scabbard, Tommy cut delicately through the air, marvelling at the twenty-six-inch blade. He'd saved for weeks, and it was the reason he packed in the twelve quid-a-week cushy job as a trainee import clerk to work as a labourer in a cold and wet pallet yard for twenty-two quid a week.

Once, a school psychologist had written a report on his *deferred gratification tendencies*, a term Tommy had to look up in a reference book. It meant Tommy was weak to temptation. His interpretation—if it's good enough for Adam and Eve… He glanced at the headline of the previous night's Liverpool Echo, 'Rampant teenagers charged in court.' Setting the newspaper aside, Tommy's mind drifted back six months.

Every Friday payday, he'd get off the bus in Wavertree High Street to pay another instalment off the thirty-pound price tag in Scully's Wavertree Emporium. It was a glorified buy-and-sell pawn shop with goods such as second-hand fish tank aquariums, gardening and power tools, air guns, bicycles, typewriters and the samurai sword, bought cheaply by Scully and if necessary, sold back on a drip-by-drip basis.

Scully allowed Tommy to lift and admire the sword, but never to brandish it. On his visit to pay off the final instalment, Blue Face Maloney and his crew were inside the shop. Blueface was arguing with Scully. Tommy had stepped outside and waited near the Picton Baths entrance while this was kicking off. Within minutes, the commotion had gotten louder, and stepping forward, he'd seen the gang jump over the counter, Scully held in a stranglehold by an Afro-Caribbean brute. The rest of the crew were wantonly helping themselves to airguns and anything at hand. One lad had opened the till and was stuffing notes into his pockets. Tommy decided to camouflage as one of them.

Running in, shrieking wildly, he vaulted the counter, grabbing the box that contained the sword. He'd paid hard-earned money for this fucker. Reaching, he grabbed a bicycle from a stand and passed it over the counter, one lad taking it keenly. Tommy snatched at another and again passed it.

Everyone was in too much of a frenzy to notice the stranger. Taking another bike outside, Tommy jumped on it and raced up Wavertree High Street with the sound of police sirens behind him. His acquisition was worthy of a samurai sword owner. At least the payments had been honourable… The poor owner, Scully, had been found dead in the back of the shop, his neck broken.

Six months later, in his bedroom, Tommy's mind conjured a fantasy as he chopped off Chris Lawler's fat head before putting Mad-Mick out of his misery. Cautiously, as though lifting a rock that shouldn't be, he framed the image of the scarecrow man in his mind. Can't just stay in my dreams—'give me bag and money'—okay, let's have a sword fight, and I'll chop your stinking head off.

With the human race safe for the time being, there was business to do, deals to make, and money to be earned. The bugle would not sell itself to the young Yank of Childwall.

Down at the shops, Tommy bought himself twenty Players No 6 and a box of Swan matches from Jake's newsagents. He scanned the headline in the Daily Post for mention of the dead scarecrow man; not one line. Turning through the first few pages, he spotted another reference to 'rampant teenagers' and decided to buy a copy.

The article on the Childwall school break-in reported that members of the Mad-Mick gang had been caught red-handed following an alert by residents, one of whom was quoted, 'It's getting to be like Northern Ireland around here. You get a school break-in by one gang, the police turn up and sort this, and another gang turns up. It's like the Falls road. And they are all using and selling drugs.' The reporter had labelled them 'teenage tearaways,' many were still in custody on remand.

'I'm not selling or buying drugs,' said Tommy. 'Might be a hairy-arsed tearaway, though.' A young girl had stopped and was listening to Tommy. 'Hello, little girl, I am Tommy Tearaway, and I have a hairy arse; what is your name?' He crossed his eyes and the girl ran off giggling.

Over the road, he saw Joey giving lip to an elderly woman. 'Cheeky little bastard,' she said as she dragged her bin bag from a pram and into the launderette. On seeing Tommy, Joey backed off towards his wall.

'I told you, I'm getting our Mad-Mick!'

'Going to break him out of nick, are you? Shut up and listen. I need you to go and see Suggoski again.' Joey looked at the sports bag.

'Decided not to give your bird one?'

Tommy ignored this. He opened the bag and discreetly showed the bugle to Joey who snatched it before leaping onto his wall. Cheeks bulging, he blew out several rasping notes. Despite himself, Tommy had to smile. He saw Joey as one of the crows in the Disney cartoon film Dumbo, 'Well ah once seen a house fly…' He shook his head.

'Get down, soft lad, put it back in the bag.' They walked to the bottom of the Greenhills. Tommy had passed the bugle back to Joey.

'How much?' asked Joey.

'Dunno, a fiver?'

Joey scratched his chin, fingered at the keys. 'You know, I'd have it for myself if I had the money... From the high school again?'

'No, somewhere else. It's yours for a fiver, but I'm telling you now, you go blowing it on your wall, you'll get your collar felt very quickly. Could end up in the same cells as your Mad-Mick and his crew.'

'I heard about that. Our Mick got away though; he knocked a bizzie out. He's been hiding in another cousins' house in Netherly…'

‘Do they call him ‘Mad-Mick’ in the family?’

‘Are you kidding, would you say it to his face?’

‘No chance.’

‘I suppose they do, but only when he’s not around.’ Joey examined the bugle. He saw a few dark specks near the mouthpiece. Scratched at them. Dried blood—from Davey’s cut hand. Joey placed it back into the bag. ‘Let’s go and see the Yank. Anything over a fiver is mine?’

‘Deal. But make sure to tell him not to sell it to any of his schoolmates. I repeat, he cannot sell it to anyone from King David’s school.’

At the gatepost, Tommy watched Joey in discussion with Suggoski. He saw them shake. Back down the path, Joey was delighted.

‘Eight squid,’ he bragged. ‘Think he’s fell for you, Tommy. He shifted all them tennis sticks from yesterday. Said he could have made more if he’d a net to go with them.’ Tommy held up a hand for silence.

‘You happy with the three squid?’

‘Too right.’

‘Not going to tell tales to any cousins of yours?’

Joey shook his head.

‘Good. Here’s some advice. Chris Lawler and his crew, you see them coming and you do one, pronto, okay?’

‘It wasn’t me who painted about his mam on the wall!’ Joey lied innocently. ‘But his whole family is selling drugs, grass they call it, made from hay or something. All their mobies have got a bag of it under the counter. Tried to get our Mad-Mick involved in selling it outside of Childwall. Mick said it can make you go blind.’

‘Whatever. You see them coming, you do one quickly.’

‘Our Mick and his mates chased them out of the school before doing it themselves the other night. Maybe that’s why he's after me… Thanks though, Tommy. Listen, now I've got dosh, me and the lads are going to see *Enter the Dragon* tomorrow at the Abbey. You fancy it?' Joey said.

'I might do, I might even get to see the whole film. Who's going?'

'About six of us. Macca's the king of the bunk in.'

'He only looks about ten… Anyway, why do you need the money if you all bunk in?'

'Got to have some scran at the pictures,' explained Joey.

Tommy nodded.

'I'm barred for life anyway. Can't even get in to see a kids' film, even if I was paying!'

'We'll talk about this later. But listen. I want you to do something else for me.'

'Sound, Tommy. Whatever you want, mate.'

'Wait here for five minutes while I go and get a net. You're on for halves.'

Joey rubbed his hands. He was going nowhere.

Six quid heavier, Tommy waited for Davey at the High School tennis courts. Despite the scorching heat, he decided to warm up, hitting the ball back and forth against the wire mesh. He kept a close eye on the sports bag holding his dosh, one of the binoculars, towel, melting Marathon bar and (for now at least) chilled bottle of Coke. You had to be careful with so many robbing bastards around.

Outside the tennis courts, a gang of kids were performing synchronised cartwheels. There were games of football on different parts of the field. From over the Childwall Valley Road, he could see two teams having a proper match on the all-weather pitch next to the children's swing park. There were several motorbikes and scooters parked up near the pitch.

And here was Davey, a large plaster covering his left hand. 'You ready to get your ass run ragged?' asked Tommy, bouncing the ball. Davey said nothing as he took up his position on the tennis court.

Ten minutes into the match, Tommy was shattered. He had to stop for a Coke and a smoke.

'You didn't say you were a frigging pro!'

Davey laughed, 'Been playing since I was a kid. I even had lessons. Me mam and dad, they play for the Cadwa team.' This was the Childwall And District Workers Association club.

Tommy said, 'That's where I met Linda, the Cadwa disco.'

'Oh yeah? Well, I joined for a while to see if there were any decent birds; there weren't, but I just stayed anyway.' Tommy dabbed the towel around his head and passed the Coke bottle to Davey.

Spitting out the coke, Davey complained, 'Warm coke! How can you drink warm Coke? Oh, and that reminds me... Here's your prescription ID thingy.'

'Smart. I'd forgotten about that. How old am I?' His date of birth read 2 Feb 1957. 'It's great being nineteen, thanks Davey.' Davey grinned.

'One thing you need to remember though.'

'What's that?'

'Whoever you show it to, try not to let them read the medication bit.'

'Why not?'

'It's for the pill.'

'The pill?'

'Yeah—copied it from my sisters. It's the oral contraception pill...'

'Fuck me!'

As they contemplated hot Coke and pills, Tommy said, 'Uh-oh, my Spidey senses are tingling.' They heard a commotion from the swing park on the other side of the road. Several young girls were screaming. 'Our Patricia could be in there,' said Tommy as they packed away and headed over the road. There was no sign of Patricia, but several of Mad-Mick's crew were dancing in delight as Nobby—Tommy thought he'd been collared in the police raid on the school—poured liquid from a brown jug onto the plastic seat of the swings. The rest of the crew cavorted as a plume of smoke rose from the dripping and melting swing seat.

'Shit,' Tommy told Davey, 'they've brought the acid from the school, let's get back over the road.' They headed back when Tommy stopped to watch the lads playing football on the all-weather pitch. Looking closer, he saw they were strangers to Childwall, and that there was something peculiar about the nearest lad in goal. Dipping into the bag, Tommy aimed the binoculars at the goalie.

'Have you seen this?' he said to Davey, passing him the binoculars. 'That bloke in goal, he's only got one frigging arm.'

'Oh yeah,' said Davey. 'That's er… what's his name now…' he clicked his fingers, 'Moved into Page Moss from Halewood, I think. I've seen him coming and going through Court Hey Park. Sparky! That's him.'

'Looks armless to me.' Tommy could not resist.

Groaning, Davey disagreed. 'I'm not so sure. I heard my mother talking to the other mothers in the road. Telling each other to keep all the young girls away from him, as well as away from the park.'

'They need reminding to keep away from Court Hey Park?'

'It's not that bad, I've played golf in there with my dad.'

'Well, you're probably lucky to be carrying long iron bars. But anyway, who's the other lads he's playing with? They must be all frigging loons to have a one-armed lad in goal.'

'Haven't got a clue. Maybe he's fetched them down from Page Moss?' Davey continued to watch the footballers through the binoculars.

'Look at this—St John's Angels—it's sprayed on all the bikes.' Tommy took the bins. He saw the Angels motif. When he glanced back to the swing end of the park he saw Nobby as though at attention near the gates, waiting for someone. The young girls had long since run off screaming. Someone entered, wearing a German army helmet and khaki uniform. His black AirWair boots were laced just below the kneecap. He was dragging a huge rusty chain.

'Shit, no one messes with the Angels, unless your name's Mad-Mick,' said Tommy. He passed the bins back to Davey. Mad-Mick was dressed for battle. Someone was going to have their day spoilt. Behind Mad-Mick, several crewmembers appeared, tooled up with an assortment of baseball bats, planks of wood, and more bottles of acid.

'Davey, have you ever seen anyone getting battered—I mean getting the shit literally kicked out of them?'

'No.'

'You're about to mate. Let's fucking do one, now!'

Davey turned to face Tommy, and, taking the binoculars, he saw a magnified version of Mad-Mick.

'Shit,' he said.

'We're going to walk away, back over the road, whistling like we haven't got a care in the frigging world. Do not, I repeat, do not shit and run. If he looks across and sees us running, he might have something against us.' Away from the park, they strolled quickly back across Childwall Valley Road, and over the wall to the High School playing fields.

Lighting a ciggie, Tommy decided they had to move further away. 'Up on the bridge.' They moved up the embankment to a safe, hidden point on the disused railway. It was the spot where Tommy had lifted the scarecrow man over his shoulders. Through the shared binoculars, they watched the scene below unfold.

Over twenty of Mad-Mick's crew were in the park and getting closer to the football pitch. Incredibly, both teams were carrying on playing, blissful of the lurking danger. Except Sparky: he was backing from the goalpost, inching to the high iron railings.

'Why doesn't he shout out, warn the others?' asked Davey.

Still unaware, the ball was kicked high in the air, and one lad timed his jump to meet the ball—but instead of the soft leather, a ten-foot chain whipped against his head, knocking him out cold; Mad-Mick spat at him, wrapping the chain around the lad's neck and dragging him, choking, to the top of the goal posts.

On cue, the rest of the mob waded in, slashing, clubbing and kicking at the fleeing footballers. Several made it out and over the fence. One managed to get to his scooter, starting it up before racing out of the park gates. Others were tearing towards the high-rise flats nearby. Most were taking a terrible hiding.

The lad with the chain around his neck was hauled high up into the goalpost as Mad-Mick wrapped the chain around the crossbar. Letting go of the chain, he grabbed someone else and delivered a nose-breaking head butt. He grabbed yet another lad by the hair and dragged his screaming head down to waist level. Mad-Mick began delivering full-bodied kicks against the lad's head as though repeatedly volleying a football.

All around, the massacre continued like a choreographed horror show.

Davey vomited shreds of carrots and hot black coke.

'Easy now,' said Tommy. He focused the lenses onto a pool of blood that was enveloping another lad's head, as he lay motionless. Throughout this mayhem, Sparky had stayed perched on the iron railings.

'He's got two frigging big brass bollocks, that Sparky mate of yours.'

Still retching, Davey took the binoculars and saw Mad-Mick, brandishing a small bicycle chain. He swung this around his head as he charged at Sparky. Animated, Sparky leapt over the railings and over Childwall Valley Road—dashing and darting amongst the slowing traffic as drivers pulled over to witness the carnage. Safely on the opposite side, Sparky stopped and dropped his kecks and bills to his knees, waving his bare arse at a furiously ranting Mad-Mick. Police sirens were approaching. It was time to leave.

'I think we should go home,' said a green-tinged Davey.

'Yeah, agreed mate.' Tommy hesitated, staring at Sparky who was waving his one arm at his own arse before waving back at Mad-Mick. 'That's a walking, one-armed dead man.'

Retching again, Davey asked, 'But why do they do it?'

'Dunno, territory? Because the other lads are not local to Childwall, because they're not from round here.' Davey shook his head.

'I've got to get off. Feel sick. I need a shower. Meet you on the Greenhills tomorrow?'

'What time?'

'I don't know… Give us a bell about twelvish?'

'Okay,' said Tommy. He didn't have a shower at home, but at least he'd had a bath, only a few hours ago, and Davey was a bit minging.

Near the shops, Tommy looked down at the Childwall Valley road, wondering if some curse existed near the disused railway bridge and its surroundings, something possessed. The Lawlers and Mad-Mick inhabited the locality.

Tommy entered Jake's newsagents. He scanned the jars of sweets.

'Two ounces of sherbet lemons and a quarter pound of apple tarts, please, Eunice.' The shop assistant weighed both measures into the scales and bagged them. Tommy eyed the chocolate selection and remembered the brown stain in his sports bag that had been the Marathon bar.

'Give us a big box of Roses as well please.' Eunice raised her left eyebrow at him; this was an unusually expensive purchase from Tommy.

Back home, Patricia was sitting outside the doorstep. He handed the bag of sherbet lemons over, tantalisingly, but for some reason, she wasn't overjoyed.

'Tommy, I'm getting scared. There've been terrible noises in the attic. I had Butch, but he ran into your room, hiding. I was trying to tell me mum, but she doesn't hear anything anymore. It was dead loud, a terrible banging noise. I'm scared, Tommy; I've never heard anything like it. I think there's someone up there.'

Danger? He headed upstairs into his room. Butch was cowering in the corner. Tommy grabbed the sword from under the bed.

'Butch—with me.' Butch's tail was tucked between his legs. Tommy stood beneath the attic hatch trapdoor. He climbed onto the doorframe, pushed the hatchway open with the sword, and listened. The attic was empty. Danger over. He put the sword back under the bed and headed downstairs, looking for his mam. She was sitting in the garden, still wearing her dressing gown, staring into space.

'Mam, pressie for you. Your favourite.'

She smiled vacantly.

Unseen, ghost-like, Tommy's dad appeared behind them, dressed in a smart suit and somehow more aged. He gently eased them closer together.

'Carol, he's only doing what's good and proper. Give him something back, hey, sweetheart? Come back to us for a little while?' Tommy's mam took the box of chocolates and smiled.

'Thanks, son. And you rest in peace, Michael….' Tommy turned, and the image of his dad had faded into nothing. An ice-cold shiver ran down Tommy's spine. It wasn't the image of his dad who had spoken. It was his Granddad—who'd died nine months ago.

9
LITTLE SISTER

Despite the heat, Tommy felt chilled. He headed to his bedroom. He stared at the Master as he lit a ciggie.

'What the hell have I just seen?' Butch looked up at him, whimpering. His tail tucked between his back legs. 'Frigging useless you are,' Tommy said. He blew smoke at Butch but regretted it. 'Come here fella, it's okay, come on.' Butch stepped up onto the bed and rolled over, paws in the air for Tommy to scratch gently at his belly. 'You smell like a dog.' He swatted playfully at Butch's snout, who reacted with his own gentle growling and playful nips at Tommy's fingers. Tommy stood and put the ciggie out. He stared out the window. His mam was still holding the box of Roses chocolates. She hadn't opened them. At the top of the stairs, Tommy called for his sister.

'What?' She shouted back.

'You want to take Butch to the park?' Butch's ears perked up, he jumped off the bed and stared intensely at Tommy. Patricia entered the room with the lead and collar in her hand.

In Score Lane Gardens Park, thanks to the continuing scorching, cloudless day, Tommy could see for miles down the valley below. The binoculars helped. Squinting, he could make out the power station from Fiddlers Ferry in the far-off distance in Widnes. Below, he could see the sprawling mass of Childwall Valley Road and the new Childwall council estate. The children's swing park, where the mayhem had been witnessed earlier, was in plain view.

The gates had been blocked off and the police were patrolling. It was a crime scene. To the left was the wooded and notorious Court Hey Park. Linda's house lay just beyond.

Patricia had let Butch off the lead and he was fetching a tennis ball. Slowly, they headed to the All Saints Church end of the park. Passing by garden fences, the opportunity for pegging crossed Tommy's mind. He remembered why these were relatively safe; a lot of them were owned or rented by police officers from the newly built Belle Vale police station.

'Shall we go to the stables?'

'Nah, can't take Butch in there. He'd see a hundred tins of dog meat wearing a saddle.'

'What do you mean?'

'What do you think dog meats made of?'

'No! It's not horses… is it?'

'Only dead ones… Come ed, shall we go through the graveyard?'

'No, I don't like it in there.'

All Saints Church and the graveyard dated to the fourteenth century and were listed in the Doomsday Book. There was supposed to be an underground passage from the Church to the nearby Childwall Abbey pub, a bolthole for monks escaping the Dissolution of the Monasteries. The pub was rumoured to be haunted. Tommy had been knocked back several times trying to buy a pint in the Childwall Abbey pub.

He'd been embarrassed on his second date with Linda, when the landlord asked for ID. Tommy had told the landlord to go and screw himself along with the ghosts of the monks, which didn't impress Linda.

Patricia had spotted horses from the riding school in the paddock between the park and church grounds. She put the lead back on Butch and was whistling over to a tall piebald mare eating from a trough in the far corner. The horse ignored Patricia. Butch barked and pulled on the lead. He stood on hind legs against the fence as if to encourage the horse to come and play. From a distance, they heard motorbikes approach. Made skittish with the noise, the horse's head bobbed before it trotted to the far side of the paddock.

Tommy took hold of the lead and pulled Butch. He wrapped the lead around one of the legs under a nearby bench. Patricia followed and sat, staring at the passing bikers.

'You ever thought of getting one of them motorbikes?'

'No, why?'

'It seems like every other kid has got one now, mopeds aren't they?'

'Never ever been tempted. Noisy fuckers.'

'There's more and more of them… How old do you have to be to get one?'

'Seventeen. You can get a moped with an engine size below 50cc, with a provisional license.'

'Are you going to start again with driving lessons?'

'I suppose, when I can afford it.'

'Why do the mopeds get called fizzies?'

'Main brand of them is a Yamaha FS-1—sounds like fizzy.'

'They're not as bad as the ones with the big handlebars.'

'Malaguti's.'

'Yeah, those are the nosiest. Why you've never wanted one?'

'Patricia, I wouldn't even get a lift on any of them.'

'I'd love to go horse riding,' she said.

'Why?'

'A few of my mates do it in school. They've got rosettes for it. Julie O'Malley has got one for crossdressing.'

'What?'

'It's for making the horse go where you tell it to.'

'Not for dressing up like a man?'

'Silly! You have to control the horse—make it run faster or slower, and make it jump when you tell it.'

'She sounds like a right cowboy to me.' Tommy felt another pang of anguish. Linda's sister had numerous awards for horsemanship displayed in the parlour of their home. Would he ever be there again? Would Linda grow tired of the old arguments, realising she could easily do better with someone else? He scratched at the baby fluff hairs on his chin.

'Tommy, what are we going to do about our mam?'

Tommy stared at his sister. He found it hard to reply. 'You shouldn't be worrying about things like this.'

'I know, but who's going to fix it? Our dad can't.'

'Don't speak bad about our al fella.'

'But Tommy, he can't, he's always dreaming about taking us all away with that job in New Zealand.'

'I know…'

'He keeps telling me we'll be okay if we move, telling me to tell me mam. Why doesn't he tell her himself? I can hear them talking, usually shouting at each other. And you trying to shag Linda.'

'Hey—frigging hell, stop right there—do you know what that means!'

'I am fourteen, Tommy.'

'Ah, for god's sake.'

'You should stop pushing her.'

'What?'

'Stop pushing her too hard. We've been away for too long, you can't expect to get back and do what you like.'

'So, my little sister tells me what to do?'

'I want us all to be happy, Tommy. You aren't, she isn't and I'm not. What shall we do about me mam?'

Tommy stared at his younger sister. This was not a sibling to be bought the occasional sweets and fobbed off with whatever he had robbed. 'Patricia, you've grown up.'

Patricia nodded. She knew this.

Butch was taking a shit in nearby bushes. He whipped up the grass with his hind legs to cover it up.

'He doesn't do that in our garden,' said Patricia.

'It's because he thinks this park is too posh for him,' said Tommy.

'The Liverpool Collegiate Grammar School for boys was too posh for me…'

Patricia tilted her head back. 'Just thinking… Our Drama teacher says you have to find someone… what did he say… someone who you can aspire to, make you want to do better.'

'That's why I've got a poster of Bruce Lee on me wall.'

'No, I mean someone real, someone who can say things to you to make you feel different, make you want to be better than you are now.'

'Uncle Darren's clever, and Uncle Brian in Walsall, but…'

'They don't inspire you though… Hasn't anyone you've met made you think differently?'

'Well… If there is someone out there, I haven't met them yet…'

Tommy lit up a ciggie and had a slow, ponderous smoke. Patricia was staring through the binoculars at the horses in the paddock.

Quietly, Tommy said, 'Everyone had an expensive blazer, an expensive tracksuit for games. Ben *bastard* Sherman shirts, silk ties. Do you know I've never had a pair of footie boots? Can you imagine how it feels to try and get on the school footie team wearing a second-hand tracksuit from Greaty Market and a pair of flimsy pumps? I felt like a pauper from the day I walked into that school. We had to write all our work with a fountain pen. Mine was handed down from me Grandma's mother!'

'Is that why you started sagging off and all the fighting?'

'Yeah, I suppose it was. We used to get the bus into town, and think… ah, bollocks to it. Let's not bother. We used to walk around the museum all day. Back in school, the best way to cope was either being the class clown, or the hard case. Sean Duncan was the class clown.'

'And you became the hard case?'

Tommy picked up the binoculars and examined the police activity in the park below. They were making a forensic sweep. Maybe Mad-Mick's crew had killed one of the lads they'd attacked. Tommy stared at his sister.

'Not that hard,' he said. Both were silent for a short time.

'It's not so bad getting the free dinner ticket in the Comp,' said Patricia. Tommy thought back to the separate short queue he had to stand in outside the school office—the 'scruff' queue, as it was known.

'Most of the kids I know get a free school dinner,' said Patricia.

Tommy lit another ciggie. Thought back. The first school he had broken into.

It wasn't long after meeting Linda at the Cadwa club. He needed money to take her out to the pictures—show her a good time. He'd walked aimlessly around the Fiveways until ending up outside the school gates. With a quick jump, he scampered over, heading to the school canteen and finding an open window. Inside, he'd made his way into the Headmaster's office. A quick search revealed a weighty Sony 630 reel-to-reel tape-recording deck. Sellable. In another cupboard, he found a six-inch-thick roll of school dinner tickets labelled 'LEA—School Meals—prepaid,' each had a designated voucher number '12'. Free school meals were designated '0'.

'These will do!' he'd said out loud.

The proceeds from the tape recorder, five quid from Scully's Emporium in Wavertree, and the slow trickle sale of the dinner tickets had kept him in funds for several weeks. Maybe it was time for a revisit… 'Do you fancy coming with me back to Christ the King school?' asked Tommy.

Patricia put the lead back on Butch. 'No chance. I know you've been back there loads of times. I'm not getting involved in your robbing.'

'Didn't say that when I gave you the dinner passes, did you?'

'Tommy, the money I made, I gave it all back to you.'

Heading home, Patricia ran ahead with Butch. Outside, she stopped and waited for Tommy. 'If his job comes through, will you come with us to New Zealand? Tommy—it might happen.'

'What, me dad's daydream? There's no way… do you think I'd leave Linda behind?'

'Tommy, she has already left you behind. Can't you see that?'

What the hell…

10
LOVE THY NEIGHBOUR

As Tommy woke, he was vaguely aware that noises from the attic had been present but not part of his dreams. Although he'd had no nightmare images of the scarecrow, a future without Linda had been a recurring theme, leaving him hollow and lonely. *She's already left you.* The memory brought a lump into his throat.

Glad to get away from his bedroom, he'd rung Davey and arranged to meet within the hour. He'd packed Davey's new boots into his haversack and fetched them out as Davey approached along the disused railway line.

Despite his revulsion, Davey was fascinated with the way Mad-Mick had demolished the poor lad whose head had been kicked like a football. Tommy demonstrated the technique.

'You need to bring the head down first.' He feinted a dig at Davey's belly, 'That always brings it down—reflex. Next, when the heads down,' he grabbed both of Davey's ears and pushed his head further down. 'Ears or hair doesn't matter.' He took a step back, pulling Davey towards him, head at waist level, 'Poise and balance,' he said, aiming a slow-motion kick at Davey's head. 'Dead easy.'

'Sick though,' said Davey.

'Totally agree, mate, but good to know the technique, hey?' Tommy felt an urge to share with Davey what had happened with the scarecrow man. The absence of newspaper reporting and local gossip was concerning. Was it a dream? He recalled the cliché—*let sleeping dogs die*... lie... or whatever.

Rather than confessing, he decided to advise. 'Listen, Davey, I was thinking the other day about danger, about what to do if you are in big trouble.'

‘How do you mean?’

‘Well, say you’re out and about, a walk in the park, and from nowhere, there’s a big docker in your face threatening you, say he has a knife in his hand.’

‘Why would a docker come at me from nowhere?’

‘Well, say he did…’

‘But why a docker?’

‘A big bloke—you know, that’s what you call a big ugly hard case.’

‘I’ve got an Uncle who works on the docks, and he’s only small, not bad looking, pretty sure he wouldn’t pick a fight with anyone.’

‘Oh my God… okay, let’s say you are suddenly in real danger—what do you do? Do you try to reason with him, talk sense with him?’

‘Do I talk with this docker who’s holding a knife and threatening me for no reason?’

‘Well… yeah?’

‘Well, if it did happen, I think I’d leg it as fast as I could.’

‘That’s what I’m talking about!’

‘I don’t get you, Tommy…’

‘For fucks sake… you’ve only got two choices, right? You immediately leg it, or you land one on him as hard as you can.’

‘But… I wouldn’t want to fight with a big, ugly, knife-carrying docker.’

‘But you might think it was a good idea to try to reason with him. Attempt some logic to, like… diffuse the situation.’

‘Tommy, I’m not getting this, mate. If this big bastard docker wants to stab me, I leg it every time, every day of the week, no ifs or maybes—my name is Goff and I’m getting off…’

Tommy shook his head. He’d confused himself, so he made a last attempt, partially to understand his reasoning better.

'I know I'm not explaining this properly, but I decided the other day that something happened that made me stop and think that to... well, stop and think for too long when you are in danger is err... wrong. You get your retaliation in first bang—that or you leg it.'

'Yeah, I get that, Tommy. If you can, disable the danger and if you can't, get out of its way. I can't see any mystery or deep Kung Fu wisdom in that. Plus, I don't know of any dockers that live around here.'

Tommy considered; Davey had a point there.

They crossed Chelwood Avenue and into Walsingham Road.

'You fancy the movies again tonight? Oh, and before I forget, here's two-fifty—half for the bugle.' He handed the money over. 'Joey Finn and his mates are going to the Abbey.'

'They're not nearly old enough; it's an 'X' certificate! None of them look eighteen.'

'Doesn't matter, they won't be paying either. I remember last year when *The Exorcist* was on, took Linda and...'

'I went with the lads from our road. That was one seriously scary film!'

'Frigging right, I didn't sleep for a week. Kept dreaming of Regan lying in my bed, head twisting around and all that. It was about the time I found our Butch. He's slept in my room ever since.'

'I hated the bit with the silhouette of the demon on the wall—whoa!'

'Linda made out she wasn't bothered, said she thought it was funny watching me, well, shit me self. But I know for a fact she asked her sister to sleep with her that night. The jammy bitch.'

'Know what you mean, Tommy. Ken Gee reckons it didn't bother him, but his mum told my mum he woke up screaming every night for a week afterwards. They were talking about how it should be banned.'

'I thought you might have started to turn your swede all the way round when you were spewing yesterday... Thing is, violence and that on the pictures, I bet they can't make anything worse that what we saw.' Davey nodded and they pondered.

'Anyway, I was telling you about Joey Finn,' remembered Tommy. 'He was there in the balcony circle, think he'd bunked in for a full week of it. It gets to the green spew scene—half the audience was baulking. So, there's Joey and his mates, front row of the circle looking down at the stalls. They've only brought in bags of mushy peas. Mixed them with wet curry.'

'They didn't lash it down?'

'They had a bagful each—lashed the whole lot over the heads below. There was frigging murder!' They laughed easily at the image.

Tommy stopped mid-laugh. He stared at Davey. 'How come you know Linda?'

Davey stopped laughing, his expression anxious. 'Told you I used to play tennis in the Cadwa.'

'Yeah, and you said you went there looking for birds.'

'That's right, I did. And I told you there wasn't any decent, and I know, that err... you know, Linda is ah... decent.'

Keep digging, thought Tommy...

'My mum and dad were in the bowls team as well. Linda's dad is the Captain, and her mother is the Secretary. I saw Linda a few times on awards night. I think you were with her on one night.'

'Ah...' said Tommy, quietly relieved. 'I remember seeing you there now. Snotty pair of bastards them two. Keep trying to get Linda to dump me off. She's over in Gay Paree for thirteen days. Sixth form school trip.'

'She's on that as well?' said Davey. 'Thingio's on that trip…' he clicked his fingers, 'Danny Clarke—Clarkey. Do you know him?'

Tommy had stopped walking again. He sparked up a ciggie. 'Shit' he said. 'Her frigging 'ex'. I hate that fucking prick!'

'Well, that's all right, isn't it?' suggested Davey.

Tommy stared at him. 'You reckon? Bastard *Gay Paree* in the sunshine with…'

'Tommy, you said her 'ex.' She's jibbed him for you. She looked happy with you when I saw you coming down the Greenhills until you bumped into Mad-Mick's crew.'

Tommy shook his head. Davey wouldn't understand—how could he when even Tommy couldn't understand his relationship with Linda…

That bastard lanky streak of piss was the problem. He made a mental note: 'Visit Danny frigging Clarke as soon as the school trip is over.' Maybe introduce Clarkey to a sharp samurai sword.

Stopping halfway down Chelwood Avenue, Davey said, 'Do you want to say hello to some of the lads here? You'll remember a few from Christ the King.' He could see Tommy was still sour. 'We're off camping on a farm in Wales in a few days' time. Me, Ken Gee, Ricey and Jack.'

'I don't know Jack,' said Tommy. 'I know Ken Gee and Ricey. I had a pint in the Corrie with them once. I've heard they're both... you know... fruits.' Tommy raised an eyebrow.

'This is Ricey's,' said Davey, as they walked up the path and rang the doorbell. They waited and got no answer. 'We'll give Ken Gee a knock. I was telling you about when we last went camping. Ricey and Ken Gee always had torches on hand for one nudie book or another. It would have cost them a fortune in batteries. They must have saved it up for a year… you won't want to know about the state of their sleeping bags at the end of the week. Borrowed Mr Morrin's hose to wash them down.'

'Who's Mr Morrin?'

'Local farmer, we always stay on his field.'

A young girl, aged nine or ten, approached. 'You're Tommy Dwyer, who wee-weed on the fire,' she said. 'My big sister used to love you. She's got a picture of you on her wall.' Tommy blushed.

'You might be on a few walls around here. You remember Claire Mullins from school? This is her little sister. Aren't you Jane?' Tommy dug into a pocket and fished out a ten-pence piece.

'Here you go, little Jane. Get yourself an ice cream. And tell your Claire I said hello.' Jane ran off, squealing delightedly. 'Has Claire grown a decent set of…?' asked Tommy. Davey simulated giant melons, and they laughed.

Davey knocked on Ken Gee's door. His mam answered. Smiled at Davey. She stopped smiling as she recognised Tommy. She had started to shout upstairs, 'Kenneth, Davey's here…' whispered, 'With Tommy Dwyer.' She stared at Tommy, took a deep breath for composure, and painted a smile back in place.

'Won't be long before you and Kenneth go back to the Holt sixth form. Up you go, dear, after, you know…' she pointed at their shoes. Davey smiled and nodded to Tommy, miming 'take your shoes off.' As he reluctantly slipped the pumps off, Ken's mam gave Tommy a sober appraisal. 'I don't suppose you'll be entering sixth form?'

'Why should I?' he said.

'Well, to get qualifications, for one good reason.'

'What makes you think I don't already have any qualifications and no plans for getting any more?' Tommy was getting pissed with this skinny snotty mam looking down through her nose at him – making judgements. Davey shifted, his eyes begging Tommy. Mrs Gee smiled.

'Kenneth passed four O-levels this year. And err… how many did you pass, if any?' Tommy felt like sticking his fist into her face.

'None this year,' he said. Mrs Gee smiled—she knew this.

Tommy replied, 'But last year, I got eight.'

Mrs Gee laughed into her palm, awaiting the punch line.

Tommy stared back, poker-faced.

'Now come on—you're saying eight O-levels—not getting mixed up with CSEs…' Tommy stared back. Mrs Gee stopped giggling. Wiped at non-existent fluff on her dress. Looked at Davey accusingly and asked, 'And what examination board did you sit the exams with?' Her polite smile suggested she had got him. Davey saw this and feebly tried to intervene before Tommy waved him aside.

'Let's see … English Lit and Language, Geography, Art, Maths, Physics, History…' he paused. 'Just thought on. I'm lying to you,' he smiled happily. 'I haven't got eight O-levels. I've got nine. Eight with the JMB—you know the Joint Metrication Board? Well, for the social and economic History of Britain, I fancied having a go with both the JMB and the AEB—you know, the Associated Examining Board—so with the two Histories, I scooped nine.' He slapped his forehead. 'There I go, lying to you again! I also took the French with AEB, seeing how a massive twenty per cent was oral. Mrs Gee, thinking of oral stuff, parlez-vous Francais a un degree?'

Mrs Gee's jaw began to sag. Tommy continued, 'Got eight, grade As, but only a C in Maths—this was always my worst subject, but there you go. So, Mrs Gee, you were saying that Kenneth passed how many O-levels?'

Tiredness filled the corners of her eyes. 'He's upstairs,' she answered with a thin smile as Davey was staring at Tommy, determining whether this was for real or bullshit.

Up the professionally decorated stairs. They heard music—volume on low. It was Slade's 'Mama we're all crazy now'. They knocked on Ken's door and heard shuffling. A key turned (no crude wooden wedges) as the door opened, and the red-faced, squinting head of Ken Gee popped out, almost bald. Tommy was taken aback—skinhead? No, he decided, just plain baldness. Ken squinted—missing his prescription glasses.

'Oh, it's you, Davey,' blind and deaf Ken—didn't hear his mam. He looked to Tommy like a giant balding hamster.

Inside the bedroom, Tommy saw Ken Gee revising for a Biology exam with an emphasis on female genitalia. He was squinting at Tommy, looking more like a mole than a hamster.

'Major Dwyer, from the ministry of the wank here. Sir, we've had reports you have been, uh, at it?'

Ken and Davey froze. Both shushed Tommy and checked the door to see if Mrs Gee was within earshot. Davey locked the door while Ken retrieved his glasses from the rumpled bed.

'Bloody hell,' he whispered, 'it's Tommy Dwyer!'

Back out in the bright sunlight, heading for Davey's house, Davey stopped. 'That was a bit tight in there, Tommy.'

Tommy shrugged. 'Who gives a shit? You should have seen what I did with his mam's pink toothbrush. Cleaned the rim of the bog very nicely. Snotty frigging bitch.'

Davey winced. 'That stuff about the O-levels. That was all bullshit—yeah?'

Tommy stopped and stared at Davey. 'What you reckon Davey, think I'm too thick to pass nine exams?'

'I don't know Tommy. I know you'd walk any music exam. I find it hard to work you out…' Tommy shrugged; he appreciated the honesty and wanted to drop the subject.

Davey persisted, 'It's not like in your house around here. I mean, don't get me wrong, I think you're sound and all that. But we don't like, well, we don't swear in front of our parents—don't even answer them back. Mostly. I live a mile away from what we saw in that park—and I've never seen anything like it at all! I knew it went on, but… It's like back at Christ the King; you know what I mean? We all still go to church.'

'Listen, I'm going to piss off home, okay?' said Tommy, getting annoyed again.

Davey stood in front of him. 'Tommy, I'm telling you the god's honest truth. When mums and dads are around, can't you just well…'

'Tone it down? Yeah, I suppose I can do that sometimes.'

Davey nodded hopefully and opened his front door. Listening… The house was empty.

Tommy took in the opulence: the white leather three-piece suite, hardwood dining table and chairs, and professionally fitted carpet with no cigarette holes. He browsed a set of silver-framed photographs in a glass cabinet and focused on a wedding montage.

'Our Diana—you remember her from school?'

Tommy shivered. He had a flashback.

Christ the King Junior School.

Davey, aged eight, was wearing short pants and a thick, oversized woolly grey jumper. While the girls played skipping games and chanted to the rhythm, a tall girl two years older than Davey cornered him and began slapping his bare calf with a twelve-inch wooden ruler. He tried to push back, but the girl was bigger and stronger. Two schoolteachers on playground patrol purposefully turned their heads and walked by.

A crowd of school kids gathered, forming a circle as Davey's sister Diana continued to slap his calf. Tommy's little sister Patricia rushed over to help but was pushed to her knees.

As Tommy shed tears from the pain and humiliation, the crowd and the skipping kids chanted.

'Tommy Dwyer peed on the fire,
The fire was too hot
so he peed on the pot,

Tommy stared helplessly into the nearby headmaster's office as the school Head, Mr Lord, turned his back on the display outside:

The pot was too round,
so he peed on the ground,
The ground was too flat
so he peed on his hat'

The pain registered in tears, and despite an effort, Tommy wet himself in the full glaring spotlight… *Humiliation in the playground.*

Tommy came back to the present.

Meanwhile, Davey was saying, 'We've still got crates of ale left over from the wedding. Fancy a lager? Nice and cold, not like your warm Coke.'

Tommy nodded, wiping his brow. Sneakily, he checked his pants, pretending to check his zip. He'd kill for a cold lager. With Davey in the kitchen, Tommy looked again at the wedding photos. Carefully opening the cabinet, he chose the main photograph—happy bride and groom emerging from the church—the newly rebuilt Christ the King Catholic church. Blowing gently on the glowing ember at the end of the ciggie, he moved it towards the beaming Diana's face—shivered—remembering again.

The morning prior to the humiliation.

The school assembly hall. Full school in attendance.

Children were cross-legged on the wooden floor. Young Tommy and his classmates were near the back, and a young Davey was sitting and fidgeting nearby. A few rows ahead, Davey's sister Diana was tapping the hall floor with a wooden ruler. Tommy's little sister Patricia was nearer the front with her class.

On the stage, Mr Lord was in full flow, 'And of course, I'm delighted to pass the hearty thank you from our own dear Father English, who was delighted, absolutely delighted with the attendance at our own church yesterday. You all thankfully remembered this was one of our most special days of Holy Obligation.' The teachers and schoolchildren smiled.

'You will remember his message—'Bed-wetting is a sin!'' Teachers nodded to each other. 'Bed-wetting is wrong!' Mr Lord continued, looking sternly at the assembly. 'All remembered the special day… except maybe for the Dwyers, who turned up at the school gates yesterday as if it was a mere normal day of the week. Are they here with us at all this morning?' *Two hundred eyes swivelled and zoned in on Tommy and Patricia.*

Davey returned to the room. 'Please don't, Tommy,' he said.

Tommy had his head lowered, eyes closed, hand behind his back, hiding the photo frame. 'Don't what?'

Davey pointed at the ciggie. 'No one uses them in the house. The garden?'

'Okay, yeah.' Davey passed the chilled bottle of lager and swapped the proffered bottle with his own.

'Taste this—got lime in it.'

Tommy took a sip. 'Lime? Never had lime in lager. My god!' He sipped more, getting back into reality. 'Davey, this is good.'

Davey smiled and went back to the kitchen. Tommy quickly placed the frame back into the cabinet. The photograph was undamaged. He moved to the kitchen. Davey was pouring a half inch of lime juice into his bottle of lager. They headed out into the back garden.

The heady smell of violets and roses was abundant. Over the privets and bushes, Tommy was amazed to see the garden backed on Court Hey Park. He scanned the broad expanse of greenery… Court Hey Park, a place Tommy had always avoided.

Davey said, ‘Seeing the park outside surprises everyone coming into our garden.’

‘It’s like some weird Doctor Who Tardis thing,’ said Tommy. He headed closer to the railings at the end of the garden. Scanned, getting his bearings. ‘Corrie boozer—it’s over that way. The brook runs along that line on the far side.’

‘That’s it.’

‘You never get any hassle here? Kids pegging?’

‘What? No way… not as far as I know. My clean bills and socks are always tucked away in my room.’

‘Not your smelly bills, soft lad, they go for sexy knickers, decent jeans, things like that.’

‘Well, no, don’t think so…’

‘Never seen any big kick-offs, crews meeting here?’

‘Actually, for the past few weeks, I have seen quite a few gangs meeting up here. My bedroom overlooks it.’ Davey pointed up to his room. ‘Now I think on, there have been a lot of police patrols late at night, their headlights bounce around my bedroom walls. But, well you’ll know, since the beginning of this heatwave, all sorts going on. Muggings… and the likes of what we saw yesterday. It’s getting closer…’ Tommy nodded, greedily finishing the drink.

Davey fetched another two bottles of lager, and they squatted in the shade of a crab-apple tree. Tommy dug into his haversack. Hefted out the binoculars. He handed them to Davey.

'Be useful in my bedroom these, could see what was going on around the whole park.'

'Well, you can now.'

'I wasn't asking to borrow them…'

'And I wasn't offering, you tit. I told you I had the two sets of bins. These are yours, Davey. Half-ies mate.' Davey looked thrilled. He offered his hand, and Tommy shook it.

Another two bottles later, both were relaxed. Nearby in the park, golf balls were being whacked, dogs were chasing each other, and kids were playing. Tommy lit another cigarette.

'You said you'd been away?' asked Davey.

Tommy nodded silently. 'You know me Grandma died. Mam's mam. Lived in Walsall with Uncle Brian, the one who sends me the posters, near Birmingham. My mam was… is, in a really bad way. We only went for the funeral, but she couldn't leave. Not in the state she was in. Had to stay there with me Uncle until she got better. We were there for the whole month.'

'That's sad. But, is she okay now?'

'Not really. She doesn't say anything; she just seems to stare into space. Our Patricia's doing her best.'

'But what about your dad? Did he go with you?'

'My al fella? No. He never got on with my mam's side of the family.'

'What does he do, your dad?'

'He's in the merch'

'Sorry? The Merch?' Davey scratched his head.

'Merchant Navy. Steward on the ferries, Felixstowe to Ostend. Two weeks on, two weeks off. He's been waiting for like, forever, on a job offer from some New Zealand shipping company. Been off too much lately. He's gone on the sick.'

'Does he help with your mum?'

'He tries, but he lost his al fella—my Granddad—nine months ago. Fucked his head up.' Tommy thought back to the scene in the garden. Had he seen a ghost? He decided not to mention it. He knew he'd have trouble sleeping again that night.

'I'm sorry, Tommy. I don't know what to say… Hang on.' Davey headed back into the house, emerging five minutes later, carrying a tape player and recorder combo. He slotted a cassette inside and pressed play, setting the volume to max. The first track was Peter Sarstedt's—'Where Did You Go to My Lovely'. They settled back down, listening.

'It's hard for both of them. Thought getting my mam back home might help her come out of it. Maybe her and my al fella getting back together…'

'And has it been like that?'

'No! Worse if anything and I'm thinking it's all my fault… There was another reason I wanted to get back…'

'Linda?' Tommy nodded.

'With her going away, I thought her mam and dad had won and she'd finished with me… Frigging hell. I'm getting full of doom and gloom here!'

Davey stood, leant across and put a hand on Tommy's shoulder. Tommy nodded as the tape started playing David Cassidy's 'How Can I Be Sure'. Both tracks had a French melody. Tommy was pleased; he had always mixed emotions about David Cassidy since the first night in the Cadwa disco, dancing with Linda to the 'Get Dancing' song by Disco Tex and the Sexolettes. She'd said *all the girls think you're the spit of David Cassidy*. Bopping, clapping away, he hadn't been sure whether to take it as an insult or compliment.

Davey headed back inside to get more ale. Tommy strained to get up, wobbling.

'This heat's getting to me,' he said as he knocked back the dregs from the bottle. Davey passed another. Tommy rolled the iced chilled bottle across his face, savouring the tingling sensation on his cheeks.

'Best make these the last, hey?' said Davey with a distinct slur. It was strong German lager.

'Well, you've had my life story. Your turn now. Tell me about this camping business.'

'Been going there for the past three years now. On a farm in North Wales, a place called, well, it's spelt H.E.N.L.L.A.N., but it's pronounced Henklen, you know, local Welsh like, with the K?'

'Davey, you are a frigging linguist mate.'

Davey laughed. 'Jack, you don't know him, his dad's a cousin of the farmer—Mr Morrin. Jack's doing a course at a farming college in North Wales. He's off now for the summer. Going to be a herdsman or something. Jack's big brother and Jack is big himself, Big Eddie—you've heard of him?'

Tommy nodded. 'Yeah, heard loads of tales about him. He still knocking around, is he?'

'Not knocking around as such, he's now a top motor mechanic. The tales I know about are all true. Eddie drops us off there and picks us up. He used to stay camping on the farm when he was knocking about. He doesn't half put his foot down driving! Mr Morrin is sound. We help him do odd jobs. The first year I went, there had been a big fire on the farmhouse; some local, Mad-Dog, was involved.'

Tommy shook his head slightly. Did Davey say a mad dog had caused a fire? The heat was getting to them. 'There's a local girl, Rhonda, who works for him; Mr Morrin's stepdaughter, she's sound as well.'

'Hang on, a mad dog caused a fire?'

'Nah, some local hard case, nutter, they call him 'Mad-Dog,' had a fall out over Rhonda, tried to burn the main barn down.'

'How old is she?'

'About our age, seventeen, eighteen.'

‘She got a decent set?’

‘Nah, never looked at her that way…’

‘What other way is there? It's not so bad with little ones, but big, bouncy ones are drawn to my eyes. They stare at my eyes.’

They laughed for too long. Composing himself, Davey continued. ‘Mr Morin *showed us his shotguns* last year. That’s hard to say… Jack said he used to let Big Eddie shoot with them. There’s one story about Eddie when he was sixteen. He was camping there with his mates, and after a session in the local boozer—the Llindir Inn—they gave him this mad dare. There’s a massive cattle barn with this huge haystack inside. They used to climb halfway and jump off. They had competitions to see who could jump from the highest point. So, this night back from the boozer, they’d been arguing why it was only Eddie had been allowed to use the shotgun with Mr Morrin. The fact that the family was related was dismissed. Eddie gets pissed off and tells the other lads it’s because he’s the only one there that was not just a snotty kid. So, this other bloke says, if you’re so big and grown up, why don’t you prove it and show us how you jump down from the top of the haystack?’

‘I’ve heard this tale! The one I heard was that he jumped off this hill.’

‘It wasn’t a hill—but I’ve seen the haystack and believe me, it’s a long way from the top.’

‘Well, did he?’

‘Yep. Silently climbed to the top of the haystack and jumped all the way down.’

‘Well, was he okay?’

‘Buried him right there on the farm!’

‘Oh, piss off Davey!’ laughed Tommy, unsure.

'Course he was okay. It helps if you are six and a half feet tall, though. By taking the jump, he's shown them how much more of a man he was.'

Despite the heat and booze, Tommy thought about this. 'But, logically, he'd be the last person I'd let near a gun. I mean, if he's that frigging stupid enough to risk his neck just to show off to his dickhead mates, I mean, come on! He let Eddie shoot the gun because he was Eddie's al fella's cousin. End of story.'

Both lads laid their heads back against the tree. Davey snored gently. Yawning, Tommy looked over the garden privets to the park. 'Got to find my way around this park,' he thought, 'Ins and outs… could be a lifesaver.' He made a mental note as he sat back down next to Davey and quietly fell asleep.

That night, drunk, Tommy and Davey queued outside the Abbey cinema. After boozing and waking in Davey's garden, they'd gone to the Fiveways pub to while away the time until the eight o'clock start of the main film.

A life-sized cardboard poster of Bruce Lee in a fighting pose adorned the foyer. Tommy's scrambled brain was working overtime on schemes to rob this. If Blueface Maloney had turned up again with his crew, the only resistance Tommy and Davey could offer would be to spew all over them. They'd met Joey outside, idling innocently near a fire door exit with several of his young mates who had bummed ciggies off Tommy.

'We'll go in the stalls,' said Tommy, 'Just in case Blueface turns up again.'

Davey nodded.

Tommy spotted two of Joey Finn's mates in the queue ahead, Leo and Macca. Leo was the tallest of Joey's mates and could, on a good day with the wind on his back and the sun behind him, pass for eighteen. Macca had given lip to the ancient disabled cinema commissionaire, known fondly as Igor… The war veteran had an obvious false leg, together with a twisted spine. He was a miserable old bastard, loath to take the slightest hint of lip.

Macca produced a postcard and said loudly, 'Telegram for Mongo, telegram for Mongo…' Those in the queue who had seen the film *Blazing Saddles* laughed knowingly.

Igor was getting irate. 'You cheeky little bastard, wait till I get hold of you!' Macca was dodging attempts to snatch the postcard.

'Watch this, Davey,' slurred Tommy. 'Joey's man Macca is going to cause a dispersion.'

'What's a dis-per-tion?' asked Davey.

'Shush—just wait and see.' Davey closed an eye to focus on the proceedings. Waiting to buy their tickets were two queues. On the left were scally types waiting for the thirty-pence stall tickets. On the right-hand side, posher kids and couples were queuing for the fifty pence upstairs circle seats. A thick maroon rope link barrier separated them.

Macca, still dodging the slaps, coughed up a terrible brick of phlegm and spat into the commissionaire's face. There was an angry outcry from the women in the posher queue that circled Macca. 'Igor' wiped at the drool in fury and took out a tin whistle to summon backup.

Someone shouted, 'Pick the bones out of that!'

With a practised ease, Macca whipped the belt off his pants—the belt was a thin metal chain. He swung this first towards the women, then at 'Igor's' head, forcing him to back off. More queuers were getting animated, taking sides with Igor.

Unnoticed, the silent Leo slipped past the ticket kiosk, blending with the crowd at the 'Refreshments For You'. Eyeing the usherette as she led off a small group, he sneaked to a side door fire exit and pushed it open to allow Joey and the rest of the crew a free entrance.

Halfway through the film, a bleary-eyed Tommy woke in total disorientation.

'Where the…' blinking, he felt Davey leaning into him. A globby trail of slobber had attached from Davey's mouth to Tommy's sleeve. Davey was snoring gently. Tommy rubbed his eyes and detached himself from the drooling' Davey. He saw a man standing behind him, shaking his fist at someone in the circle above. The audience was whistling, calling for the man to sit. Tommy nudged Davey to wake him. Wiping his mouth, he looked up to see Joey Finn and his mates emptying large bags of crisps from the upstairs circle onto a furious bloke in the stalls below. People were standing and shouting. The theatre was bathed in bright chandeliered light, causing the image on the giant screen to disappear. From the corners of the theatre, there was a massive outcry.

'You heard about the kid in the stalls, watching the film with his mam?' asked Tommy.

Yawning, Davey shook his head. 'The mam says to the kid, you want a tub of ice cream, son? No thanks, says the kid, the nice man up there keeps dropping these crisps and popcorn down to me. The mam looks up and sees a leper in the circle seats above, picking his nose.'

Davey shook his head, groaning. The whole cinema was in uproar.

That night, Tommy's sleep was again disturbed. He was bouncing on the bed on top of Diana—but she became Davey, wearing a wig. As this image faded, a dull thumping, booming noise was coming from above. Where was Butch? Tommy rolled over and fumbled below the bed for the sword. Someone or something was in the attic. The bedroom window flew open gusting the curtains, which billowed around the room. A blue light entered through the window sending strange-silhouetted shadows off the walls. Sitting, wide-eyed, Tommy saw a giant head appear outside. This was not the *Wizard of Oz* and it wasn't the 'scarecrow man'. The giant head sprouted an Afro hairstyle—the one they called Blueface Maloney was at large. Reaching inside the tiny room with a giant hand, Blueface grabbed past Tommy at the headboard and pulled it towards the open window. Tommy was paralysed with fear and drenched in sweat. He called feebly, with the voice staying in his throat—'Butch…' The giant hand reached for Tommy's minute right arm and placed it gently down on the windowsill. Maloney raised a giant axe, swung and chopped off… nothing.

'What's this?' he demanded, flipping at the empty sleeve. Tommy's right arm was missing. 'That's no good for me,' said Blueface furiously as he stomped away, crushing the trees in neighbours' gardens. The blue light faded.

Bolt upright and dripping with sweat, Tommy got up and opened the window. Checked through the gardens with a sweep of the binoculars. All clear. There was an acrid smell of sweat, vomit, piss and Chinese takeaway food. Something wet and slimy was covering the floor. He checked his foot: a pungent mixture of vomit and sweet and sour food. Shaking it off both feet, he opened the door and whistled for Butch.

'Come here, fella, good boy,' he called quietly. 'Come on, there's hot din dins here for you.' The spew was still warm.

11
BUTCH AND WALES

The small bedroom was ablaze with sunshine again. Desperate for a piss, Butch risked a slap by nudging Tommy's sleeping head and licking his ears.

For Tommy, waking in the bright light was excruciating. Dehydrated and badly hungover, he smacked his dry chops, considering the awful thought that Butch had *shat* in his mouth. He slapped the dog across the head. They both urgently required a bathroom.

'Frigging hell,' he said, as he had a flashback to the Fiveways pub. Had he and Davey gone back there on the way home from the pictures? He sat and gazed at the big posters on the wall. Neither Mr Bruce Lee nor the Master looked impressed. Tommy took his watch from the floor and shaking it clean from a dangle of carrot saw that it was two thirty. He'd slept for over fifteen hours.

Out of bed and stretching, Tommy glanced at the windowsill and wondered what the hell Ken Gee's glasses were doing there. Vaguely, the memory of arranging to meet Davey, Ken and Ricey—somewhere, sometime—flitted in and out of Tommy's mind. Butch disgraced himself; he couldn't keep it in and cocked a leg up, pissing against the side of Tommy's bed. Tommy kicked him up the arse, hurting his foot more than the dog's arse.

He went to the bathroom. When he flushed, there was a loud hammering and thumping from the attic. Rather than diminish, the thumping grew louder, like heavy metal chains dragged through the pipes from the attic into the bathroom.

'Water hammer,' said Tommy. 'That's the noise Patricia has been on about.' He'd heard the noise on a lower level interrupting his dreams. 'We need a plumber. Who can afford a plumber? Need to give Uncle Darren a call.' The banging, hammering continued for a full five minutes.

'Mother,' he shouted at the top of the stairs.

No answer.

The house was empty: just Tommy, the dog and bad plumbing. Butch yelped to him pleadingly to be let out into the garden. Tommy tidied the mess of takeaway food containers, went to the kitchen to hunt for food, and let the dog out. Despite the remains of the takeaway, he couldn't remember eating the day before. His stomach knew.

The contents of the fridge were paltry: one half-empty tin of condensed milk and one broken egg. Butch, back in from the garden, was wagging his tail hopefully. The larder cupboard was also bare, except for a tired-looking box of cornflakes. The box was light and there was no milk. Still, Tommy emptied the contents into a bowl: barely a handful. As Tommy aimed a spoon, one of the cornflakes flew from the bowl and fluttered back into the cupboard. Butch cocked his head.

A corn flake-coloured moth.

Tommy looked back in the empty larder, where he once hid when they had first moved to the house when Tommy was five.

He used to sit in the dark cupboard for hours, imagining he was in a spaceship travelling to the moon or stowed on a sea ship heading for deep jungles. His travels ended abruptly one day when he felt a cockroach crawl across his hand and up into his sleeve. Somehow, the cupboard door had jammed tight and he could not kick it open. Shaking his arm wildly, screaming, he felt the walls closing. Crushing to his chest, as though underwater and unable to breathe, the cockroach entered higher into his shoulder, his neck, his mouth. He screamed 'Mother' as the door was ripped open.

'I've been looking everywhere for you, Tom!' said his mother, helping him out.

Tommy clung to her, panting for breath. 'There's a monster in there.'

Looking inside, his mother skewered the bug with a breadknife before spreading it across a piece of bread. She took a bite, offering it to Tommy, 'This is what we do to monsters.' Horrified, he ran off to hide in the garden.

He later realised his mother had bitten the buttie away from the squashed cockroach, but still…

A letter was dropped through the letterbox into the hall. Brightening at the thought of a postcard from Linda, Tommy rushed to pick it up. It was another red bill. Butch was whimpering again. Poor thing hadn't eaten since… when?

'Come on, fella, let's go and get some real din dins.'

At the shops, Tommy told Butch to sit and wait outside the Co-Op. As he walked along inside the shop, Tommy saw Butch through the window, tracking his movements from outside.

Eggs, bread, milk, sausages and bacon. Washing powder, bog rolls, tea leaves, sugar and three tins of dog meat, Tommy queued to pay at the checkout. With no one watching, he casually slipped a family pack of Juicy Fruit chewing gum into his back pocket. Whistling, he also swiped a bar of Galaxy milk chocolate, sliding this down the front of his kecks. Glancing outside the shop window, Tommy saw two elderly ladies gabbing away. Unnoticed, Butch had got his snout inside an open, tartan-coloured hand-shopping trolley. His head dipped back out holding a slab of butter in his mouth. As the women continued gabbing, Butch's tail was ecstatic as he wolfed the whole half-pound slab—paper and all. Tommy giggled to himself. Butch did love butter, and preferred it to margarine.

Back home, having scoffed a huge fry-up, Tommy was busy hand-washing his bills and socks in the kitchen sink. Next to the sink was a large dirty frying pan. The radio was on—Emperor Rosko on Radio One. Rinsing his socks through with clean water, Tommy refilled a pan of water and set it on the electric cooker for a fresh boil.

Draping the washed bits of his laundry over the wooden maiden in front of the electric fire, Tommy turned the radio onto full blast to hear 'Tiger Feet'. An open newspaper lying next to the couch caught his eye. The Liverpool Echo 'Wanted' column had been circled in pencil. 'Newly refurbished Wavertree Kennels offers top prices for all breeds of top pedigree dogs. German Shepherd and Doberman Pinschers in particular.'

On instinct, Tommy went to the electricity cupboard and checked the meter. Empty. 'Bastard—he's not selling my dog.' Tommy said out loud.

He'd had Butch for over a year since finding him as a skinny, starving pup hiding on the railway line under the Greenhills Bridge. Butch was more a mate than a pet. Whoever had let him go or not searched for him did not deserve such a dog.

At that moment, Davey and Ken were approaching the path to Tommy's house on Score Lane. Ken was wearing expensive prescription sunglasses and a white Rubettes-style cap.

'My mother would crack up if she knew I was here,' said Ken quietly. Davey shook his head.

'Say that to Tommy, and he'll knock you out.'

'Oh, come on, Davey, you saw what he was like last night—the way he ran off like a madman? And if he's got eight O-levels, I'll eat my frigging hat.'

'Tell you what, if he can prove he has got them, you agreed he can come camping with us?'

Ken shook his head. 'That was the ale talking last night, and with Ricey backing out. No way. I don't know what I'm doing here. I'll tell you what though—if he hasn't got them or can't prove it, he's not getting invited.' Davey shook his head. They opened the gate and headed up the path.

Hearing the knock on the front door caused Tommy to duck below the letterbox. Potentially, this could be the electricity man, the television licence man, the water board man, the policeman—even a policewoman. In Tommy's house, one was careful about opening one's door. Butch was not so cautious; he sniffed at the letterbox, woofed loudly. Tommy heard Davey's voice, 'Butch, go and get your dad, there's a good boy.' Tommy opened up.

Standing in the kitchen, Tommy, Davey and Butch were eating toast. Tommy had noted the palpable shudder from Ken at the offer of a sausage buttie—his body language expressing revulsion at the sight of socks and bills soaking in the sink, next to a dirty frying pan with a burnt handle hanging off it.

The snotty tit can go and whistle for his glasses, decided Tommy.

Patricia entered. 'Can I have some toast?'

'I'll do it,' said Davey. 'How many do you want?'

'Loads please, but butter to all the edges.' She looked at Ken. 'You look like a mole.'

'That's nice, thanks,' he said drolly. Davey pulled tongues at her. He spread the butter to each corner of the toast.

'There you go, Patricia.'

Smiling, Patricia took the toast and said proudly, 'I've got nits.' Tommy shooed her out of the kitchen, Ken giving her a wide berth.

There was a heavy silence. Davey picked up his plate and, as if to cover up for Ken's reticence, started wolfing the toast. Tommy sensed expectation; there was something the visitors were hesitant to ask. He folded his arms and stared at Davey.

'Tommy, you know you were saying yesterday about the O-levels?'

'What about them?' Davey looked uncomfortable. Tommy caught a glance between Davey and Ken.

'Hang on,' he said, heading upstairs.

'He'll say he can't find the certificates, I'll bet you,' whispered Ken.

'You'd better hope he's not gone to fetch his sword!'

'He's got a fucking sword?' Ken took his cap off and dabbed at sweat on his forehead. Butch was sat between them, his head turning to follow the conversation.

'He's taking all this down,' said Davey, nodding at the dog.

Butch looked up as Tommy came back into the kitchen. He passed a long cardboard tube to Ken.

'Have a look in there, you can tell your mam you've seen them.' Ken paused, took the lid off the tube and fished out two rolled-up certificates. He passed one to Davey and they both unrolled and read the details of the O-levels. As Tommy had said, there were seven from the JMB and two from the AEB—French and History.

'Bloody hell,' said Ken, picking up a piece of toast, 'You brainy bastard!'

Tommy blushed slightly. Maybe Ken wasn't such a prick after all. Davey looked at Ken, who gave a slight nod.

'Tommy, Ricey can't make it to Wales. His nan's ill. His mum and dad have taken them all down to their caravan in Southport. If Jack agrees, we were wondering if you fancy coming?'

Heading to Jack's house in Sulgrave Close, Ken was wearing his normal glasses. Butch hadn't been allowed to join them as Jack's mam had two cats.

'You did—you ran off with my glasses,' insisted Ken.

'I don't remember at all,' said Tommy.

'You were pissed as a fart!' explained Ken. 'We all were, but you were the *pissedest*. You were being the Master in Kung Fu, snatched them off me and legged away saying, 'When you can see without sight, it is time for you to leave, grasshopper…''

Tommy and Davey laughed at the decent impression.

'I'm sorry, Ken, I can't remember.'

The invite to the camping holiday had lifted Tommy. Ken was becoming less of a prick, and Davey was as sound as a pound. He didn't know much about Jack as yet. The week away would more than close the gap until Linda came back. There was also the vague mention of a young Welsh maid who worked at the farm—Rhonda. Rhonda to ponder! He'd heard plenty of urban myths about farmers inviting strangers to share beds with their women folk. The pleasant images were halted for a moment on practicalities.

'Just thought, I haven't got a sleeping bag or any camping gear. And how much money are you two taking?'

Dave and Ken thought.

Ken offered, 'Don't worry, I'll lend you a sleeping bag. I had to leave one at the farm last year.' Tommy shuddered—remembering what Davey had told him about Ken's sleeping bag.

Davey said, 'Need at least a tenner. Say a quid a day for ale and it's three quid each for Jack's brother and…'

'Three squid each! Frigging hell, is he driving us there on the Orient Express or something? That's twelve squid. We could buy ourselves a bastard car. Probably costs him what a squid there, a squid back—that's a total rip off. Why not jump a train?' Ken exchanged a knowing look with Davey.

'That's what we've always paid. And don't forget, we don't even pay Mr Morrin the farmer. So, we're sort of getting a free holiday,' Ken explained. 'Plus, the locals see us coming into the village with him. Not that it's rough like it is in new Childwall, but there's enough of them, and because Big Eddie's been going there for years, plus look at the size of him, it gives us protection. They don't bother us.'

Tommy could see the logic. He ran a quick mental check on how much cash he had left. He was certain it was less than a tenner. 'But have you ever offered him less?' Ken said, 'Well put it this way, if Jack agrees to you going, are you going to be the one to tell Big Eddie to take a cut in his lift money?'

Tommy didn't answer.

Outside the house in Sulgrave Close, Tommy saw the paved front garden was littered with dozens of ancient and rusting car engine parts.

Jack's tiny mother opened the front door and shouted upstairs, 'Jack, it's Davey and Ken and no Ricey. Do I know you, son?'

'No, Mrs Douglas. My name's Tommy Dwyer.'

'Ooh—like that the nursery rhyme—peed in the fire.' Tommy turned crimson. 'No need to be shy here, son; none of us get a say in what we're called. Unless you're Lulu or Twiggy… I think it's a lovely name. Here he is now, coming down to watch Top of The Pops, weren't you, lad?'

'Weren't I what?' asked Jack, stepping off the stairs and into the minute hallway. He towered over his mother at a good six feet two inches.

'You big boots, watching Top of The Pops. Just telling your mates here: Davey, Ken and Tony.' Jack nodded hello.

'All right, Tony?' he asked.

'Actually, it's Tommy—not Tony.'

'Ooh—what am I like?' said Jack's mam. They filled the seats in front of the television (apart from one seat left conspicuously reserved). For Tommy, seeing the show in full colour was still a pleasant novelty. Jimmy Saville was wearing a lurid pink tracksuit draped with several attractive young girls. Saville leered at them theatrically.

Watching Leo Sayer sing 'When I Need You,' Tommy felt a pang of loneliness. Despite sitting in the same room as four other people, Tommy was isolated—an emotional distance within himself. Christ, he missed Linda. If he had the means, he would have left then to fly off to Gay Paree—even to spend a few moments with her. Mrs Douglas broke the spell.

'You watch lads. Our Eddie will walk through that door just in time for them dancing girls.' She spoke as Jimmy Saville introduced Pam's People, dancing to 'If You Leave Me Now' by Chicago. They heard a car screech into the driveway. The front door flew open, and a long-haired and bearded Big Eddie entered. He nodded briefly to the lads, even the stranger Tommy got a nod before Eddie plonked himself down on his seat nearest the telly.

'Told you,' cackled his mother. Eddie was one hundred per cent focused on the dancing girls. Tommy estimated his boot size as a fourteen. Tommy took a size eight.

Later, in Jack's bedroom, Tommy realised Jack was a man of few words. Asked if he minded Tommy going camping with them in Ricey's absence, he shrugged. At eighteen, older than the others, the time he'd spent as a herdsman had made him comfortable with silent gaps. In The Master's terms, Jack was at one with himself. Ken was discussing arrangements, taking charge of timings and the supply of kit.

Tommy's mind drifted to Linda, and worried at a suspicion that the camping trip, instead of helping pass the time, may somehow prolong it.

Interrupting these thoughts, Tommy detected a growing stink. No one had farted out loud; the smell was definitely a body odour. Glancing around for the culprit, he saw that the others had stopped talking and were staring at him. The smell grew worse, filling the room.

'Don't look at me,' he said, 'I haven't shit.'

There was a pause, before the other three lads laughed.

'What the fuck's going on?'

Ken was almost pissing himself. Jack motioned for Davey to show something to Tommy. At the top of the stairs, the smell had grown more putrid. Holding his nose, his chest heaving with silent laughter, Davey pointed downstairs to the hallway. Near the front door was a pair of steaming boots—Eddie's size fourteens. A minging smell was rising above them. Mrs Douglas opened the living room and started cackling at Tommy's expression. Barefooted, Big Eddie emerged from the kitchen to check what the fuss was about.

'Two days,' he said to Davey. Davey looked back blankly. 'Our kid not tell you?'

'Err, no—tell us what?'

'Day after tomorrow—all here for two o'clock. If no one's here at two—tough. I drive out of that path at five past. I won't have the car on Saturday—other plans. There's only the day after tomorrow I can drop you off, and only next Thursday I can pick you up. Is that Tony lad going instead of Ricey?'

Heading up his path in the darkness, Tommy burped. The home brew he'd drunk, courtesy of Jack's farming know-how, caused him to stagger home. A local beat patrol policeman had shouted over the road, 'Everything okay, Sir? I see that you are staggering.'

Tommy had replied, 'Not bad looking yourself, mate…'

Fumbling for the house key, Tommy was keen to get indoors, maybe to throw up and check how much money he had left. Struggling with the key, he realised the door was bolted from the inside. Peeking through the letterbox, he saw his mother shooing Butch through the kitchen and into the back garden, closing and locking the back door.

'What's going on?' he said as his mother opened the door. In the living room, the black and white TV set was showing a Tom O'Connor comedy programme. The volume was off. His mother offered him a ciggie. In normal times, she would moan at him to pack in. Tommy deliberately avoided mentioning Butch.

'There's some bad news,' she said.

'What's wrong?'

'It's Butch. He had to go. Someone knocked on the door tonight and said he knew you'd found a dog a while ago. And it belonged to him.'

'Oh?'

'Yeah, they had photographs of him as a small pup and stuff…'

'Right, so some stranger knocks on the door and says, 'you've got my dog that I lost over twelve months ago, and that I've been searching for since, and here's a photo that will look nothing like the way he looks now…"

'I don't know! It was your father who spoke to him.'

'So, you're saying Butch has gone?'

His mother nodded rapidly.

'Ah well,' said Tommy nonchalantly, picking up the Liverpool Echo and reading the back pages. His mother was staring intently at him, both feet tapping at the carpet. Waiting for some reaction. He crossed his legs and patted at a cushion on the couch. He eyed his mother getting agitated, and was about to end the game, when, frenzied, she leapt up ripping the newspaper out of his hands.

She screamed, 'You couldn't care, could you, when something is taken from you—could you—could you!'

Tommy stared back. He understood this was meant as a gesture, albeit cock-eyed, to shield her son in preparation of the pain of losing something precious. Nothing had prepared her for the rending loss of her mother, which Tommy knew.

He held her close to him as she sobbed. When was this going to end?

Upstairs, patting Butch on the head, Tommy put the Beatles *Revolver* album onto the record player turntable. He listened to 'Eleanor Rigby'. Door wedged, Tommy said, 'There's no frigging way he's selling you mate.' Butch stared at him. 'I know, you'd be the King-Stud-Dog—you dirty bastard! But I like you…'

Tipping the contents of his pillowcase onto the bed, he was shocked at how little money remained. Three-pound notes and thirty pence in loose change. Enough to pay Big Eddie for the trip and ale money and ciggies for one day. Just great. Tommy emptied his mind and tried to focus on a neutral spot on the wall. *Where do I get more money?* School raiding was out—too many street patrols. Barely a moment into the half-drunken trance, the image of the saxophone entered his mind. It was a bastard of a thing to play anyway.

Yep, Suggoski would be getting a visit in the morrow—it was *Carry on Camping* time!

12
YOU SAY REVOLUTION

'This is some bastard summer!' Tommy said to Butch on the way to the shops to search for Joey. The saxophone was in the haversack. He saw his sister Patricia outside of Jake's, playing with a couple of girls.

'Been looking for you.' He handed over a ten-pence piece. 'Get yourself a lolly ice.' The other girls were eyeing him hopefully. He dug into his pocket and fished another two ten-pence pieces. 'And get your mates one too. 'Funny Faces'—it suits you.' The girls were delighted and headed into Jake's shop.

'Ah, thanks Tommy. I need one. Can I take Butch home? I hate being in the house.'

'The noise is from the plumbing, needs something doing with the water pressure.'

'It's not only the noise,' Patricia said quietly. She nodded away from the shops and Tommy followed her to the alleyway behind Jake's newsagents. 'I'm thinking our mam should go back to Uncle Brian's. She's not right, and me dad's no use with her.'

'I know.' Tommy was guilty. 'If it gets too bad, knock next door to Rene. I'm putting the electricity back on the fix, so be careful opening the front door. And listen… I'm going away tomorrow.'

'You've been caught?'

'No, not the police. Away camping with Davey and the lads.'

'Well, how long for? Where are you going?'

'It's only for a week. Farm in North Wales. Not that far away. Will you feed Butch and look after him for me? I'd take him with me if I could. Hide him if you can from me dad. I think he's trying to sell him.' Patricia nodded. 'Thanks. I'll bring him home soon to finish packing. While I'm away, he's your dog for the whole week.' Patricia perked up. 'And listen, stay away from the Greenhills and don't go near the Childwall swing park—there's been murder there.' Tommy was angry having to warn his sister.

'I know, we were all talking about it. Mad-Mick has been locked up now.'

'Well, that's good news, I suppose.' Patricia's mates had followed them to the alley and were peeling the wrappers off the Funny Faces lolly-ices.

One of the girls, older and taller than the rest, pretty and serious Julie Moorcroft, handed over a piece of paper, 'Here's the receipt. You might need this...' Tommy smiled, folded it carefully, putting it into his pocket.

Outside the launderette, a horde of pensioners was gawping at customers inside, looking in through the big window. Joey was sitting on his wall, gawping as well. Tommy recognised one of the old ladies by her tartan shopping trolley. Butch was itching to get his snout inside it again.

She was asking her companion, 'Do you think it's a revolution they're after—like in the Beatles song?'

Two kids, passing on their orange Chopper bikes, stopped to join the crowd. One had a Raw Power sound box attached to the bike's handlebars. He revved, making his pushbike sound like a small motorbike. Joey jumped off the wall to have a go, to the annoyance of the crowd. He spotted Tommy.

'You seen this, Tommy—have a go, lar!' The sound was getting on Tommy's nerves.

Ignoring Joey, he said to the young lad on the bike, 'Hey kid, do one, will you?'

'Why?'

'Cos I said so.'

'No, why should we?' The kid was staring back in defiance. The other kid on the bike, eyeing Butch, was backing away. Joey gave the sound box an almighty rev. The gawping crowd of pensioners had turned their attention from the launderette window.

Tommy got right into the kid's face, 'I'm telling you why, lad, cos if you don't get the hell out of my sight, right now, I'm going to rip that bastard noise off that posing piece of shit and stick it right up your arse…'

The defiant kid looked around, fearful. Wisely, Joey had stopped revving.

'He's Tommy Dwyer,' said Joey quietly.

Both kids backtracked, turned, and cycled away at speed. They didn't look back. Interval over, the pensioners went back to the window.

'What's going on here?' asked Tommy. He hated spoilt brats.

'It's them weirdoes who've moved into Francis Way. Students, I think.'

An old woman with long grey whiskers on her chin said to an even older, balding woman, 'I think it's devil worship… They shouldn't be allowed to use the machines in there. Should be a law against it.'

'I think it's disgusting,' said the balding woman.

'We could get a petition,' suggested an old man who, despite the heat, wore a heavy overcoat, scarf, gloves and a cap. There were murmurs of approval. He pointed a wavering walking stick at the window. 'I'll be the first to sign it! And they'll know about it.'

Tommy shook his head. 'Hey mate, aren't you too hot in them clothes?' Joey waved at Tommy—warning him not to engage with the old man. Too late.

‘Hot lad?’ he said. ‘You call this hot? When I was out there in the Burmese, fighting them Japanese in the jungle and the swamps—that’s what you’d call hot, lad, that was heat. Who do you think I was fighting for, eh? I’ll tell you who—I was fighting for King and Country. I’ll also tell you, lad, what I wasn’t fighting for—I wasn’t fighting in the jungle for this country so that the likes of them lot could come here and use our launderettes!’ The crowd again murmured their approval.

‘Well said, Jimmy,’ said the bearded lady.

‘That’s right,’ agreed the balding one. Tommy saw for the first time what everyone else had been gawping at.

Four punk rockers were folding laundered bedsheets. It was hard to determine who was male or female: two had dark green Mohican hair designs—parrot-like—and the other two sported bright orange Coco the Clown-style hairdos. All were dressed in black PVC with facial piercings and metal paper clips. They all wore white face makeup. They must have known the crowd outside was staring, but they continued folding in silent pantomime.

Tommy gestured at Joey to follow him away to the Greenhills.

‘They’re students from Japan, you know.’ Joey said to the retired soldier, causing him to bristle—waving his stick in the air, demanding someone phone the police.

Tommy and Joey walked away from the group of elderly people. When they reached the bottom of the Greenhills, Joey warned Tommy not to talk to Jimmy, the Unknown Soldier. Joey recounted an incident where he was stuck listening to Jimmy's stories until he managed to escape over a wall.

‘I’ll remember that next time I don’t want to hear war stories.’

‘Can I ask you something, Tommy?’

‘Go ed…’

'You've lived round here for years, but sometimes you'd think that you don't know what's going on. Not being funny, Tommy, but do you know what I mean?'

'Yeah, it's okay. I think that meself sometimes. It's just, mostly, I don't want to bother anyone—if I leave everyone else alone, they'll leave me alone. You know, like the Scarlet.'

'Captain Scarlet and the Mysterons, I loved that!'

'Not Captain Scarlet—you tit. The Scarlet Pimpernel—you see him here, you see him there…'

'Hmm,' said Joey. He picked a crusty scab behind his ear. 'Furry muff, none of my business.'

'Anyway, listen. I want you to go and see Suggoski again, now.'

'I can't'

'Why not?'

'He's not in. He works at his Dad's shop on Wednesday, which used to be Scully's old Emporium. I told you this the other day,' Joey said, eyeing the haversack. 'You could always go to the shop, deal with his old man,' Joey said slyly. Tommy knew Joey was aware he couldn't make a legitimate sale. He shook his head, feeling his temper flaring again.

'What have you got now?' asked Joey.

'Never mind. Are you sure you'll be able to see him tomorrow? It's important I get the money by tomorrow at the latest.'

'Taking your bird for a good time, hey?'

'No… What is the fascination you've got with my bird, hey Joey?'

Joey could see Tommy was getting pissed off. 'No problem Tommy, don't take any notice of me mate.'

'I don't.'

'Well, that's okay. Look, I'll see you here at the same time tomorrow—one o'clock, we'll go and see Suggoski?'

Tommy nodded, and headed back home with his head down. Outside the house, he was cheered at the sight of his Uncle Darren's van.

Darren was washing his hands in the bathroom sink. A toolkit was underneath the attic door. Winking 'hello' to Tommy, he flushed the toilet, and they stood listening… all clear, water hammer sorted.

'I don't suppose you've got a ghost fix in that toolkit,' asked Tommy.

'What?'

'Just that, the other day, I thought I saw something in the garden. I thought it was me al fella at first, but it, well, I thought it was me granddad…'

'My dad, who we buried nine months ago?'

'My mam called him Michael.'

'I think the heat's getting to you, son,' said Darren sadly.

'I know, but with me mam saying it—she definitely called him Michael.'

Darren reached across and put an arm on Tommy's shoulder. 'We've all been though a bad year, son. Maybe you more than most, with losing two grandparents. Have you ever thought of speaking to a priest about it? It helped me. I can take you now to see my parish priest if you want?'

'No thanks,' said Tommy. 'I'll deal with it…'

13

MY PAL JOEY

At one o'clock the next day, Tommy opened the haversack and showed the saxophone to Joey.

Snatching it, Joey examined the instrument in detail. 'Ah, Tommy, I want this for meself. Haven't got much, maybe two squid, but I could give you say, a quid a week?' He was almost pleading as Tommy shook his head.

'I would if I could Joey, but I need the money today, mate.'

'Not for me—for my al fella.'

'Your al fella's in nick!'

'I know, but I could take this into him. He told me he used to play one of these in a skittle band years ago, when he was a kid. He'd be made up! Please, Tommy, sell it to me?'

Tommy considered. 'No. I know for a fact you'd be blowing it on your wall—you wouldn't be able to help yourself. See what you were doing with that kid's bike and the Raw Power thing yesterday? See what you did with the bugle? If you can make noise, make someone hear you, you will, and you do. And as for giving it to your al fella, he's not a Redcoat in Butlins holiday camp, is he?' He knew he was being harsh. Maybe it was the mood he'd woken with; he kept waking to thunder and the rattle of the water hammer, but he was determined to explain harsh truths. Besides, he needed the cash. He was due at Jack's at two o'clock—in one hour. He hadn't fully packed.

'A nick that's full of bizzies coming and going. Where do you tell them you got this, cos they will ask? Tell them it's from savings on Green Shield stamps? It's frigging stolen goods—you know that. Recently stolen. Again, you've got to tell Suggoski he can't sell this to any schoolmates.' Joey reluctantly placed the sax back in the bag.

'A quarter is yours,' said Tommy to brighten the mood.

Negotiations were short and sweet. Staring down the path, Tommy wondered if Suggoski ever took the yarmulke off his head. Back down the path, Joey was smiling.

'Twelve squid! That's eight for you and four for me,' said Joey, holding the crisp tenner up to the light as if checking it hadn't been newly printed. They both heard a noise like a gunshot and ducked, then a car engine revved on the busy road.

'Give me that. Here's your three quid. Don't try to be acting soft with me—I said a quarter, not a third you cheeky little bastard. Don't they teach you anything in school?' The heavy car revving was getting closer.

'Me, in school? They seek Joey here, they seek Joey there, they seek the Joey Finn-Pernel…' before he could finish, a car screeched to a stop in front of them and reversed back onto the kerb, blocking their path.

Tommy's first thoughts were, *bizzies—I'm fucked.* His second thought was, *I'm okay. Poor Joey is fucked.* Chris Lawler was getting out of the battered car, followed by a smiling Nobby and Sean Duncan.

Driving cars now, thought Tommy. *They've evolved.*

Joey had dashed, but was tripped by Butch's outstretched leash—Butch was frantically trying to tear away and run at the car. Nobby raced forward and kicked Joey full force in the head. Butch strained again in the other direction, growling—ready to pounce on Nobby.

'You best get that wolf under control,' said Chris Lawler. A knife dropped down from his sleeve into his palm. He flicked it open, and a six-inch blade shot out. 'You're not dealing with a stinking hobo this time, Dwyer. How many have you killed so far?'

‘Not so many you’d notice. Some carry bigger knives,’ said Tommy. Both teenagers squared off, staring at each other. Sean Duncan moved closer and stood between them.

‘Got him for us, hey, Tommy lar?’ he said. ‘Best not do this here, hey?’ He opened his arms and gestured at the busy traffic that was already slowing as drivers looked to see what was going on. ‘Best stick to the plan.’

Sean opened the boot of the ancient Ford Zephyr and Nobby dragged Joey off the ground by the scruff of the neck. Tommy saw the curtains move in Suggoski’s front room, and for the first time in his life, wished someone would summon the police.

Between them, Nobby and Sean heaved Joey up rag like and brutally into the boot, slamming it shut.

‘He was giving you money,’ said Chris. Tommy gently crushed the tenner in his palm and pulled Butch towards him, grabbing his collar and fingering the note inside of it. He produced the lolly-ice receipt from his pocket, ripping it into small pieces.

‘Tried to sell me a dodgy pound note.’

Chris watched the paper drifting away with one gozzy eye, the better one still on Tommy. ‘Get in the car, Dwyer,’ he said. ‘You’re coming with us.’

‘We’re taking him to ker-ker-Crosby beach,’ said Nobby. ‘Got a ter-ter-tow rope, gonna…’

‘We’re gonna lash him to the back of the car and towrope the bastard around the beach,’ said Sean.

‘You with us, or you with this prick?’ asked Chris, pointing to the car boot.

Tommy had to think quickly—no time for meditation bullshit. He wasn’t in danger. His sword would help.

‘What do you think? Can’t stand the cheeky little bastard. Been trying to rip me off.’ Tommy felt guilty relief that he had taken the tenner off Joey. 'Think—quickly,' his mind racing. 'Let's come with you? I'll ditch the dog.'

Chris stared back hard and slyly at Tommy.

'He robbed my ber-ber-bins,' said Nobby accusingly. 'I want them back.'

'You still on Score Lane?' asked Sean. Tommy nodded. 'It's only around the corner. We don't want to be sitting in the car next to that anyway. They go mad in the heat, Alsatians.' Butch was still growling, heckles firmly up.

Chris Lawler stared at Tommy thoughtfully, as if trying to come to some decision.

'We were going to do old stinky ourselves. You saved us the bother.'

'A man's gotta do what a man's gotta do,' said Tommy. They continued to stare at each other. An apelike intelligence shone in Chris's eyes. He turned.

'Ditch the fucking wolf, straight back out of your house—no fannying around. We've got to pick the birds up as well.'

'We're gonna finger their fannies on the beach,' said Nobby.

Tommy grabbed Butch's collar tightly and moved quickly up the Valley Road to Score Lane. His mind was racing with options… Knock next door and ring the police—that was plan A. Plan B was fetching his sword and forcing them to release Joey. Turning the corner onto Score Lane, he saw the battered Zephyr drive ahead, parking outside his house… He settled on plan B—the sword.

Patricia was skipping with her mates on the path. The postman was at the front door, handing a telegram to his dad. Tommy waved a hand to the car. 'Only be a minute,' he said; a minute to get Patricia in the house, his al fella out the way, and quickly upstairs to fetch the sword. He saw this in his mind's eye. No other options. He looked at his hand still raised in the wave. There were no tremors.

At the front door, Tommy's dad was reading the telegram.

'It's come through,' he said excitedly to Tommy.

Tommy ignored this. He said quietly, 'Patricia, get in now and take your mates into the back garden. They've got Joey Finn in the boot of the car—I need to help him. Right now.'

Shall I tell me dad? Tommy stared at his al fella—plan C? *No, this could get worse, better getting them all inside, out of the way.*

'Tommy!' his dad waved the telegram. He headed into the hall. 'Carol, Patricia, baby, it's come through. We can all move!'

Ignoring whatever the hell his al fella was talking about, Tommy ran upstairs and into his bedroom. Reaching under the bed, he dragged the samurai sword out of the sheath and took a deep breath—as a car screeched outside the house. Police sirens. Another car braked to a halt outside.

He heard his dad shout, 'They can't take me away today, not today, not when it's just come through!' Tommy slid the sword back under the bed.

From the front bedroom window, Tommy saw there were three police cars outside the house with over half a dozen truncheon-wielding policemen dragging Chris Lawler, Nobby and Sean Duncan from the Zephyr.

This was not a good time to talk to the police or tell Joey his good intentions. The car for Wales was leaving within the next half an hour. Time to slip away silently over the back gardens and head for Jack's house.

Bag in hand, Tommy headed downstairs. It looked like the whole street was out to witness the proceedings. It was safe enough to go out the front way. Tommy's dad was saying, mainly to himself, 'I thought they'd come for me...' He saw

Tommy. 'Is this anything to do with you? I hope not, lad, because we are all going away.'

'I am going right now,'

'But we're not going right now. It'll take a couple of weeks for the tickets.'

'What are you talking about?'

'It's come through, the job in New Zealand. We're all moving to Queenstown.'

'I'm not.'

'Well, why have you packed?'

'I'm going camping right now, to North Wales.'

14
SUMMER HOLIDAY

By the time Tommy reached Jack's house, the sweat was pumping out. Tommy raised a hand and saw it was shaking. Aftershock. Kidnapping, sword rescue and now Queenstown, New Zealand… What the hell!

Davey, Ken, and Jack were loading camping gear into Eddie's zoomed-up Cortina's boot and roof.

The journey from Liverpool to Henllan (the lads pronounced this Henkly) flew by for Tommy, with the sound of the Moody Blues cassette LP—*In Search of the Lost Chord* blasting throughout the car. The volume rendered Tommy's mind to stall on the day's events.

It was one and a half hours later. The final ten minutes involved the horn beeping almost continuously to warn away sheep in the blind, tight country lane bends. Eddie had pulled up outside the thirteenth-century, thatched boozer. It was the oldest in Wales—the Llindir inn. Tommy imagined the inn and grounds a hundred years ago—tinged in sepia—it had a palpably ancient history.

Getting out of the car, stretching to his full height, Eddie pointed at Tommy. 'Last to arrive, you're getting them in. I'll have a pint of best Bass…' Tommy hesitated, pulled back from his reverie, and checked his pockets. Davey saw this and handed over a fresh prescription—proof of age ID form.

'I always carry a spare on holiday. Obviously, it's in my name.'

'Thanks, Davey.' Tommy saw a battered old Morris Minor, which had pulled into the grounds, before reversing quickly back onto the lane away from the inn. He glimpsed four young men in the car. The driver had a long thin nose.

Inside, for Tommy, the boozer looked like something from an adaptation of a Dickens novel. Stepping from bright sunshine into the shadowed bar played tricks on his sight—was like stepping out of the techno-colour of Oz back into the black and white of Kansas. Farmers, capped and smoking pipes, filled the room with their heady shag and lyrical accents. There was a large, inglenook fireplace. No jukebox, yet music was being underplayed from somewhere. Ella Fitzgerald—'Summertime'. Tommy sensed a mood change, like the needle had scratched across a record—conversations switched from the laidback universal pub drawl into a loud, hostile Welsh.

'Well, screw you all—Yakky Da, or whatever,' said Tommy, quietly. He felt uncomfortable with stares from so many unfriendly faces. He urgently needed a piss.

Inside the gents, Ken was already at the urinal, shoulders bouncing, blowing his nose on toilet paper, laughing to himself at the same time.

'What's up with you?' Ken pointed to the cubicle.

Tommy finished his piss and entered the cubicle. Daubed in blue marker pen, someone had written, 'Here I sat, broken hearted, paid a penny, but only farted.' Below, in someone else's writing, was scrawled, 'It's no use standing on the seat; the crabs in here jump six feet. If you think this is high, go in the Ladies where the bastards fly.' The best was written lower—from a seated viewpoint. 'How does the Queen's corgi Wan Wan address the bitch Wun Wun when he wants to give her one? Answer equals Wan Wan would like to give Wun Wun one…' Tommy had to laugh.

He approached the bar. 'Pint of Bass and three pints of lager, please.' The landlord (it had to be the landlord—the man exuded authority) turned his mutton-chopped and bushy white-haired dome and stared at Tommy.

'Proof of age, date of birth,' he said. As Tommy produced the homemade ID, Ken, Jack and Davey shuffled behind him at the bar.

'We're with Big Eddie,' said Ken, still wiping at his nose. The landlord stared hard at Jack, nodded and started to pull pints into heavy, dimpled glass jugs.

Big Eddie entered the bar, and the atmosphere immediately changed as the regular customers relaxed.

The landlord opened his arms, 'Edward—look at you!'

Big Eddie gave him thumbs up. The pints were pulled and paid for, and the landlord hustled Eddie off to meet with the locals.

Davey was looking at a poster near the fireplace. 'Sunday night Church Disco—are you ready and humble? All welcome. DJ Keith Piperello.' Tommy knocked back half his pint in one swig.

'You okay?' asked Davey. Tommy nodded, staring at another poster on the wall—'Professional Guide to White Woman Ghost of the Llindir inn—lost soul or Siren?'

A tall, tanned, blonde-haired girl with undiscovered film star looks approached, collecting used glasses and emptying ashtrays into a small wooden box.

'Rhonda!' said Davey. 'You working here now—what's happened with the job on the farm with your Dad?'

'So, you're back… How long is this time? Is it a week?'

'Hey Rhonda,' said Ken, delighted, staring in admiration. 'You've grown up.' Rhonda put the box down on a table, blushed and straightened her dress.

'Turned eighteen in May. Good to see you all. But who is this?' She stared at Tommy.

'Our new mate, Tommy,' said Ken. 'You not working at the farm anymore?'

'Prefer it here, and the hours are better. I do miss working with my… Mr Morrin, though. I don't see him as much, but I actually get to have a lie-in in the mornings. You are thirsty!'

Tommy had swigged off the rest of his pint. 'Why does everyone call this bloke 'Mister' Morrin? Like, why don't you call him me dad, or me al fella like everyone else? Doesn't he have a first name?'

'Well, he is Mr Morrin—our biggest farmer. More so than just my dad. What don't you like about that?' The mild Welsh drawl from Rhonda was pleasant to Tommy. She wore a gentle fragrance Tommy couldn't put a name to—floral, earthy, feminine.

The inn door opened, and the brief sunshine cast Rhonda in a dazzling gold. The Welsh babbling nearby segued into a pleasant Welsh Scouse dialect, and Tommy saw in Rhonda the image of a taller, riper, blonder, Welsher, green-eyed Linda. The background 'Summertime' music spiralled.

'Are you going to the disco on Sunday night?' asked Davey, interrupting the moment. He was pointing to the poster.

'That depends now,' said Rhonda. 'Depending as how busy we are in here, see. Of course, I'd prefer working this bar than going to a Keith Piperello disco,' she said, smiling.

'Come on, Rhonda, you know you want to dance with me,' said Davey, wearing his sunniest smile. Rhonda put the pots and box onto a nearby table. She placed a hand on Davey's shoulder but turned her head to Tommy.

'Of course, how could I miss a dance with you?'

Back in the car, heading past an old mill outside Mr Morrin's farm. Ken said in a petulant tone, 'Bloody state of you two. The Jason King twins!' Jack and Eddie laughed.

'Shut it, you tit,' said Tommy and Davey together as the car pulled up at the farm and the field that would be the campsite for a week—a holiday, home from home.

Car unloaded, Jack and Ken took charge of setting up the tent. Tommy watched as Eddie drove the hundred yards to the farmhouse—beeped outside. Within seconds, two large Labrador dogs—golden and black—raced outside barking happily, followed by a tall, swarthy man in his forties dressed like a clichéd country gentleman in tweeds and leather wellingtons.

'That's Mr Morrin,' said Davey. 'He owns all the land.'

'I believe so,' said Tommy.

'Shall we go now and say hello?' asked Ken.

'Hang on, guys. You two sort out the pegs, get them in position,' said Jack, as he strolled in a circle around the tent, digging his heels in to mark the spots for the pegging and main guide ropes.

'Job number one. Get them pegs sorted, then get a brew going. Use the tins.' He stopped. Looked around. Walked near the hedgerows at the farm entrance. 'Dig a hole here for shitting in. Number two, if the main barn toilet isn't available.'

'What about a wanking hole?' said Ken, shoving his glasses higher up his nose.

'Make do with the usual fingers and sleeping bag,' said Jack, with a hint of a Welsh accent. 'Check the batteries for the radio. Essential.'

'Who's voted him in charge?' Tommy quietly asked Davey.

'Best get it done. You really don't want to piss him off.' Tommy shook his head, but followed orders.

Ken was fussing with the radio. Tuning in—zoning on a decent signal. Music was heard—Tony Orlando and Dawn—'Tie a Yellow Ribbon', Ken piped up, joining in, 'Oh, Tie a yellow Johnnie around the old bog door…' He could hold a tune. All the lads were amused.

Tommy was glad to see there were no scarecrows around the farm.

He glanced at a field adjacent to the camp, roughly the size of a football pitch. A single black horse was gazing over the perimeter wall onto the lane outside, as if expecting a visitor. Tommy walked out into the lane to look closer.

The horse's coat was black, no white markings of any kind. It had a long, thick mane and tail, with long, untrimmed silky hair on the lower legs that signalled the animal had aged beyond maturity. It stood a few inches higher than Tommy at six feet. Although there was a distinct presence and elegance about the horse, there was also something imperceptibly not right. Tommy raised a hand to stroke the horse's forehead, but almost aggressively, the head bobbed in a 'don't touch me' gesture. Tommy saw the ears had flattened backwards and the nostrils had extended. He took a step backwards.

'Whoa, Stingray. Steady, steady…' It was Davey. He clicked with his tongue reassuringly. The horse's head swivelled at the name. Both ears were standing back up, albeit floppily. 'This is Rhonda's old horse. It takes a while for him to get to know you.' He raised a hand slowly, allowing the horse, Stingray, to take a sniff of his fingers before gently stroking both sides of the black cheeks. 'He's a Friesian, an old one.'

'How long do horses live?'

'Not sure, about twenty years? Jack will know. Stingray has got some illness. Surprised he's still about. What's that actor's name, in the vampire films?' Davey clicked his fingers.

'So this one's going to be dog meat soon?'

'They don't do that anymore.' Davey was still clicking his fingers.

'Don't do what?'

'Dead horses, they don't put them in dog meat. It was banned, years ago.'

'Bet the French were made up, more horsemeat for them... Christopher Lee, is that who you're thinking of?'

'Nearly. The other fella usually with him... Cushing, Peter Cushing!'

'Davey, what are you talking about?'

'The disease—Stingray has got Cushing's disease.' Tommy took a step further from the horse.

Tent set up, bedding in order, Davey passed tins of tea. Eddie's car had left the farm without a goodbye wave or beep, and Mr Morrin was strolling across the field towards them, the two dogs racing ahead. Both headed directly to Tommy, where they began a frantic sniffing.

'His name's Butch,' said Tommy. As though satisfied with the scent, the dogs took station at each side of Mr Morrin.

'Aye lads, Jack, Davey and Kenneth Gee, isn't it? I heard Ricey's family is suffering? Please pass on my regards. And this dangerous looking type—army desertion, is it? Couldn't take to the harsh discipline of basic training, hey?' Tommy shook his head. Linda's al fella had said something similar at their first introductions.

'This is Tommy, Mr Morrin—Tommy Dwyer,' said Davey.

'Tommy Dwyer, is it? Will I need to look to my chicken wire, make sure no bales on fire with you staying here, Mr Dwyer?'

Tommy shifted uneasily on both feet. Jack started to laugh quietly, Davey and Ken joining.

'Welcome all,' said Mr Morrin—extending a hand to Tommy, who shook it slowly.

'Mr Morrin, how old is Stingray now?' asked Davey.

'Older than he should be, if truth be told. And you've reminded me, Davey, I need to speak to Ramshaw's, first thing in the morning. I've been putting it off for the past few weeks... Pains me to see him in that state, standing there staring all day long. Should have been put out of his misery a long time ago…' He shook his head. 'Get yourselves sorted, lads, then over to the house for fresh eggs and cooked meat for you. No smoking in the barn, mind. Joking aside, I'm over-conscious of a fire risk.' He said this to Tommy. 'Bring your thinking heads along too. Some rain if you can drum it up. God knows this summer has been here for long enough and my fields are as dry as a tit on a bull. Got a new theory I'd like to run by you city people.'

'Like last year's with the 'most supreme being on earth?'' asked Ken.

Mr Morrin turned to him. 'You thought of anything better?'

'No,' said Ken smiling, 'I still think it's us—humans.'

'Well, as I said last year, if you can fly over to Africa for the winter and fly back here for our summer, I'll agree with you.'

'But I can—I can get the airline tickets…'

'We've had this all before,' said Jack. 'Give it a rest Ken, we all outvoted you and agreed with Mr Morrin. Nothing's changed.'

'…Supreme, look you,' interrupted Mr Morrin.

'The most supreme beings on Earth. Jack reckoned it's a virus, Ken and Ricey and me said it had to be mankind, but after thinking about it, we ended up agreeing on birds.'

'There'd be no life on earth if there was no birds,' said Tommy. Mr Morrin passed him a sly look of approval.

'He'll do,' he said, before walking off with the dogs to the farmhouse.

All the lads were in deep contemplation as Tommy asked, 'How did he know I smoked?'

Ken and Jack looked at each other and Jack said simply, 'He's Mr Morrin.' Whatever the hell that was supposed to mean…

Smoking away from the tent (Jack had insisted the ciggie smoke was unpleasant, if not harmful), Tommy took in the whole stretch of farmland and the noise and smell of the area—cows' dung, grass, diesel oil and earth. In the distance, Tommy saw two tractors rolling across fields, all green hills and valleys. Higher and greener hills than Tommy knew back home. A shimmer of heat surrounded the machines and the raised dust.

Ken had gone through the usual drunken farmer jokes about wearing cowpats as he searched for his lost cap in the fields. Inside the tent, the heady aroma of earth, grass and canvas was as pungent as Tommy's tins of Brut.

He asked Davey, 'Will he feed us every night?'

'Will if we work for it.'

'What type of work?'

'Farming,' said Jack. 'Mucking out in the big barn. Chopping firewood. Baling hay. Maybe helping Pops, Mr Morrin's dad.'

'Mucking out… All the shit like,' said Tommy as Ken stretched up, head bowed against the roof of the tent. 'Not sure if I fancy shovelling shit.'

'Shovel on this.'

Ken blew a fart, the signal for Jack to announce, 'Okay, all out. It stinks in here now.' They left the tent. Jack opened both flaps to let the air through. He gazed at the farmhouse.

'There's Pops at the door with his cooking hat. Let's see what this new theory is that Mr Morrin wants to discuss.' Tommy realised how hungry he was.

At the farmhouse, the ancient and silent cook—a shrunken version of Mr Morrin—dished out huge globs of roast beef and scrambled eggs as the lads settled onto table-height hay bales inside the main barn. The metal ex-army plates were filled with food and clanged with the busy knives and forks. Nearby, over a dozen dairy cattle urinated like horses onto the cobblestones in their stalls.

'Now then,' said Mr Morrin, entering with the two dogs, a rifle slung casually over his shoulder. 'Thanks, Pops—and now the brew?' Pops smiled and walked away, re-entering shortly, pushing a trolley of demi-johns containing a dark liquid. Each was marked with a small skull and crossbones. 'Heady stuff, lads, need a good stomach here,' warned Mr Morrin. He picked up a demi-john and tilted it back behind his head like Jed Clampett in the TV show *The Beverly Hillbillies*, before swigging back a pint full. The lads took a tentative step towards the trolley.

Jack led off and picked up a jar of the brew. Knocked it back. Eyes rolled to the back of his head. Tommy, Davey and Ken followed. Ken almost spewed his pint straight back out. For Tommy, after a few licks, the brew slid down like angel piss. Before long, half the demi-johns were empty. A cosy, warm glow embraced the barn. The cow urine took on a serene stream-like twinkling. All the lads nodded to Pops.

Pops smiled silently, 'you're all welcome,' before leaving.

'I've been pondering on this theory of mine see, since you were last here. Said it out loud to the cows.'

'Is that cos Rhonda has gone?' asked Ken.

'Come again,' replied Mr Morrin.

Ken reddened, said apologetically, 'Er, you know, no more Rhonda to ponder?'

Mr Morrin stared ahead, poker-faced. He glanced at his rifle. The dogs glanced at each other. Jack elbowed Ken in the ribs and mouthed 'tit' to him.

Mr Morrin continued, 'Putting that aside for the time being. Are you all comfortable and fed?' The lads nodded and set aside the metal plates. 'Good. I've got this theory that can be used to explain everything. From the running of a farm to a

Prince being born to a King and Queen—and anything and everything in between.'

This grabbed their attention. 'I tried it on your Eddie—told him in terms of the running of his car engine. He didn't believe it at first and nor would I expect you lads to. By the time he left, I could see the cogwheels churning away.'

'Well, go on,' said Ken eagerly. All were waiting for more.

'It's all about the distance…'

'Distance,' said Ken 'What?'

'I'll begin with this one. How do I make a living?'

'You sell your farm produce,' said Jack.

'Aye Jack, and the success or failure depends on the distance of my products from this farm to the market stalls and the customers who buy it.'

'Okay,' said Jack, 'You have to get the stuff to the market. We know that, but I'm sorry Mr Morrin, I don't get what that's got to do with Kings and Princes?'

'Okay—let's dig deeper. Distance explains the How, but not the why of things—of everything.'

'But Kings and Queens and Princes?' Jack repeated.

'The distance between the King's sperm and the Queen's womb.'

The lads stared at each other in a shocked silence, their attention rapt. 'The difference between being born a pauper or a King's son is in the distance of His Majesties penis and a commoner's vagina. It's all about proximity.' Mr Morrin opened his arms wide, then brought his hands together slowly.

'One would like to give one, one,' said Ken.

'Have a go yourselves. A hard one this, lads, but think on it, how does distance explain the weather we're having?'

'The distance from the energy of the sun to our planet,' said Tommy.

Mr Morrin nodded. 'Very quick.'

Tommy looked at Davey. He was caught in the moment too. He stared at Jack—cogwheels turning. He saw Ken's glasses steaming.

Ken said, 'The next pint of ale, the distance between our gobs and the Llindir inn.'

'The lives of a fox and your chickens—the distance of your rifle bullet.' said Jack profoundly.

'A nice smell?' suggested Davey.

'The distance from your nose to the smell of a rose,' said Mr Morrin quickly.

'Beauty,' said Jack

'Hey—thingio, the James Bond writer…' said Tommy.

'…Mister Ian Fleming—genius,' said Mr Morrin.

Tommy said, 'He wrote something about the difference between a plain and a beautiful woman, was in the distance in millimetres from her eyes to her nose, or something like that. Think it was in *Diamonds Are Forever…*'

'It was *Goldfinge*r. They were discussing gold. Bond and *Goldfinger*. I've got all the original hardbacks. I collect books,' said Mr Morrin.

'A bad smell,' said Ken.

'The distance from your arse to my nose,' said Tommy.

'Er, in the war, say at sea, a sub against a German Destroyer,' said Ken.

'The torpedo in the sub—its distance from the Destroyer's engine room,' said Jack. They all stopped to think.

'Dreams,' said Tommy.

'Ah, good one. Usually based on what you ate and drank and experienced that day. The distance between your hidden subconscious and your perceived reality.'

They pondered until Davey piped up, 'Missing somebody?' He was staring at Tommy.

'The location of one person in relation to another. How far they are apart, emotionally or geographically,' said Mr Morrin.

What the fuck—Tommy stood. Aware some kind of synapsis connection was happening inside his head. He stared mesmerised—indeed, this was a mystery. 'Life on Earth,' he said.

'You've answered that yourself already.'

'The distance from our planet to the sun,' replied Tommy. Mr Morrin smiled happily.

'Being rich and being poor,' said Jack. Davey was struggling to get another question in.

'The King's todger and your mams vagina,' interrupted Ken—slurring distinctively.

'Hope,' said Jack.

'Where you are and where you want to be,' said Tommy. They all stared at him. Mr Morrin nodded.

'Hidden depth amongst that fierceness… Can we give Davey a chance,' said Mr Morrin.

Davey piped up, 'Theft.'

'Ah,' said Mr Morrin. 'Do you or Jack want to try this one?' He said, staring at Tommy.

Tommy answered, 'The want of what you've got, balanced against what you think you need.' Jack reached out a hand to shake with Tommy. Davey smiled.

This was a moment for Tommy. He could feel he was nicely *pissed* with the proffered brew. He took a few steps from the group, staring at the land outside the barn, feeling something stirring in his mind, as though moving outside of fog and into a new fresh clarity… As though overcome with a fusion of the delayed reaction, enlightenment and almost unbearable lightness centred in the present. Pulled one way by the day's violence, another via the opportunity of hope—would he and his family be moving to the furthest distance on Earth from Liverpool? If so, where did he and Linda stand?

Was there a hope for him and Rhonda, glimpsed despite the briefness of meetings? For some reason, switching from the right now to the near future, practicalities occurred: foremost, the realisation that his money was already short. The round of ale he'd bought in the inn had cost more than twice what he would have paid in a Liverpool bar.

He knelt against the barn door, turning to listen to the group. He missed another rhetorical question and heard, 'The tit of Rhonda and my mouth,' whispered by Ken. Jack nudged his ribs hard this time.

Mr Morrin stared and stepped back. 'No more talk of Rhonda. I'll not allow any child of mine to be slandered. Stepchild or not.' His eyes shot daggers at Ken. The two Labradors growled. Tommy got up and tried to head towards them, finding his attempt at speech had failed.

'Ken—you are a tit,' said Jack loudly as Ken backed off from the dogs.

'We'll talk more in the morrow,' said Mr Morrin. Maybe teach you how and when to use this,' he pointed to the rifle, 'only after this fails,' he pointed to his head. At least, that's the way it sounded. Class dismissed.

Tommy was gagging for a ciggie and a chance to see young Rhonda Morrin again. He pondered New Zealand and a new life versus the allures of Rhonda and her valleys and the unbearable lust for Linda. The night flashed by in a blur of a fireman pickup from Jack and a missed playful punch aimed at Ken.

That night, snoring under the canvas, Tommy dreamt of a Blue-Faced Maloney transformed into a gigantic vampire cow—udders undulating and dropping tendrils to the grass outside the tent, sucking, digging into the black earth from under the grass: the worms mating and multiplying in her udder to be squirted silently into aluminium containers, loaded via a conveyor belt attached to a lorry labelled 'school delivered milk.'

Monsieur La Fox was nearby, rapidly scratching notes with his pencil on his pad, getting his long snout closer to the action until distracted by his notetaking, he too was sucked in and mingled with the milky worms, his pince-nez, the last form to disintegrate into the earth.

All was calm and bright; all was in black and white until a long stick, thickening as it rose, emerged from the soil, with a macabre outline of a scarecrow growing and spreading as it reached man height. Stepping off the stick, the scarecrow levitated onto a tall black horse before riding into the tent. Dismounting, the scarecrow's blackened face was now right in front of Tommy's as a red right hand reached out and—on the mouth—with a rictus smile, the lips moved and said, 'Give me bag and money…'

15
HORSES AND BOOKS

Muffled, raised voices woke Tommy, an argument outside the tent. Stepping out, Tommy saw Jack had a brew of Camps Coffee on the stove. Several thick wedges of buttered bread lay on a plate. Helping himself with a nod of thanks to Jack, he looked across the field to see and hear Rhonda in a heated exchange with Mr Morrin. They stood close to the field that housed the black horse, Stingray. Tommy could see the horse was in distress, its head bobbing side to side as it did when he'd tried to stoke it the day before.

Rhonda was in apparent distress too, speaking loudly, arms waving at Mr Morrin, who stood with both hands raised defensively.

'What's happening over there?'

'Best stay out of it,' replied Jack.

Ken stuck his head out of the tent, blinking with the bright sunshine. 'What time is it?'

'Time you got out of your pit. Give Davey a nudge too,' said Jack. 'We're intruding on family business.'

As if he'd heard Jack's comment, Mr Morrin called over, 'Jack, over here if you please.' Tommy saw Rhonda storm off towards the farmhouse. Uninvited, he followed behind Jack.

'Everything okay, Mr Morrin?'

'It isn't, Jack, it's not okay at all. Rhonda's off to make a phone call to the vet. Listen up now. When she gets back here, I'm going to be driving her down to the inn. While I'm gone, Ramshaw will come to collect the horse. Deal with him if you please, and stop him putting his nose about the rest of the farm, trying to drum up more trade.'

'It's that bad?' Jack asked.

'It is. I should have made the call weeks ago.'

'Is this Ramshaw bloke a vet?' asked Tommy. Mr Morrin stared harshly at him.

'He runs the local knackers' yard,' said Jack quietly. All three stared at the horse in silence. Tommy saw Rhonda's head purposely towards them. She was wiping her face to brush away tears.

'You spoke to the vet? Confirmed what he said to me?'

'I have. I'm sorry to doubt you… I've also rung Ramshaw and told him not to bother coming out.'

'I never mentioned his name.'

'You didn't have to, Dad, I could see it on your face.' Mr Morrin opened and closed his mouth. He was blushing deeply. 'I rung Keith, he's agreed to collect Stingray and to take him… where he needs to go,' said Rhonda.

'If that's the case, what was the point of cancelling Ramshaw?'

'I'm not letting him travel there in a dead meat wagon!' Rhonda pushed her hair away from her ears and turned to stare at the old horse. Tears stained her face.

'Come on now, girl, let me drive you back to the inn,' said Mr Morrin gently, putting an arm across her shoulder. Rhonda pushed it away.

'I'd rather walk there…' Rhonda turned and headed towards the farm gates.

Mr Morrin looked at Tommy and Jack. 'Can one of you walk with her please?' Before Jack could say a word, Tommy trotted off towards the gates.

They both walked in silence for several minutes. Rhonda had stopped crying and dried off the tears with a green silk handkerchief. Tommy was wracking his brain to summon up something apt. It was no time for small talk. Rhonda spared him the effort.

'You don't have to walk with me, you know. I am a big girl.'

'I can see that…'

'I'm not usually like this, you know, Tommy.'

Tommy felt a tiny thrill when Rhonda said—remembered—his name. 'My al fella's trying to sell my dog. His name's Butch…'

'Your dad or…'

'…that's the dog's name.' They stopped and laughed. Rhonda stepped close and gave Tommy a gentle hug, kissing him lightly on the side of his neck. She was almost the same height. The tiny thrill surged inside of him. 'Thank you, Tommy. You're sweet. Now go back to your mates please, I need some time on my own…'

'You sure?'

'Yes… Why is your dad—you should call him your dad, not 'al fella,' that sounds so wrong—why is he trying to sell Butch?'

'For the money. Well, actually he's said a few times that I shouldn't get too attached to a pet. Butch, I think of him more as a friend—a mate of mine, rather than my dog. Me al fella… my dad, he's been offered a job in New Zealand, and there's no way I could take him with us. If I went with him that is…' She bent her head to one side, looking at Tommy. Tommy stared back into her green eyes. It was an effort not to kiss her. Knowing she was vulnerable, Tommy felt unfamiliar reluctance.

'I've changed my mind, I'd be very happy if you walked me back to the inn. Tell me more about your dog and family and I'll tell you all about my special friend Stingray.'

The thirty-minute walk to the inn flew by for Tommy, who felt himself slowing to drag out another few minutes in

Rhonda's company. He wracked his brain thinking of some reason for not going back to the farm.

Sensing this, Rhonda said, 'I'll have to leave you for now. I've got my usual morning in the charity shop. It's late for opening as it is. I do voluntary work there at least half a day each week. Thanks very much, Tommy, for keeping me company.'

'It was my pleasure. You sure you're up to work today? I'm sure no one would blame you for not turning in?'

'I need to Tommy, there was a delivery yesterday, whole van load of used books, they'll need to be unpacked, sorted into what's rubbish and what we can put on the shelves…'

'Book sorting? As it happens, it's exactly what I specialise in.'

'Really?'

'Honest to god. In Liverpool, I'm known as Tommy the librarian.'

'Are you? I think you're making this up!'

'Of course I am, but your al fella, sorry—dad, did ask me stay with you all morning no matter what you had planned.'

'He's my stepdad and I think you're more of a lying hound than a librarian.' Taking the cue, Tommy raised his head and howled at the sky.

Inside the dusty charity shop, the volume of second-hand books initially overwhelmed Tommy. There were half a dozen tea crates stacked with assorted novels: paperbacks, hardbacks, pamphlets, magazines and reading materials. A scan revealed a lot was so dog-eared it wasn't worth the shelf space. Three large bookshelves that occupied one side of the shop were already crammed with several hundred assorted volumes. He paced, considering.

Rhonda handed him a mug of tea. 'What you thinking, Tommy?'

‘I’m thinking there’s a load of rubbish already out here on display. Does the shop sell many books each week?’

‘More of a trickle than a steady sale, I suppose.’

‘Is there ever a clear out—getting rid of the junk?’

‘Maggie Rhea, she runs the shop, I know she’s always loath to put anything in the bins.’

‘How much do the books sell for?’

‘Ten-pence for the paperbacks and twenty-pence for the hardbacks.’

‘But you’re in charge this morning?’

Rhonda nodded in agreement.

‘Okay, we’re going to have a tidy up…’

For the next two hours, Tommy shifted through the existing three bookshelves, rearranging the fiction into alphabetical order—separating the paperbacks and hardbacks. Tommy used his knowledge of the local Childwall library classification into types of nonfiction: history, religion, arts, sciences, technologies, and language. Now arranged in neat order, the nonfiction, along with a children’s section, conveniently took up one of the bookshelves.

As the work progressed, a growing stream of customers passed in and out, many complementary of the improved book order.

In the kitchen area at the back of the shop, Tommy was appraising a long fold-up table. He sat on it to test its weight resistance.

‘What you thinking now, Tommy?’ asked Rhonda as she made another pot of tea.

‘I’m thinking it’s time for a book sale, outside of the shop.’

‘I’m not sure Maggie will be happy with that.’

‘Happy with what?’ A short elderly woman entered the kitchen and stared at Tommy through the thickest-lens spectacles he had ever seen. The magnification gave her features an owl-like quality.

'Hello, Maggie. This is Tommy, he's helping today.'

'Are you responsible for the new arrangement on the bookshelves?'

'Er, yep, I suppose I am.'

'In that case, I'm glad to meet you, young man.' Tommy shook hands warmly with the shop manager. He was happy to see a smile on Rhonda's face.

'I was thinking, maybe take this table outside to the front of the shop.'

'For your book sale?'

'Sort out the books in the tea chests, stack them up on the table. If it's okay with you, Maggie?'

'Absolutely. I'll write up some display cards. Liverpool is it?'

'Yep, Scouser…'

'Well now, Rhonda, can you fetch up a Scouser every time you're in please.' Tommy and Rhonda laughed as they shifted the table to the front of the shop. Manhandling the six chests outside, Tommy found three fitted neatly underneath the table.

Sorting through the first crate, he picked out a bundle tied with an ancient silver ribbon. He counted twenty volumes, with the same light blue faded covers. These were clearly not everyday book formats, more of a Victorian almanac or pamphlet.

'Rubbish,' he said to Rhonda as he gave a cursory glance at the first cover. *David Copperfield The Younger* by Charles Dickens of Blunderstone Bookery. Faint illustrations adorned the book title. Curious, he checked through the twenty volumes; each contained a chapter of text. The final part was twice as thick and included an illustration on every other page. From deeper inside the crate, Tommy fetched three expensively bound volumes: *Master Humphrey's Clock, Oliver Twist,* and *Pickwick Papers*, bound in a light tan leather cover and unblemished. The growing idea he was holding something rare and possibly valuable made him giddy.

'What's the matter, Tommy? You've gone pale!'

'Rhonda, go and get Maggie. I think the shop's takings will be up today. These all look like Dickens' original works.'

'Oh-my!' said Rhonda, a hand raised in front of her open mouth.

'Oh-my is right. These look like the dog's bollocks.'

16
MAD-DOG MAN

Tommy woke to the smell of coffee. Stretching outside the tent, on another scorching bright day, he saw Jack had a percolator on the stove along with eggs, boiling in a pan. Ken woke yawning, farting—before coming alive and racing for the dugout shit hole.

Mr Morrin approached, accompanied by Davey and the two Labradors. The gloom from the previous morning was replaced with a beaming smile aimed at Tommy.

'Had some excellent reports about you, I'm glad to say. Good work yesterday, by all accounts.'

Ken and Jack had listened to Tommy's explanation of his absence from the farm the previous day with incredulity as if he'd made up the story of the rare book to pass off a day's skive with Rhonda.

Expectantly, only Davey had made positive remarks. 'Have the books been valued yet?'

'Have to clear it with the donors first, if they find them. When that's through, there's a dealer in Chester frothing at the bits to get his hands on them. Go to auction, I imagine. It'll make news headlines around here.' Tommy saw a look pass between Ken and Jack.

'Well done Tommy,' said Jack quietly. A smiling Davey patted Tommy heavily on the back.

The morning flashed by in a montage of digging, planting, picking, packing, rounding sheep, collecting eggs, mucking out and painting the window frames around the farmhouse.

It was the third day on the farm. All the boys worked hard, shirtless, tanning from white to red, from brown to mahogany. Tommy didn't smoke much.

There was no sign of any change in weather; it was still relentlessly hot. Throughout the morning, Tommy drank three whole pots of water—the demi-johns expunged, dregs of the moonshine the night before swilled out—cool clean and fresh. His piss was as hot and clear as the cows in the barn. Tommy leaned heavily against a shovel—clear sweat pumping from his body. Toxin free as though having spent an hour in a sauna. His eyes were a clear blue.

At six pm, Pops stood purposely outside the farmhouse, a trolley of hot food ready. All were spitting feathers for a pint. After the meal and brew, Tommy and Davey took turns to spray the cold cattle shower over each other near the entrance to the cowshed.

Walking back to the tent, Tommy confided in Davey, 'Been thinking it more and more—in fact, sounds mad, but I've had an empty head and it's getting lighter. I think the time spent with Rhonda yesterday has made me feel a whole lot better. I'm loving it here—no big mad rush—no bullshit.'

'Apart from the cow shit. Everyone was jealous. Ken was going on so much about you spending time with Rhonda that Jack had to tell him to shut up. 'Pathetic little boy,' he called him.'

'Nice one, Jack... Anyway, I'm thinking maybe me al fella could be right. Could be a better life away from it all.' Tommy worried where he should sling his ciggie. He pegged it out, half burning his thumb and forefinger.

'Today, for the first time, I can think of Linda and not feel like I've been kicked in the balls. Now it's down to a mild bellyache. More looking forward to the next thing: like a pint tonight, or this disco in the church hall—more so than Linda getting back from Paree. Distance shit.'

'He does make you think—tried to tell you...'

‘I know, mate. My head’s still up my arse, but it does feel somehow clearer… Can’t explain it.’ Tommy relit the ciggie.

‘Davey?’

‘What?’

‘Did you give her one?’

‘Who?’

‘You know who, Davey.’

‘Did I fuck—I’d have told you—told the lads. You don’t mean Rhonda. You’re talking about Linda. Just say it,’ said Davey

‘I’ve still got this, thought in my head… About someone else shagging her. I’ve also got this fox in my head.’

‘What?’

‘It’s stupid, I know, but it keeps coming back in dreams—like he’s… I don’t know, cleverer than me…’

‘Tommy, I think you’ve got an issue with trying to prove something. You don’t have to, mate…’

‘Okay, but, she hasn’t let me give her one and if…’

‘Tommy, stop thinking too much, mate.’

‘I, but… maybe you’re right, Davey lad.’ Tommy relit the ciggie, inhaling deeply.

‘What happened on the way to Jack’s? You haven’t mentioned it once—you looked like a bag of shite.’ Tommy told Davey about Lawler’s kidnapping of Joey.

Shaking his head, Davey interrupted, ‘But Joey’s cousin?’

‘I know—how the hell are they going to go to war against Mad-Mick?’

‘Hang on, Mad-Mick and all his crew are inside.’

‘Even so—you can’t mess with them. There’s something going on with the Lawler family as though they are taking over Childwall.’

‘There’s enough of them, must be making loads of money selling drugs from their mobies.’

'Something bigger is going on. I don't know exactly what it is... Just hoping they get put away for what they did, what they were going to do to Joey…'

'Leave them all to it, Tommy—just look after ourselves…'

Tommy nodded. *Good point.*

'I'm getting so pissed off with all this… shit. For god's sake—I promised me Grandma on her dying bed, promised meself—I'd do… be something better.'

'Well, you are going to the sixth form, 'A' levels and stuff, that's a definite option for doing better?'

'I don't know, Davey. Sometimes, I know exactly what I'm doing, or should be doing, or what I should have done… My head gets screwed up… More so with this New Zealand stuff.'

'Let's take it easy and see what happens, hey mate? We are on holiday.' Davey paused. 'Tommy, maybe you should have said something to the police when they turned up outside yours. Even to just let Joey know you were only trying to help?'

Tommy pondered. This had been nagging his conscience. 'I know, Davey. That probably would have been best. But Suggoski, he saw what happened. And I did tell our Patricia they had him in the boot. I think I did anyway.' Tommy scratched his head. 'At least, I know I never did anything wrong and I did intend to help him. If I had spoken to the bizzies, there's no way I'd have got away in time to come here.'

'That's true,' admitted Davey. Mr Morrin interrupted, rifle in hand, as he approached the campsite.

'Ready, Jack?' A hundred yards away, Pops was placing a target board in the middle of the field next to the main barn.

Tommy asked, 'How come only Jack gets to have a shoot?'

'Show me some of this,' Mr Morrin tapped his head, 'Over the next few days and we shall see.' Tommy was about to argue, but Davey and Ken shook their heads.

Jack said, 'I'll catch up with you later at the inn.'

'Ah, that reminds me… Be wary in there tonight—keep your eyes open and ears peeled. An old acquaintance of mine is rumoured to be back near these parts. Goes by the name of Mad-Dog.'

'Mad-Dog?' said Tommy, looking at Davey.

'Is he out now? Thought he got three years?' asked Jack.

'Somehow convinced Her Majesty of his good behaviour and reformed character.'

'Surely he'll be barred from the inn?'

'Never did anything inside for the landlord to warrant that. Plenty outside, though, as I know to my cost.' Mr Morrin stared at the barn. 'Tried to burn me out after sacking him, he did.'

'Is he hard, like?' asked Tommy.

'Hard enough,' said Mr Morrin. 'Never had that long nose broken. Not yet…'

The thirty-minute hike to the inn was a pleasant stroll in the evening sunshine. Passing the old, deserted mill, Tommy eyed the climbable gates.

'Nothing in there,' said Davey quietly.

'Don't you be getting any ideas here Tommy,' said Ken. 'It's a small village, and everything that goes on is known about. We've never had any trouble here…'

'Mainly because Jack and Big Eddie have been with us,' said Davey.

Entering the bar, there was that palpable hush again, as though they were trespassing into a no-go zone. Without Eddie and Jack in company, the locals let it be known the Scousers were not welcome, talking in an exaggerated, loud Welsh. Off in a far corner, three teenagers stared at them with hostility. The lads heard clearly, 'It's them thieving Scousers again.'

Davey said, 'I'll get them in, do you want to grab a table outside?' Tommy, after a cursory glance for Rhonda, nodded to Ken. They walked outside.

Rather than sitting at a table, they set up on the short dry-stone wall, taking advantage of the cool shadow.

'Didn't see Rhonda in there,' said Ken. Davey joined them with three pints in the heavy dimpled glass jugs, on a tray.

'Rhonda's late for her shift at the bar,' he said. 'I hope Jack hurries up and gets here. Didn't like the look of that crew in the far corner.'

Tommy said, 'I'm going for a piss.' He put his pint on the wall and walked back into the bar. He headed straight for the crew in the corner: three lads, maybe a year or two older than Tommy, one bigger and stockier than the others. He had a skull and crossbones tattoo on the back of his right hand. They fell silent as Tommy approached—staring with hostility.

'All right, boys,' said Tommy quietly. The locals looked at each other. 'Name's Tommy Dwyer. Here on holiday from Liverpool, as you may have guessed.' Tommy was trying to establish who was the leader, who to focus on. He decided it was the tattoo artist.

'These your buccaneers, hey pirate Pete?'

'Only buccaneers I've got are on my bucking head mate, and they don't like to hear comments about thieving Scousers, okay?'

Not as openly hostile, the locals continued to stare at each other, avoiding eye contact with Tommy. 'I don't want any trouble, lads, but just so you know, if there is any trouble, I'm up and ready for anyone of you, fuckers. So, if you want to carry on staring at each other like you're watching a bastard tennis match, carry on. If there's any more of giving me or my mates the daggers, I'll take any one of you outside and I'll knock your fucking heads off, okay?'

The locals all looked down at their tables. The tattooed lad beamed red with humiliation—yet, beneath the surface, Tommy detected some other emotion—as though the confrontation had been expected, anticipated…

Tommy got another round in at the bar. Again, he was forced to acknowledge his dwindling money. A visit to that old mill had become necessary. Tommy's instinct was telling him there were goodies. The round cost ninety pence—the ale was not cheap. Seeing Rhonda approaching the bar, Tommy's mood lightened. Eyeing the silent crew in the corner, she said, 'Saw and heard what happened over there. Aren't you the brave one now.'

Tommy shrugged. He saw the tattooed lad getting up and heading to the phone box in the corner. Looking over, Rhonda nodded at him. 'He'll be ringing his cousin—Mad-Dog, he calls himself. Both not out of jail for two weeks yet. Bad people. I'd be careful if he comes around now.'

'Never mind him or his mad cousins, are you going to this disco tomorrow?'

'Oh, I'll be there all right,' said Rhonda, smiling. There was that floral fragrance again, which Tommy would have happily trailed along like a Bisto twin. 'What is that perfume?'

'Violetta Penhaligon. Do you like it?'

'I love it.'

'Keith Piperello gets it to me from Italy.' Tommy raised an eyebrow. Cocked his head—*may I?* He reached out to take her hand; Rhonda smiled and nodded approval. Held out her wrist to Tommy's nose. He took a deep appreciative pull on the fragrance. They locked eyes gently. Who the hell was this Keith Piperello?

A local farmer was waving his empty pint jug at Rhonda. Their eyes unlocked. 'Speak to you later, Tommy…'

Outside, knocking back his second pint, Ken produced a pack of playing cards.

'Rummy,' he said, and started to deal the cards out.

Within half an hour, Tommy had lost another quid, mainly to Ken who, in Tommy's opinion, was an expert cheating bastard at the game.

'Deal me out,' he said, standing. Tommy sparked up a ciggie and turned to see a tall, mean-looking man next to him, his long nose twitching like a dog sniffing a bloody steak.

'Got a light there?' The man was invading Tommy's space. His breath was awful.

'Can't see your ciggie,' said Tommy, taking a step back.

'That's the next question, isn't it? Give me a cigarette.' Davey and Ken had stopped talking and were flashing warning signals to Tommy. The three lads Tommy confronted had left the bar and stood outside staring at the Scousers. Their leader accompanied the locals.

'Are you deaf?' asked the man. Tommy saw crude, prison-type blue flower tattoos on his neck. Mister Mad-Dog. Out early due to good behaviour. 'I heard you were up for knocking heads off. Is that correct?' He took a pace forward—right back into Tommy's space. The three lads were looking more at ease, grinning at Tommy. Mad-Dog was in his mid-twenties, at least six foot, two inches taller than Tommy, and stocky. Long-nosed indeed. Tommy saw Mad-Mick's dangerousness in this man's persona. 'Not so fucking big, boy, are you now?' said one of the lads. What the hell was with the 'Mad' names? Mad-Mick, Mad-Dog…

'Stop it—all of you—now.' Rhonda had appeared outside of the inn doorway. 'I've called my dad—he's on his way here.' Mad-Dog stared at her with hatred.

‘I hear you lot are staying on this one’s farm. I’m going to burn down the fucking lot,’ he said, a hand reaching into a back pocket. Tommy saw he was now holding a cutthroat razor. The blade was pointing at the floor. Tommy felt his bowels loosen. Fight or flight.

‘You’re near to shitting yourself, aren’t you, Scouse? Never come up against anything like me… Your worst nightmare, eh?’

‘Not quite,’ Tommy lunged his forehead, delivering a massive butt to Mad-Dog’s nose, but he’d seen it coming and ducked away to swiftly step aside. The razor flashed past—an inch from Tommy’s nose. Distance. Time slowed as Tommy paced around Mad-Dog. Six locals surrounded Davey and Ken. Tommy aimed a kick at Mad-Dog’s balls, but again, he’d seen it coming and danced out of the way. He switched hands with the razor.

Maybe it's time to run, thought Tommy when, in a plume of gravel, a Land Rover screeched to a stop, braking yards from them and the dust. Mr Morrin and Jack appeared.

Enraged, Mr Morrin rushed forward and grabbed hold of Mad-Dog, lifting him off his feet. Jack was standing solidly square against the six local lads, easily towering over all of them. He took a left hook swing, turned right at the hips—a second left hook swing and two of them were sparked out. Three seconds. Tommy was silently awed.

Mr Morrin had now flung Mad-Dog across the car park, his razor tossed aside. He stood raging above him, ‘Assaulting my daughter again, is it?’ He booted Mad-Dog in the face. Tommy saw the big nose spluttering and dissolving into a red mess on his face. The tattoos on his neck appeared as red rose flowers.

Mr Morrin headed back to the car, fetched out the rifle, cocked it and Rhonda was in his face, 'No Dad—he's not worth it.'

'Step aside.'

'Dad, no—he only grabbed my arm. He was asking if these lads were staying with you. You will go to jail like he did—he's not worth it—it's what he wants.'

Tommy saw the locals had disappeared, including the two Jack had sparked out. Mr Morrin was shaking, the gun aimed at Mad-Dog's head.

Tommy stepped forward and pushed the aim of the rifle from Mad-Dog's head. 'He's not worth it.'

Slowly, Mr Morrin regained his composure. 'You stay away from here. Far, far away.' Mad-Dog was half standing, leaning forward, the blood gushing out of his nose. He waved a hand at each of the lads as though taking note of their faces, before staggering off to his Morris Minor parked nearby.

The landlord was standing outside.

'There's a large malt here with your name on it,' he said to Mr Morrin.

'I'll just have the one. A very large one,' he said, his body language relaxing.

'Never had any trouble here before Tommy came,' said Ken. 'Some people seem to attract it, wherever they are.'

'Tommy never brought the Mad-Dog shit on us,' said Davey.

'I'm not so sure. What did he mean by you 'Knocking heads off?' You started this!' said Ken. 'Trouble doesn't have to travel far to find you!'

'You know what happened—he tried to burn Mr Morrin's farm down. And he's just grabbed Rhonda—not for the first time by the sound of it,' said Davey.

'That's true,' said Jack, 'That had nothing to do with Tommy, or any of us.' The lads headed back into the hushed bar, Ken staring hard at Davey. Tommy was breathing hard, adrenaline pumping.

Mr Morrin was talking quietly with the landlord—his mutton-chopped sideburns even bushier than the day they arrived. Another man entered and stood with them, tall and stout with a bright red nose—testimony to a fondness for fine liqueur. He was holding the rifle with a competent ease. Mr Morrin made introductions.

'Now, lads, you'll know this is the landlord, Selwyn Thomas. Been running this place since it opened in the thirteenth century. The oldest pub in Wales, see.'

'I prefer the word inn. Thank you, Mr Morrin,' said Selwyn.

'And this big chap here, this is Sergeant Bradley of the local constabulary.'

'And I'd prefer retired Sergeant if you please,' he said, staring at Tommy. 'I know Jack here, and your two faces do look familiar. Not in a professional manner, I'm glad to say, but I haven't seen you around here before tonight. Could be said it was you who started off this commotion?'

'This is Tommy Dwyer,' said Jack, adding, 'Ken and Davey.' Mr Morrin had knocked back his scotch and interrupted—waving a hand at Tommy

'All my guests on my land,' he said. 'You can't be shaking any blame on this one—not when Mad-Dog is around.'

'Well, that is true,' admitted the Sergeant. 'I'll be making a call to one of our lads to go and have a quiet chat. Make sure there's no nonsense about being threatened with firearms.' He placed the rifle on the bar next to Mr Morrin. 'I think another stiff round for us all would be the end of this matter.'

'I told him he was barred for life,' said Selwyn. 'Saw him getting hold of Rhonda's arm and warned him I'd have the police on him.' He fetched cut glass tumblers and poured a heavy drinker measure in them.

'That'll be my last one,' said Mr Morrin, knocking back a drink. 'I have to drive, you know.' Selwyn gave him a knowing wink. Mr Morrin picked up the heavy tumbler.

'Maybe one more,' he said. He held the glass in his hand, deep in thought. His face took on a puzzled expression, which switched to realisation, 'Damned fools!' he said—slamming his hand on the bar.

'He set it up—sending his idiots in to provoke these idiots. This particular idiot,' he pointed to Tommy, 'he wanted any excuse to start trouble.'

'They were going on about thieving Scousers,' said Tommy defensively.

'And you took the bait. Invited yourself to a knife fight with just your fists—idiot!'

'I didn't know.'

'Son, you need to use this,' he tapped his head. 'Before anything—before any action you take involving a confrontation.' Tommy shook his head.

'I didn't know what was going to kick off.'

'...And where there's a knife, you go one better and have one of these at hand.' Mr Morrin picked up the rifle. Knocked back his whisky. Looked at Tommy, tapping his shoulder sympathetically. 'Never mind. Store it in there, son, for future reference. Never underestimate the consequences of a threat.' He put the glass down on the bar. Tommy reflected as Davey stood shoulder to shoulder with him. *I knew anyway—I already knew...*

Sergeant Bradley asked, 'How about a bit of history for the lads here? A bit of culture to save the night, what do you say Selwyn?'

'I could tell you tales about this place that would make your hair turn as white as mine.'

'It's supposed to be haunted, isn't it?' asked Ken. All eyes were on the landlord, except Tommy's, who emerged from his thoughts to track Rhonda as she collected empty glasses, smiling lightly as she stared back.

'Dewi Roberts tells it best in his book, Old Villages of Denbighshire and Flintshire.'

'I love a ghost story,' said Ken. Selwyn nodded. Pulled himself a pint of Bass. Took a swig, then rolled up the sleeves of his heavy white cardigan. The inn appeared to diminish and to focus in on his bushy head. He closed his eyes and palmed his hands together as though in silent prayer. Nodding, he began his tale…

'Over two hundred years ago, it was. The events that happened right here.' Locals gathered closer to the bar with an expectant hush. 'For over two hundred years, a ghost of a woman has haunted the Llindir inn. The name of the ghost is Sylvia—and she always wears a white or blue dress. Alive, she always wore a smile to all and every customer who came here to slake their thirst. Being childless, she devoted herself and her love to the happiness of the inn and her husband, a former Captain sailor. He was in charge of the inn—before my time. It's said he grew tired of the life of an innkeeper and the sea nymphs called him back to the waters. Made him miserable. Barely civil to any of his customers and became determined to leave. Sylvia tried to stop him, using her womanly wiles to tempt him to stay home, which worked for several long days and weeks. But the call of the nymphs took a powerful hold, and he left the inn in the dead of the night whilst Sylvia slept.

'When she woke and found him gone, she vowed to avenge herself by taking in a lover whilst her husband was away. One night, a storm struck the vessel the Captain was Mastering, and he was shipwrecked off the coast of Anglesey. Tired and forlorn, he made his way back to this inn and in the dead of night, he walked through that door and witnessed his naked wife in flagrante delicto.'

'Shagging,' said Ken quietly.

'…and in a fit of rage, he tore his wife and her lover apart, limb from limb. Their bodies were found the next day. The Captain was never to be seen or heard of again. Some say he had drowned on the shipwreck and it was his restless and tormented spirit that came back here that night…

'It is the ghost of Sylvia that walks through the inn, some have seen her sobbing silently for forgiveness, others have seen and heard her rage as a banshee in revenge to the sea nymphs. In sadness, she wears a white dress. In her fury, she dresses in blue.'

'And is it true it's only other women who see her?' asked Jack, who had heard the same tale dozens of times, but was happy to play along and feed lines to the landlord…

'Do I look like any female to you?' Selwyn replied. The bar had fallen into total silence.

'Do you mean, you've actually seen her yourself?' asked Jack.

'Every night after I bolt that door, she passes me by…'

The hushed, stilled atmosphere in the bar was broken by a tall, fragrant lady with an American accent, 'Does she give autographs?'

Mr Morrin smiled ruefully as he left the bar.

Coming from the Llindir inn, eleven-thirty, all as pissed as judges and into the darkness of the lane leading back to the farm, Jack advised them to look away from approaching car headlights.

'What?' asked Tommy. Almost on cue, a car approached—headlights on full beam. Tommy didn't look away and for the next ten minutes, stumbled blindly through the darkening lane, using only the proximity of the other lads as a guide. Tommy stopped and took in the sheer blackness and silence of the night. Checked his pockets. Funds enough for two more nights. Money stashed somewhere in that mill?

After a half-hour walk, they all stopped to take a piss near the bottom of the hill. Tommy lit a ciggie and ensured he closed one eye to keep his night vision intact.

'You reckon it was a load of bollocks, that ghost tale?' Davey shrugged.

Ken said, 'It doesn't do his business any harm. There're always American tourists in there.'

'The mill we're coming to, that's supposed to be haunted as well,' said Jack.

'Hey, just think, we could have had the white woman following us…'

'And meeting her lover at the mill,' said Davey. They laughed quietly. Approaching the dip in the lane that led to the mill, a ground fog appeared.

'Stay close to the hedge—single file—all close in together,' said Jack. Entering the rising fog, Tommy felt a chill. He reached forward and was comforted by the feel of Davey's jacket. 'Keep talking lads,' said Jack.

'This is getting spooky,' said Ken. 'Shit, I keep thinking of *The Exorcist*.'

'Shut it, you tit,' said Tommy.

'The bit when her head turns around. What if she's in our tent when we get there?' The image crystallised in Tommy's head. The mood spread.

'Guys, I'm not joking now,' said Ken… Silence. Darkness. The fog dissipated as they passed the mill and approached the entrance to the farm. They could see the welcome lights on at the main farmhouse. 'I'm not going in the tent first'.

Jack moved forward and opened the flaps. There was no possessed young girl. He lit the lamp, and they took a collective sigh.

17
CLEANING THE PIPES

Waking to the animal-like aroma of coffee—Jack had got out of bed early again—all the lads discussed the events of the previous night with what ifs. In the midst of the discussion, a police panda car pulled into the farm road and stopped outside of the farmhouse.

The familiar sensation of flight or fight surged through Tommy. He saw a uniformed policeman emerge from the car, followed by a waving Sergeant Bradley. Tommy exhaled.

A short time later, as the police car drove from the farm, Mr Morrin approached. He was clean-shaven and looking smart in tweeds and a Homburg hat. He was holding a walking cane decorated with brass edgings.

'Now then,' he greeted the lads.

'Are you in any trouble?' asked Jack, eyeing the passing police car.

'No, not at all. Just a courtesy call, that's all. They tell me Mad-Dog spent the night in a hospital bed in Denbigh and was awoken by his parole officer who threatened to have him locked back in jail if he shows his face around these parts. Should be the last we see of him.'

'Good riddance,' said Jack.

'Now, as it's a Sunday, anyone for morning Chapel?'

The lads all shook their heads. 'That's okay. There is no day of rest on a working farm. Okay, two tasks, please. There's a whole vast tub of whitewash on its way here now. When it arrives, I'd like two of you to get busy on those outside walls. Need a good cleaning first—something for the paint to hold onto rather than the weeds. Hasn't had a good coat of paint for five years now and there's no reflection when driving in at night. But first, I need two of you to accompany me to the village—to load the wagon with hops and barley and unload at the inn.'

'What—I didn't know Selwyn brews his own ale there?' asked Davey.

'No, it's a drop-off point for local brewers. Monthly meeting there to swap business news and for a good drinking session too.'

Tommy nudged Davey, 'We'll go with you, Mr Morrin.'

'You okay with that?' asked Mr Morrin to Jack.

Jack nodded, but Ken didn't look so happy. 'Okay, Davey and Tommy, let's get the wagon loaded now.'

All nodded. The sun was out and it was becoming another scorching day. 'It'll pass the time before you get to the disco tonight,' said Mr Morrin, smiling. Tommy and Davey followed him to the main barn.

As they drove out of the farm in the open wagon—loaded with heavy sacks—Ken stared morosely at them.

'Good type is Jack,' said Mr Morin. 'Coming here full time when he's finished his training. Make an excellent farmer. Good sober head on him... Unpleasant night last night. Hopefully not too many of those,' he said, staring at Tommy.

At the inn, the landlord directed Tommy and Davey to a converted stable at the back, 'Drop them in there, lads. May have a nice surprise for you when it's done. Will you be stopping Mr Morrin as well? Bit late for Chapel.' As if on cue, bells rang from the nearby St Sadwrn Church.

'That's the eleven o'clock morning prayers service,' said Mr Morrin. 'Market straight after it for me now, Selwyn. Will you boys be okay for walking back?' Tommy and Davey nodded. They toted the heavy sacks from the wagon, dragging them inside the storeroom. Tommy was hoping the surprise Selwyn mentioned had something to do with Rhonda.

'Cleaning the pipes day, isn't it?' said the landlord mysteriously as he walked away.

'What's he on about?' asked Tommy.

'No idea, mate.'

Dusty and already sweating heavily, Tommy and Davey entered the inn from the back entrance, through the rustic kitchen and into the large bar. With the front door bolted, and none of the lights on, the bar was in gloomy darkness—all except one of the heavy curtains were draped closed. Tommy felt an involuntary cold shiver.

The Doctor Hook song 'Sylvia's Mother Said' started to play in his mind, the chords ominous. The single open curtain permitted a beam of light targeted directly at the landlord. He was pulling a pint into the now familiar dimpled glass pint jugs. Tommy experienced déjà vu as the inn again took him back through time.

He closed his eyes and in his mind sensed spirits from a distant age passing by him—hustling around the bar. A woman dressed in white silently pleading with a miserable stone-faced mutton-chopped man that could pass for Selwyn—the hair slightly less white. The man was ignoring the woman, raising the glass up into the light…

'Nearly there, lads,' said Selwyn, as he poured the pint into a large bucket below the bar. The music stopped in Tommy's head as he yawed back to reality.

'Best fertiliser money can buy that,' said Selwyn. 'People pay me good money to take the slops away. Nearly as much as they'd pay for a proper pint.'

'How come you're throwing the ale away?' asked Davey.

'That's your nice surprise lads. I'm cleaning the pipes—pulling the dregs through. Can't sell it with any trace of the cleaning fluid.'

'Oh, okay…What's up, Tommy?'

'Eh, how do you mean?'

'You, you look like you've seen a ghost.' Tommy stared at Selwyn, not stony-faced any more. 'Maybe I am…'

'You wouldn't be the first,' said Selwyn as he started to pull another pint. 'Ah.' He held his pint jug to the light before taking a sip. 'That will do for this pump, lads—all ready for you now. Hope you've eaten a breakfast?'

'I hope that's not a hint for me again,' said Rhonda appearing from the kitchen area. Tommy's chill lifted.

'Hello, Rhonda,' Tommy and Davey said together.

'You make sure the cleaner is flushed through; don't want a bad stomach to spoil the day and the night, now.' Tommy and Davey nodded in dumb agreement. 'You haven't got a clue what he's doing there, have you?' Tommy and Davey nodded.

Selwyn explained, 'Simple lads. Matter of taste, see? The yeast builds in the pipes over time. I usually run cleaning fluid through every fortnight—give them a good sluicing. If you clean the line thoroughly as time goes on you will get to a point where there will be hardly any yeast to remove at each clean. This is when you've reached a pinnacle with your line cleaning.'

Tommy and Davey had never heard of this.

'Got to get the balance right. Strong stuff first—one pull, straight into the bucket. Dilute the cleaning fluid, pint by pint, until it's all through. There's at least two pints of real ale that has to be pulled though—ale that would normally go to waste see. As Rhonda said, always best not to take a chance on getting a dodgy stomach. I slop the first of those two pints, but the second, such a waste, hey lads?'

'Ah,' said Davey, 'That's why you sometimes get served with a 'bad pint?''

'That's it. The less you clean the pipes, the more build-up and contamination the ale is. Many landlords baulk at the loss of dead money that the cleaning costs. But besides anything else, the Denbigh Brewers Club is meeting here this afternoon, and they are all in the top ale connoisseur class in Wales. Couldn't risk them tasting a bad pint here.'

'That's why you charge so much for your ale?' asked Tommy.

'Thirty pence a pint isn't bad,' said Selwyn, waving a finger at Tommy. 'You get what you pay for.' He took the pint jug to his lips and slowly, methodically downed it in one. He punctuated the action with a mighty belch.

'That stink,' said Rhonda—wafting at the odour in the air. Tommy and Davey had their eyes wide open. They counted twelve pumps—six pints each, four each if the landlord was to join in. Beginning with Rhonda's arrival, their day got better. Tommy pointed to a pump labelled 'Magnet light ale.'

'I feel strangely drawn to that there, pump,' he said.

'Eh?' said Davey.

Rhonda laughed, 'If I had a pound for every time I've heard that.'

Seeing the greedy eyes, Selwyn held a hand up, 'Do I have volunteers here lads?'

'Does the Pope shit in his hat,' said Tommy.

'I'm for it as well, you know—not just a pretty face around here,' said Rhonda as she dug Tommy in the ribs. 'No blaspheming here on a Sunday, please.'

An hour later, Tommy, Davey and Rhonda were sat on a bench outside the inn. The boys were nicely tanked. Tommy and Davey had put away three and a half pints each. Selwyn had gulped four—the greedy bastard—with Rhonda making do with just a pint of mild. 'Don't know how you can drink so much this early in the day,' she said. 'That one pint has done it for me. Don't you go telling Mr Morrin about me drinking this early, now.'

'I won't—you can tell me anything—do anything, it'll always be between you and me.'

'And me,' said Davey, smiling. Rhonda looked at them both—a mischievous smile on her face. Davey blushed and glanced at Tommy. 'How come you haven't got a fella? Maybe you have, but…'

'Who said I haven't? Got any number of men who come here trying to court me.'

'Yeah, but I've never seen you with anyone special, like,' said Davey.

'Well, there's Keith. He came to pick up Stingray instead of Ramshaw, the knackers man.'

A respectful moment of silence passed among them. Tommy broke this by asking, 'What's the latest with the original Dickens books?'

'Still waiting for clarification on who donated them.'

'You'd think whoever had them would have known how valuable they were?'

'Maybe, but some people think more of the benefit a gift can bring rather than in taking any credit for the giving…' Tommy and Davey nodded.

Davey asked, 'This Keith fella, with the horse box. Who is he?'

'From your neck of the woods—Wirral. Italian American he is, or his family is. You could say he's my regular fella. Runs a riding school nearby. Takes turns as the local DJ too.'

'You could say? Is he or isn't he your fella?' asked Tommy.

'Well, let's say I feel safe with him. No funny business…'

'Eh?' said Davey.

'Is he Beirut?' asked Tommy.

'Beirut?'

'Er, prefers men to women?'

'Ah… You'd better ask him. Due here now he is. Very handsome, but never made me feel… pestered… He writes jokes on the gent's toilet walls, he tells me. Drives Selwyn mad. I think he's starting to suspect, as they appear after he turns up, putting his disco posters on the wall.' Tommy and Davey nodded.

'Rhonda,' said Tommy. 'How come you left the farm to work here?' Rhonda stared back soberly. 'That's if you don't mind me asking?' he added.

Rhonda paused thoughtfully.

'You shouldn't ask that, Tommy,' said Davey.

'No, it's okay. I don't mind talking about it. Especially since what happened last night.' Tommy and Davey sat up expectantly. 'It was partly my fault what happened with my dad and Mad-Dog…'

'How do you mean?' asked Tommy.

'Well, for years, there was always talk—suspicion about what had gone on between him and my real dad… Went missing when I was just five, he did. My stepdad, Mr Morrin, arrived one day with a solicitor holding land registry papers and took over the farm. Ten years or so later, Mark Dylan, that's Mad-Dog's real name, turned up at the farm claiming it was his land—nephew of my real dad.

'The solicitor came back and they had a meeting here at the inn. A mess at first, but they'd all ended up shaking hands, with Mad-Dog getting a stake in the lands. He'd been the farm manager for about a year after I turned sixteen. Before that, he'd always been friendly with me. Complimenting me on things. They called him Mad-Dog because of the way he rounded the sheep so expertly—he did it better than any of the dogs could—his initials as well—MD.

'There was talk of him taking over the full running of the farm as my dad got older. I suppose I was flattered, and I suppose I was enjoying this grown man flirting with me. It felt right, especially with him having those prospects of taking things over. It felt natural. But after my sixteenth birthday, I could feel a change in the way he looked at me. He became a bit tongue-tied and blushed every time we spoke.'

'This is after you turned sixteen?' said Davey. He looked at Tommy.

'As the days went by, I found myself seeing him watching me from a distance, and I felt maybe I had done something wrong to make him so awkward with me. I tried to make conversations with him at every opportunity until one day, my dad pulled me aside. He asked me why I was throwing myself at his Herdsman. Called me a Temptress, he did.

'I denied it, but looking back, I could see he was right. I heard them having a raging argument one night outside the barn. I heard my dad telling him to keep away from his little girl, and I resented him for that. I thought I hated him at the time. I was not a little girl to anyone… The next day, my dad was out at the market, and I was alone in the main barn milking the cows. I sensed Mad-Dog behind me, and there he was, standing too close to me… He covered my eyes and started to… kiss the back of my neck. He started to whisper things in my ear—very, well, intimate things… For a short while, I kind of… liked it. But then he began spreading his hands all over. Not gently, but pawing at me… I got scared and told him to stop, but he carried on and started to rip at my dress. I pushed him off and made to run away, and he called me a 'prick teasing bitch,' and came at me again.'

Tommy turned away in shame, staring down at the floor. Wasn't this what he thought of Linda—a prick teasing bitch?

'He ran at me and ripped more on my dress. I started screaming just as my dad and Pops came rushing into the barn.

He spotted my ripped dress and ran at Mad-Dog, and they had a terrible fight.

'I ran and begged Selwyn to let me stay for a while. Mr Morrin—I'd stopped calling him dad—came to the inn the next night with Sergeant Bradley. My dad's face was bruised, and he had a black eye. He wanted me to talk to the Sergeant and make a statement, but I didn't want to. The Sergeant asked if he could talk to me alone. We sat here, on this bench, and he told me Mad-Dog had a similar history on other farms in Wales. Three times, he had been sacked for 'interference.' On the last farm, he was accused of trying to molest one of the dairymaids. He had threatened to burn the place to the ground if the owners went to the police.

'Charged, but not found guilty. He had lied about his references to get a job with my dad. I agreed to make a statement about him. That night, my dad discovered the main barn had been set on fire. He rang for both the police and the fire brigade. They saved the cows. Sergeant Bradley had picked up Mad-Dog near the old mill—he stank of petrol.'

'Did he admit to lighting the fire?'

'He denied it at first, but then he said if any other charges against him, interfering with me, were dropped, he'd plead guilty to the arson.'

'Why didn't he get charged for both?' asked Tommy.

'Something to do with the insurance. As if I'd provoked him into the arson, as though it was partly my fault with my teasing… I've never felt comfortable with my dad, Mr Morrin, since. We never mention it to each other. And, there he is, turning up last night.'

'I'm sorry, Rhonda, maybe if I hadn't spoken to them three dickheads the way I did…'

'No, Tommy, he was on his way anyway, set his cousins up to provoke you. When he walked in the bar, he asked me to step outside with him to talk. I said no, and he grabbed my arm and showed me a razor—cutthroat one he had in his hand. Told me he was going to sort out some Scousers that were staying at the farm then come back to mess up my face.'

'Fucking hell!' said Tommy.

'Didn't tell my dad that bit though. He really would have shot him.'

'And what's your plans? Just to stay and work here at the inn? He could always come back,' said Davey.

'Wouldn't you be safer at the farm?' asked Tommy.

'Here?' Rhonda laughed drily. 'Stay here in this one-eyed village, where everyone still looks at me with that knowing look. This village is not for me. I've saved every week. Within six months, I'll have enough put by to travel. I'll have my training complete as well.'

'Where will you go?' asked Tommy, resisting an urge to take Rhonda in his arms.

'Spain… Spain at first. Be as hot as here, won't it? Spain for a few months, then around Europe. Me and Keith have talked about it loads, he speaks Spanish as well as Italian. He put me on the training courses. I'm doing a residency in teaching English as a foreign language at the University in Bangor. Start in September. Three months course, after that I'm off. Six more months, and goodbye Henllan for me.'

'And what does Mr Morrin think of that?' asked Davey.

'Oh, he's not happy. Offered me the farm to stay, he has.'

'And you're not tempted by that?' asked Davey.

'He thinks I am. Thinks I'm a temptress, doesn't he, now.'

A minibus pulled up outside the inn. Several paunchy men alighted. 'Here comes the brewers and Keith,' said Rhonda. A grey-haired young man was tethering a tall white horse. Tommy couldn't decide if the man's hair was dyed or a natural grey.

'You want to say hello to Keith?'

‘I need a piss,’ said Davey. Tommy walked past the overweight brewers and admired the horse. Keith kissed Rhonda hard on the lips, and Tommy felt jealous.

‘Keith—this is Tommy. From Liverpool he is.’ Keith stood back from Rhonda and offered his hand.

‘Nice horse,’ said Tommy. ‘You get this from teaching?’

‘That and a few other skills,’ said Keith. ‘I’m late. Has Selwyn done with cleaning the pipes?’ Rhonda and Tommy nodded. Keith gazed at the brewery club members entering the bar. He spoke with a Scouse accent mixed with American Italian overtones.

‘Where are you from?’ asked Tommy

‘Me, well, I suppose, here there and everywhere. Most recently from Denbigh via Bromborough. Scouse, huh?’ Tommy nodded. ‘You coming to my disco tonight?’ He stood forward—blocking Tommy’s view of Rhonda.

‘Too right,’ said Tommy, aware a rivalry had been established.

18
YE OLD MILL

Heading back to the farm, Tommy and Davey discussed Rhonda's tale.

'She never mention this before?' asked Tommy.

'Nope, we all had an idea of what happened with Mad-Dog, but no details. Looks like you bring out the truth sometimes, Tommy.' Tommy nodded. They stopped to take a piss against hedgerows. Tommy's thoughts turned to his dwindling money.

'Davey lad, we've got a short detour on the way back.'

'The mill?' asked Davey.

'Your starter for ten,' said Tommy

'There's nothing there.'

'How do you know? Ever been inside?'

'It's always been empty since we started. I've seen the odd van going in and out but always taking things away—never taking things in. Won't be any cash there.'

'Well, do you fancy having a quick look to confirm?'

'I suppose, but we'll have to make sure we are all clear.'

'Frigging hell, Davey, you going to give me an egg-sucking demo next? I need some more money.'

'Tommy, I'm telling you, there's no cash in that old mill. And anyway, I've got money. You know I'll lend you whatever you need, mate.'

Tommy stopped. 'Thanks, Davey lad. But it's like the mountaineer fella who was asked why he climbed the mountain…'

'Because it's there,' said Davey, smiling.

'Correct, now here's the plan…'

Standing outside the entrance gates, Tommy lit up a ciggie and checked that no one else was around. Davey had stationed himself behind hedges on a field high up the lane. From there, he could see both ways and whistle a warning to Tommy if anyone approached.

Tommy sized up several metal bins that held overflowing rubbish near the gates. Using one as a prop, he was up and easy over the high gate.

There were clear signs of dereliction in the old mill yard. He passed by, looking into the empty windows at rubbish-strewn flooring. Huge rats scampered openly. All of the doors he tried were open except one at the far end of the mill courtyard. The door was marked 'Site Facilities Manager.' Pushing against the door, he found it firmly locked. Taking a quick look and listening closely for traffic, he confirmed there was still no one else around.

Tommy knew that breaking a locked door was not just a matter of brute force. It was a technique of angle and the speed of the assault. Taking three strides away, he started forward quickly, raising his leg, twisting at the hips, and his heel punched though the lock like it wasn't there. 'Open sesame,' he said, entering the office.

Inside, an assortment of tools hung on wall racks, hammers and chisels. Lunch wrappers and empty food cartons showed signs of activity. Rat traps and baits were heaped in a neat pile on a worktop. Tommy stepped outside and listened. The only sounds came from scampering rats. Nothing else. Back inside the office, searching, Tommy focussed on a locked cupboard. He selected a hammer and chisel and made short work of the lock. Inside, under a tartan blanket, Tommy unearthed a long narrow box. Hinged along one side, it looked like it could contain a snooker cue or expensive fishing rods.

Or, perhaps, fingers crossed… a rifle. Keeping the rats at bay would have required more than mere traps and poison. He placed the box onto a worktable and saw it had a small lock at the top. Who locked up a fishing rod?

A tap with the hammer and chisel and bingo—the box opened. Inside, Tommy delightedly picked up the long air rifle—labelled 'Webley Falcon .22 MM.' There were several small cardboard boxes, each containing a dozen pellet cartridges.

'You beauty,' said Tommy, tracing a finger around the polished wooden stock. 'Sorry, Davey, but this would freak you out. Now, how the hell do I get you home?'

Outside from the mill, Tommy stashed the rifle and bullets in a large bin bag, hiding it behind a load of rubble. Davey approached. 'Anything?'

'Nah, you were right, Davey—waste of time, mate.'

Davey nodded and said neutrally, 'Didn't want to mention it, but I thought there might have been a rifle in there that you'd find. We've heard shooting from inside the mill a few times when we've been here. Seen a maintenance bloke out with Mr Morrin, hunting.'

Tommy's initial instinct was to stay quiet, but he looked at Davey and found he couldn't continue the lie. Besides, how the hell could he sneak this back to Liverpool? He pointed toward the rubble where he'd stashed the rifle.

'You knew, didn't you… in the black bin bag.' They took another good look around. Coast clear, they dug out the rifle and headed off the road into a nearby field.

'Binoculars would have been handy,' said Davey.

'I was thinking exactly that,' said Tommy. Davey cocked the rifle and loaded a pellet. It dropped out of the barrel end.

'Looks like you've got to hold it level,' he said, reloading. He held the stock level. Closed the rifle. Aimed…

'Tree on the far right.' Davey sighted and fired. Nothing happened. He bent the stock and the pellet fell out again. 'Shit.' He felt and found a safety switch near the trigger, reloaded, and fired; a soft 'ping' sound from the rifle and a small piece of bark was blown from the tree.

'Fucking hell—Davey Crocket is right!' said Tommy, impressed. 'My turn,' he said, grabbing the rifle. 'Clint style, locked and loaded.' He cocked it, placed the cartridge in and fired off a quick shot at nothing, reloaded and fired again—hitting the same tree Davey had aimed at. Smugly, he blew down the barrel. They shook hands.

Pulling away, Davey said, 'Don't forget, it's nothing like the real thing that Mr Morrin has. It's only an air rifle.'

'But would it hurt though?' said Tommy.

'No one would want it pointing at them,' conceded Davey.

'Need to stash it somewhere handy.'

'Back outside the mill?' suggested Davey. Tommy nodded, and they headed back to the mill and wrapped the rifle and pellets in separate bin bags near the rubbish outside of the mill gates.

Strolling back to the outside of the farm wall, Tommy and Davey whistled nonchalantly as Tommy finished a ciggie.

'Where've you two been?' asked Jack. His bare arms were covered in the white paint. 'Some of us have been earning our keep here.' He and Ken looked bushed.

The length of the farm wall had been scraped clean and a start made on the painting.

'Just admiring the scenic view,' said Tommy. Brusquely, Jack handed Tommy and Davey a roller brush each.

'Well, you can both admire that. We're off to get a brew.' Tommy took the brush, and carried on his whistling as he applied the whitewash.

Ken approached, 'You've been boozing at the inn, haven't you? Slobbering over Rhonda.'

'May have been.'

'Jack—you seen this—both of them stinking of ale!'

'I thought I could smell it,' said Jack, nodding.

'Ken, what bollocks is this? I need an absence chit from Captain Jack there before I have a pint?'

'What if that mad fella and his mates were hanging around by the bar again?' said Jack to Davey.

'We all heard what Mr Morrin told us this morning—Mad-Dog won't be able to show his face anywhere near this village.'

'But what if he, or those other three lads—his cousins or whatever—what if they got a grip of you? More trouble, hey,' said Ken angrily.

'The only thing they'd get a grip of would be this…' Tommy raised his hand in a fist, scowling, his lips tightening, nostrils flaring. 'Bang in their bastard nose!' he smacked his hands together. Jack and Ken stared at him. Jack shook his head.

'I don't know, Tommy, maybe Ken is right and trouble does follow you.'

'What?' Tommy was enraged. 'I'll give you fucking trouble, you big prick.' He raised his fist and shook it at Jack's face. 'You're not in charge—and neither is that frigging tit.' Davey moved between Jack and Tommy. *Jack was impassive*, he sighed.

'That's true Tommy. Got no answer for that.' He turned. Tommy calmed, flight or fight easing, adrenaline slowing; he regretted showing Jack his temper.

'The landlord, Selwyn was cleaning the pipes,' said Davey. 'He invited us in…'

'I know what happens there,' said Jack. 'I've helped him a good few times.' Ken was still staring angrily.

'Is that all you can say? He's threatened me. And he's just threatened you as well…'

'Tommy hasn't threatened me,' said Jack.

'I'm sorry, Jack,' said Tommy. 'I shouldn't have snapped at you. It's… well… the past couple of days have been crazy for me… You know what I mean?'

Jack nodded.

'But he is a fucking tit,' he said, pointing at Ken.

'Come on. Pack this in. Too hot now anyway. We'll finish the walls off tomorrow.'

'Could have come and got us a free pint as well,' mumbled Ken.

19

PRE-DISCO-FEVER

The freezing shower in the hay barn was a delight as the lads took turns scrubbing the sweat, paint, dust and general crap off their bodies. Two minutes in the sunshine was enough to get dry and then sweaty again. All agreed on an afternoon siesta. Tommy and Davey got a few hours kip in the relative coolness of the tent, with Jack and Ken having a sleep on the hay in the big barn.

Waking at five, Tommy headed for a walk by himself, nodding hello to two young girls on horseback—huge scary beasts to Tommy. One was chestnut brown, the other a shiny black colour.

With a mixture of pleasant and pre-emptive thoughts, Tommy ambled to the mill and retrieved the air rifle and pellets. A fifteen-minute jog—passing the two horses—and he was near the village church hall where the disco was soon to be held, choosing a good spot near thick bushes. He stashed the bin bags containing the air rifle and cartridges away from the public path. Johnnies—just in case, he said to himself… If Mad-Dog were to turn up, he'd find himself outgunned.

Back at the camp, the tent was empty. He headed to the main barn and saw that all the lads had their best gear ironed and spruced, thanks to Pops. The sour mood from earlier had gone. It was a pity the tiny radio had died.

Ken donned a purple velvet jacket and two-tone trousers. He had grown three inches with his stack-heeled shoes. As the light played on the trousers, they flashed purple and blue.

Pops kept repeating the word 'Purple,' saying it in a high-pitched Scouser style—'Per-Pull.' Jack, Davey, and Tommy pulled on their flared Flemings jeans. Davey put on his black and white Budgie jacket while Tommy and Jack wore simple, short-sleeved shirts.

Back in the tent, Tommy doused himself in Brut splash-on lotion, hairspray and deodorant. Ken daubed himself with Hai Karate after-shave, and Davey splashed on Old Spice aftershave. Poking his head into the tent, Jack sneezed loudly.

'Christ, smells like a whore's handbag in here. Can't you lot do that outside?' Ken farted and shook his leg to disperse it down his trousers.

'Lads,' said Jack. 'We need a plan for tonight. Besides his stink, I can smell trouble on the horizon. We all want to enjoy ourselves, but we need to stick together. I've rang a few lads I know, told me they were coming anyway and were a bit pissed they might be called upon not just to enjoy themselves. Mr Morrin is sending a few of his farm hand lads—keep an eye on Rhonda.' Tommy noted this was the longest dialogue he'd heard from Jack. He was satisfied his earlier preparations were well-founded.

'That's it. We all stick together. Any sign, any hint of trouble, we group up... Now, let's get outside of this.' Magician-like, Jack held up a huge can of Watneys Party Seven—seven full pints of best ale.

'And this!' said Ken, holding up a slightly smaller, but nonetheless impressive, Watneys Party Five. Ken whipped out a tin opener and expertly cracked holes in the huge cans.

'Crack it both sides on now,' said Jack. He prised open the cans on adjacent sides and all the lads sat outside the tent to tank up. Fresh batteries for the radio had been discovered and Roxy Music—'Virginia Plain'—was in full blast. The disco Fever was rising...

As Mr Morrin and Pops approached, Pops again fixed on the word 'purple'. Both were carrying proper rifles and shotguns. Mr Morrin eyed Ken's two-tone pants and stack-heeled shoes.

'See what you meant, Pops. Bloody hell—didn't realise Roxy Music was in the village, let alone on my lands.' Pops smiled.

'Quick word here. As I've already said to Jack, had reports there may be a Mad-Dog running around. Can't see him showing his face in the church disco—not his style—but I want you all to be extra careful. He has his family and all their cronies. Who knows what has been planned… Be extra vigilant, as we are going to be here tonight.' As he spoke, he cocked his rifle and inserted two cartridges; he nodded at Pops, who gave a nod back.

Something is coming down tonight, thought Tommy.

'Be careful lads—and enjoy yourselves.'

20
DISCO INFERNO

Outside the church hall, Tommy saw the black and the chestnut horses he had passed earlier. Both were tethered up and munching at a bag of hay.

Inside, the hall was bathed and swaying in disco lights. Red, yellow, green and blue traced across the dance floor, walls and windows. Thirty young adolescents milled about a soft drinks stand. Churchwardens had set up two tables to dispense orange squash and real lemonade. Maggie Rhea from the charity shop gave Tommy a happy wave of hello. Tommy made a mental note to ask her for the latest news on the Dickens novels.

The Osmonds' 'Crazy Horses' song was playing. A small ring of girls was swishing their heads in time with the synthesised rush of the music. At the DJ turntable, Keith Piperello waved a big thumbs up at Tommy and Davey.

Tommy's disco fever receded as his Spidey sense tingled. He clocked the exits. One at each corner. The northwest the most direct route back to the farm. A balcony overlooked the dance floor, which housed the church choir. Tommy headed that way. Davey, Ken and Jack queued for the orange squash. Acknowledging the 'No Smoking' signs, Tommy cupped his ciggie inwardly. From the balcony, he had a clear view of the hall below. No sign of Rhonda.

Four tall teenagers entered. Tommy sensed recognition from one staring up at him. Part of the six-man crew that had turned up outside the inn? More and more lads entered. The ratio of boys to girls was now three to one. Tommy eyed Jack as he queued again for orange squash. He was easily the tallest bloke in the hall. Tommy took some reassurance from that.

Rhonda entered the hall. She strode like a gust of fresh air. ‘Magic’ by Pilot was playing. She was wearing a white dress reminiscent of the billowing one Marilyn Monroe was remembered for. Every male head swivelled as she glided across the hall, waving hellos.

‘Absolutely edible,’ said Tommy. Pegging his ciggie out, he headed down the balcony to get in the queue to speak to her. Ken was practically slobbering. Jack and Davey were at her side. Davey took an arm and led her into the middle of the dance floor.

Tommy saw Jack clocking the four lads at the drinks table. A tall, young farmer type approached Jack and they shook hands warmly. The lad looked like he could handle himself.

‘Well, that’s better, five of us at least now.’ Tommy said quietly to himself.

The Osmond dancers surrounded Davey and Rhonda in the middle of the dance floor. Both could move. Tommy felt a pang of jealousy and headed over to the DJ Keith. The proximity of the speakers meant he had to shout into the DJ’s ear. Keith was beaming at Tommy’s request. He took off his headphones and gave him another big thumbs up.

‘Good call Scouse, some re-al music.’

Heading over to Rhonda as ‘Magic’ played out, Tommy took Rhonda’s hand.

‘My turn,’ he said to Davey.

The boom of the DJ’s microphone was bouncing off the walls. ‘Okay kids, this next one is a request from our guests from Liverpool—for Tommy and our own Rhonda, it’s Disco Tex and the Sex-O-Lettes and ‘Get Dancin.’’

The wardens on the squash tables stood and swivelled their heads at the mention of the ‘S’ word and gaped open-mouthed at the DJ.

As though it had been thoroughly rehearsed and choreographed, Tommy and Rhonda danced, bumped and clapped hands together. In Tommy's eyes, Rhonda became the centre of the universe—both were Masters. For three minutes their sheer vitality and unison was a delight for those gathered in the church hall.

And then it kicked off.

Someone hit the fire alarm and six teenagers surrounded Jack and his farmer friend. Punches started flying. Davey and Ken rushed to help. Other lads headed towards them; Tommy wasn't sure whose side they were on and before he could move, the three lads from the inn stood in front of him. One kicked him hard in the left knee causing him to drop. Two lifted him by his arms, and the one with the tattooed hand-delivered a lung-bursting punch to Tommy's stomach, then smacked an uppercut into his drooped jaw. Almost blacking out, Tommy came again to his knees. Through skewed, blurred vision, he saw the two horses now inside the church hall—skittish and spooked by the lights, music and mayhem. The wardens were trying to get a hold on them. Younger kids scampered out of the way for the exit doors.

Keith had stopped the music and rushed over, helping Tommy to his feet. He held up his fists to ward off the three lads from Tommy. Rhonda was screaming and trying to scratch at the tattooed lad's face. He slapped her face hard. Helpless, this hurt Tommy almost as much as the punches. The black horse got closer, putting Tommy in danger of getting trampled. Keith managed to get a hand on a rein and was trying to calm it—the horse and the attackers, all at the same time. Davey joined them—fists raised and ready to hit out.

Timing carefully, Tommy rolled under the horse. Helped by Davey, he staggered to his feet and limped to the northwest fire exit. Kicking open the door, he gasped for breath outside, before slamming the door closed again. His left knee was starting to swell.

'Plan A Davey lad. I'm going to dance on them fuckers,' he said, as the fire exit burst open and out came the black horse—with DJ Keith on his back.

'Scouse, hold on here, need to get you aways.' He held out a hand to Tommy, who hesitated. 'Your friends are okay in there. Jack has backup. But you are fucked. You can't walk, man. Help him Davey.' Tommy saw the battered old Morris Minor parked nearby. Mad-Dog at large. Reaching out, Tommy took the DJ's hand and with a great effort, pulled himself across the horse's neck.

'Head that way,' said Tommy pointing to the bushes outside of the church grounds. At a canter, the horse was led to where Tommy had stashed the rifle. Davey ran alongside.

'Hold on,' said Tommy, getting off the horse. He reached in and retrieved the rifle from the bin bag coverings.

'Man, I say you hold on!' Keith slid off the horse, and held a hand in Tommy's face. 'What you thinking of, Scouse?'

'The fuckers hit Rhonda as well—you saw that, now help me back up!'

'Scouser,' Keith was interrupted by the sound of approaching sirens—police on their way. 'Hear that?' He reached out a hand to take the rifle. 'Scouser, she's not Felina, you are not Marty Robbins, and this is not El Paso.'

Davey nodded as he took the rifle off Tommy and passed it to Keith. What?

Tommy fell to the ground, vomiting—empty heaves. When he looked up, the Morris Minor had gone. A police car and a fire engine were outside the church hall. There was no sign of Keith or the black horse.

Davey was speaking to Jack outside the Hall. Hobbling, Tommy headed towards them.

Outside, all of the kids were standing around. One of the churchwardens was holding a bloody handkerchief to Ken's nose. Jack and Rhonda were now speaking quietly to a police constable. Davey approached him.

'Jack said we need to get away from here Tommy, right now, back to the farm.'

'You mean, get me away?'

'Well… yep.'

'I've done nothing wrong.'

'Tommy, Jack knows about the rifle—the DJ Keith told him.'

'So what, I've done nothing wrong here!'

'Let's get back…' before Tommy answered, a policeman approached.

'You okay, son?' he asked Tommy.

'Fine,' said Tommy.

'Just need to take down a few of your details if you don't mind.'

'But what for? I've done nothing wrong.'

'That may be, but we are checking on everyone that's not from here. And I can see you've been hurt. Just a few questions if you please…'

'You answer one of mine first,' said Tommy

'I'll try.'

'Okay… One of the locals… You know them all?'

'Mostly.'

'Well, who the hell is Marty Robbins?'

'Marty Robbins… He's that country singer, isn't he? Cowboy like.'

'Country singer?'

Another policeman had joined them. He said, 'He's smashing, he is, sang 'El Paso!''

'That's the one.' They started singing:

'Out in the west town El Paso, I fell in love with a Mexican girl'.

They were interrupted as a senior police officer was approaching purposely. 'That's enough, you two. Tommy Dwyer of Score Lane Liverpool?' He stared at Tommy.

'Er, yeah, that's me.'

'I'm arresting you.'

'What for, it wasn't me…'

'Kidnapping for a start. Handcuff him. Cells for you tonight.'

21
FATHER FORGIVE ME

The police station cell was cold, damp, and harsh. Echoes from adjacent cells bounced from wall to wall. It was a busy night for the local Constabulary. A singing drunk was working through his repertoire of Irish protest songs, favouring 'The Fields of Athenry.'

Hunched on a sparse wooden pallet, Tommy mulled over the humiliation of being carted away, handcuffed in full view of the church hall. Davey and Rhonda had protested. Jack stood with his arms folded, whilst Ken… Tommy was sure he'd detected satisfaction in that mole-like weasel face. He'd seen an ambulance take Mad-Dog's tattooed cousin away.

Two of the lads who'd started the attack were in the same cellblock, one demanding a call be made to his parents. Tommy looked at his hands. The ink the arresting Sergeant had used to take his fingerprints would not wash off. His shoelaces had been removed.

'Shit, I was going to hang myself with those,' he'd said.

After his fingerprints were taken, Tommy stood against a white wall marked with height indicators to have his photograph taken. From there, he was led to an interrogation room, where a tired Sergeant sat behind a chin-high rostrum.

'Can you tell me your name, date of birth and current address please?'

'Tommy Dwyer, fifteenth of April, nineteen fifty-nine.'

'You're seventeen, correct?'

'Yes.'

'In that case, you are entitled to have an adult with you at all times during any questioning. Is there anyone you want to call right now? Parents?'

'Can you call Mr Morrin, he's a farmer in…'

'I know who Mr Morrin is, do you want to call a parent, a solicitor perhaps?' This dismissal of Mr Morrin gave Tommy pause.

'What am I getting charged with?'

'We aren't going to be charging you. There's bobbies on the way here from Liverpool to come and collect you. We are just holding you for a few hours. You can wait until you are back local to call a solicitor. Up to you. My senior officers may want to question you here. I'll say again, you have the right to have an adult present.'

'I've got nothing to say.'

'The charges are very serious.'

'And I'll say again, I've got nothing to say.'

'Please yourself.'

That was an hour and a half ago. Shivering, worried, and dying for a smoke, Tommy tried to massage relief into the hurt knee. He heard footsteps outside, and a shutter opening on the cell door.

'Stand away from the door with your back against the far wall.'

Tommy stood and limped to the far wall. Keys rattled, and the door was opened. A tall, youthful-looking policeman nodded to him. 'Hurt your leg?'

'A bit.'

'You want to show me?'

Tommy reddened and tried to roll his trouser leg up past the swollen knee. He hesitated, reluctant to pull his pants down. The policeman saw the discomfort.

'I'll see if I can find some strapping for that. And a pair of shorts maybe.' He beckoned with a finger. 'Follow me.' Obediently, Tommy followed the policeman down a length of corridors away from the cell block to an interrogation room.

Inside, an older policeman with a haggard face was smoking untipped cigarettes. The smoke permeated the room. By the look of the ashtray, he'd been here a while. Momentarily, the nicotine rush was a pleasure for Tommy.

'Sit down.'

Tommy sat at the table. 'I'm Inspector Marlon of Denbigh CID, and this is Constable Rees on rotation from Rhyl, isn't it?'

The constable nodded, taking up a position near the door behind Tommy. 'Already caused us some commotion here you have… The phone hasn't stopped ringing, has it, Constable?' The Inspector was lighting another cigarette from the tip of his previous one. Red mottles of frustration were showing in his cheeks. There was a knock on the door.

He stood. 'Let them in,' he said impatiently. The constable opened the door, and Mr Morrin and Sergeant Bradley entered.

'I wouldn't have agreed to this. It's not right,' the Inspector said to Sergeant Bradley, as he and the constable left the room. 'Fifteen minutes—that's all. And the constable stays outside the room.'

Mr Morrin took a seat opposite Tommy, pushing the ashtray away with distaste. For the first time, Tommy saw Mr Morrin not in his usual smart attire. If anything, he looked somewhat dishevelled.

'I'll go and find coffee,' said the Sergeant, dropping a box of matches and a packet of Players No.10 on the table before leaving them alone in the bare room.

'Thanks for coming,' said Tommy. Mr Morrin wiped his hands across his face. He looked gaunt and tired.

'I was here anyway. Talk to me, Tommy. Tell me about you?'

'I'm Tommy Dwyer. From Liverpool. What do you want to know?'

'They say confession is good for the soul. This place may be less so than a church, perhaps. I know who you are, but give me an idea of what you are?'

'I, uh, don't know what you mean?' This was becoming uncomfortable.

'What are your hopes, lad? What are your plans, workwise? What are your plans for the next few years—assuming you have your freedom?'

The unease was growing in Tommy. 'If I have my freedom?'

Mr Morrin patted his shoulder. 'I know you will, lad. I'm on your side. But, humour me—tell me what's going on in there. What are your secrets? I'll tell you mine. Share with me, Tommy.' He tapped his forehead; Tommy took a deep breath and decided to speak honestly.

'I've got a choice: move with my family to New Zealand, or I'm supposed to be going to a sixth form College. Do my 'A' levels, after that, I don't really know.'

'Big choices indeed. It's said travel can exercise the brain more than education. But you said supposed to go to College—what does that mean? You don't want to—or that you don't know if you should?'

'It's hard to explain…'

'Try me.'

'Well, for a start, there may be a problem with the qualifications I'm supposed to have.' Tommy had never admitted this to anyone else—he could barely acknowledge it to himself.

'Explain?'

'Well, to get in the sixth form, you need at least five decent O-levels…'

'And have you got these qualifications?'

Tommy paused. 'We don't have much more time,' said Mr Morrin. He fished out a silver hip flask, took the lid off, guzzling down a large swill. He passed it to Tommy who sniffed the contents. 'Best French brandy. Warm your cockles,' said Mr Morrin. Tommy necked the hip flask. A warm glow flowed into his belly and spread to his arms and legs. He lit a ciggie.

'Bad habit that, especially if you live on a farm. I'm certain it's not good for you. Can I have one please?'

Tommy passed over a ciggie and struck a match for Mr Morrin. He took a couple of pulls before pegging it and passing it back to Tommy. 'You hesitate with your truth?' he said to Tommy. 'I understand.'

'Can I ask you a question?' said Tommy.

'Please, go ahead.'

'When you came in, you said I was here anyway—what did you mean?

'Manners now, answer my question first. Do you have these qualifications?'

'I've got the certificates…'

'Ah, I'm beginning to see.' He took another long swill from the hip flask. Passed it back to Tommy. 'So, someone sat the exams for you—a bright lad you paid—hey? Not unheard of around here. A lot of locals go in for that sort of thing, for taking driving tests and such like.'

'No, nothing like that. My Uncle works in a printing company. They've got the contract for the examining boards.'

'HMSO—Her Majesty's Stationary Office?'

'I don't know about that, but his works print off the exam certificates. That and film and music posters. I passed the exams, but only just. My Uncle printed me new ones—all with a higher grade.' Feeling lighter, Tommy took a long pull on the brandy.

'And does anyone else know this?'

'No, only me, my Uncle, and you.'

Mr Morrin nodded. He put the stopper onto the hip flask. 'Then I don't see any problem. Do you need to exaggerate the truth?'

'It's just that, well, most of my life I've felt I wasn't good enough…'

'This your thoughts or someone else's that they put in your head?'

'I don't know… I suppose, maybe, a bit of both.'

Mr Morrin nodded, taking another hit from the flask. 'Catholic, was it? Catholic schoolteachers?'

'I hated going to the church…'

'Religion has a lot to answer for—there been so much misery, death, and destruction over the ridiculous premise that my God is better than your god. Young minds don't have the brainpower to filter out the propaganda they force-feed you. Making children go to a Confession is a sin. How can a young mind harbour the Catholic guilt?'

'I don't know…'

'Makes me sick. Priests and their own teachers are worse still—re-enforcing it—driving it into your head. Did you know that brain in your head isn't fully developed until you are twenty-five years of age?' Fists clenched, he slammed them against the table. 'We should all be made to worship the sun. We can see it and feel it every day of our lives. More so over the past month… Now…' He took deep breaths, calming… 'Putting that aside. Tell me the truth. Are you innocent to, what is it, kidnapping?'

'I killed a man.'

Mr Morrin stared into Tommy's eyes. 'Tell me…'

A surge of relief washed over Tommy. He confessed. In hoarse whispers, he told Mr Morrin of the unprovoked dog attack, the scarecrow man, the demand for his bag and money, the brief struggle… Mr Morrin listened, a finger against his lips. He paced the room thoughtfully. He whispered as quietly as Tommy had spoken. 'Did you set out that morning with the intention of killing someone?'

'No.'

'Would he have hacked you with that blade?'

'More like a sword. It was a machete, for chopping bushes down.'

'I know what a machete is. Are you certain—he wasn't just scaring you—just wanting your wallet?'

Tommy had never carried a wallet in his life. Folding money went into his arse pocket. In his mind eye, he dismissed this irrelevance and recalled the sharpness of his perception on that morning, the high-resolution details of the patches sewn into those trousers at the knees—the red right hand raising behind his head…

'I'm one hundred per cent certain.'

'But what if you had run away—ran as fast as you could?'

'He was about to throw the machete at me, I would have got it in my back.'

'But say you managed to dodge it, and you ran away and told the police, and they caught him and put him in jail. Hey Tommy?' Mr Morrin had his right eyebrow raised.

'Maybe, but he would have got out one day and maybe…'

'Maybe if my Aunt Joan had balls, she'd be my Uncle John—we can maybe all day until the cows come home. Did you do the right thing? Did you do what was good and proper?'

'Yes.'

'And did this man get what he deserved?'

'Yes.'

'Did you do your community a service by ridding it of this foul creature?'

'Yes…'

'Then that's the be all and end all and no one will mention it ever again. For all time… Amen.'

Mr Morrin pulled Tommy towards him in a tender hug that Tommy realised was exactly what he needed. Standing back, Mr Morrin coughed gently, straightened his jacket, and adjusted non-existent cuff links, becoming business-like.

'Okay, this other matter, these so-called charges, kidnapping is it?'

'Mr Morrin, on my life! I was with the lad who got dragged off into the car. We were out together, but this crew turns up in a car—all tooled up—they'd been after Joey for days, and I had to make out I was with them, on their side—I had to. They followed me back to my house, where—well, I've got this sword under my bed, but the police came and instead of me, they rescued him. This was on the morning we came to your farm.'

'So, it wasn't that you were running away or anything?'

'I told my sister what was happening as they sat outside the house waiting for me.'

'Tommy, I believe you. You should have explained that to the police. And this lad who was assaulted—will he back you up?' Tommy thought. He'd avoided that question.

'He should do, but he's only a kid—and he was terrified.'

'I don't doubt it. Okay, only a few minutes left. Business. Do you have a family solicitor?'

'Er, not really.'

'No disrespect, but I didn't think so. You'll be entitled to all sorts of legal aid, but there's a sharp man I know, handles my affairs. He'll be here shortly. Listen carefully to what he says. You've got two of these and only one of these.' Mr Morrin pointed to his ears and mouth before checking his watch.

Gears meshed in Tommy's mind.

'You said you were here anyway—meaning, besides coming to see me. What's going on, Mr Morrin?' Both stared at each other. Mr Morrin raised an eyebrow, pressed a finger against his lips—shushed, pointing at the door. Tommy nodded. They had an understanding.

'Oh, it's just a small matter of Mad-Dog being found dead on my property…'

'What!'

'Oh yes, came back to finish what he'd started. Carrying this big jerry can of petrol to burn my house down he was, as he'd said he would, that night he tried to slash your throat.'

'And you've killed him!'

'Not my pleasure, I'm sad to say.' He leant close to Tommy's ear, his voice dropping to an icy whisper, 'but it was my idea to place the jerry cans nearby his body…' He raised his voice. 'Pops shot him in the head—self-defence mind. Came at Pops with a razor. He's in the cells here right now, Pops is. Been arrested he has.'

22
I HAVE SINNED

Inspector Marlon and Constable Rees were back in the interrogation room. The Inspector sat in front of a stunned Tommy. He'd pocketed the cigarettes and matches, and was lighting one of his own untipped brands. The constable again took up station behind Tommy.

'Just so you know, if it was up to me, I wouldn't have allowed that to happen.'

'Allowed what?' asked Tommy looking up. He felt numb. Mad-Dog dead! The image of the razor blade that had flashed past his face loomed in Tommy's mind. The numbness passed. *The bastard had deserved what was coming to him. He'd have shot the prick too*. Mad-Dog and his *bastard* nephew.

'Are you listening to me? I said I would not have allowed that to happen—retired Sergeants calling in favours with Inspectors…'

'I don't know what you're talking about, but I do know mad dogs get shot.' Tommy stared back, holding full eye contact with the Inspector.

'They have been tonight, and you are up to your neck in it. I can smell it. I know your sort. If there was no trouble in front of your face, you'd be pulling up stones to see what was lurking underneath. Trouble goes with you hand in hand. That cosy little visit… I understand you've been staying on our Mr Morrin's farm?'

'So what?' Tommy attempted to calm his breathing. *Trouble didn't have far to travel to find you…*

'And I've also heard there's been a run in between you and a few of our locals over the past few days.' The Inspector's fingers were tapping the table. The man was building up to a head of steam.

Tommy said, 'I thought you weren't allowed to do this—question me without an adult here on my side?'

Bewildered and enraged, the Inspector practically spat at Tommy, 'Damn your eyes, you Scouse bastard, piece of shit, you're in my world now; I'm allowed to do whatever I fucking want!' His cheeks were turning red. Tommy glanced back, hopefully to the constable behind. The constable avoided eye contact. Now pushing the table from him, standing and snarling, the Inspector lashed his chair away and slammed both palms hard on the table. His hands clenched. Tommy instinctively leant back.

'Kidnap on your own doorstep—and then violence follows you sheep-like into our village—or own church hall! Murder in Henllan!' This was shrieked at Tommy who was now finding it difficult to swallow.

The Inspector's temper was impressive. But before he could continue, there was an urgent knocking. The constable opened the door and the Sergeant who'd taken the fingerprints entered.

'Colleagues from Liverpool have been on the phone again, Sir. And there's a mister Rex Goldsmith—the lad's solicitor. He's demanding the right to have a chat with his client prior to any questioning, Sir.'

Shaking his head in disgust, the inspector ground his cigarette out—his eyes boring deep into Tommy's.

'Bring him in, but I want more time with this one. I want all of his TICs. He doesn't leave this station without my say so.'

To Tommy's relief, the police officers left as a tanned solicitor stood calmly by the door. The best-dressed man in the station, and from near and far—in a black tuxedo, white silk shirt and spotted dickie-bow. Rex Goldsmith exuded a positive aura of authority and sheer posh aplomb. Taking a confident look left and right of the outside corridor, he closed the door and sat facing Tommy, placing an expensive leather briefcase on the desk. He took out a set of documents. Reaching out, he offered Tommy his hand.

'Rex Goldsmith—solicitor of law. Pleased to meet you.' Tommy shook the hand and found he was able to swallow again.

'Tommy Dwyer. Very pleased to meet you too.'

'I'm sure. Let's get the administration of the way first, hmm? If you agree to me representing you in this matter, and I urgently advise you to do so, you will kindly sign here, here and here. Plus, all of your personal details on this form.' He produced an ancient fountain pen and scrawled three 'X' marks across the legal paperwork. Without reading it, Tommy signed all the documents. 'Good. Now Mr Morrin has provided me with brief details regarding your circumstances, and I can happily say you are free to leave.'

'What?'

'Your choice: stay here in a voluntary capacity, or leave right now.' Tommy stared at the papers he'd signed. 'Oh, don't be concerned by those. Purely routine. You've given me the power to act on your behalf now and in the future. There is no arrest warrant out for you, simply a request that you assist in police enquiries regarding an alleged incident that happened in Liverpool a few days ago.'

'So, I can just get up and walk out?'

'You can. The Inspector was all for keeping you here unduly, but I've set him straight on that matter. He'd have arrested all of you lads who were staying on the farm—had you not been at this disco.'

'Well, I'll go then…' Tommy stood, eyeing the door.

'I was hoping to persuade you to stay for a little bit longer. Mr Morrin—your patron here, his family—is facing serious charges, and I was hoping you could assist in some way. Perhaps a statement? I understand you have been recently threatened by the ah, deceased, one Mark Dylan—A.K.A. Mad-Dog?'

'Whatever you need.' Tommy sat back down.

For the next half an hour, Tommy recounted his activities since arriving at the farm, focusing on the threats of Mad-Dog and his cousins. The solicitor took careful notes, re-emphasising the threat Mad-Dog had made to Tommy about returning to the farm to set it ablaze.

'I have statements signed by your friends, the landlord Selwyn Thomas, retired police Sergeant Bradley, and by Mr Morrin's stepdaughter Rhonda, detailing the threat they heard issued to you on the night of an altercation outside of the Llindir inn—can you confirm this please?' Tommy read the statements. Davey and Jack had both signed a report. There was no statement from Ken Gee.

All had declared, in their own words: 'I distinctly heard Mark Dylan say to Tommy Dwyer—I'd move from that farm if I was you, I'm going to finish off the job of burning that bastard farmhouse down to the ground and any bastard who's inside it at the time.'

Tommy signed his own pre-prepared statement. This was good. The bastard had deserved what was coming.

'Okay, we'll see the Inspector now, unless he has plans to keep us waiting. My advice to you is to simply answer only to confirm what is in the statement. Anything else, anything he tries to bring up, you will say, 'I have no comment, other than that which is in my statement.' Clear?'

Tommy repeated this silently to himself.

The interview with the Inspector was a formality. Tommy stuck to his comment, 'Nothing more to say.' The Inspector barged out of the room after five minutes, upset at having a plum murder charge and committal taken out of his grasp.

'Thank you, Tommy. Can't have been easy. I understand there's a lift home available early tomorrow morning. Ken Gee's parents have already picked him up, with the others waiting for Jack's brother Edwin.'

'So, I can go?'

'You can. I will plan for someone from a good local firm to accompany you to see Belle Vale police, in order to make a voluntary statement for the separate matter you were involved with. If any officers approach you I strongly advise you to remain silent until you have legal guidance. I'll see if I can arrange some transport.'

'To get me back to Liverpool tonight?'

'That's not quite what I meant. You will almost certainly be called back here as a main witness if the case goes to trial. I'm hoping with the evidence we have, the charges will be dropped.' Tommy nodded, taking this in.

'I'll do whatever I can to help Mr Morrin.'

'That's kind of you. Mr Morrin has arranged for you all to stay the night in the Llindir Inn; you'll find all of your friends there, apart from Ken Gee, of course. Do you have any more questions for me? Anything you are unsure about?'

'What was the 'TIC' the older copper was going on about? Made me think I've caught fleas since I've been here. That wooden pallet and the rag of a blanket in the cell was minging.'

'Ignore him, Inspector Marlon enjoys his dramatics. He can see any charges against Mr Morrin dwindling away. He was looking for any 'taken into consideration,' to add to his 'solved' crime list. A lot of people who have been arrested are persuaded to provide TICs, especially with the promise of a sympathetic hearing in a Court of law. Of course, you've kept your nose clean since you've been here?'

'Of course,' lied Tommy, thinking—now how do I get that rifle back off that Keith fella and take it home?

23
NIGHTIME INN

Outside the inn, Tommy was shivering in the cold night air. He tried the door handle. Locked. He rapped on the window. He could see the lads standing around the bar. The landlord, Selwyn, was in deep conversation with Sergeant Bradley. Jack talked on the phone at the bar before passing the receiver to Davey. The roaring fireplace looked inviting. All other customers had long since left after the ten thirty last rounds. Rhonda unbolted the door.

'You okay, Tommy?' Instinctively, Tommy wrapped his arms around her. They kissed briefly.

'Fine, glad to be out and about. Were you hurt?' He stepped inside and headed for the cigarette vending machine.

'No, nothing to worry about, except for my dad. Just waiting for him, he's still at the station. How's your leg?' Tommy rubbed his swollen knee. He put a handful of loose coins inside the machine, pressed a button and picked up a box of sixteen Players No. 6.

'Bastard ciggie machines are a right rip-off.' He lit a ciggie.

'Selwyn doesn't make a penny off them. Costs him money to hire the machine.' Tommy nodded. There was a lot unsaid. Keith approached. Jack had his back turned on Tommy, listening to Selwyn and the ex-policeman. Keith purposely reached out a protective arm around Rhonda.

Staking his claim, thought Tommy. *Screw him, and where the hell is my rifle...* Davey came over and handed a pint of lager to Tommy. Both moved towards the open fireplace.

'Well?'

'Well, what?'

'Well, what happened? Are you getting done for what happened with Joey?'

'I thought I was going to be. The Liverpool bizzies had a warrant out for me, but when the local cops rang them, they found out it was dropped. They were pissed—they lost their bonus or promotion or whatever the hell they got for catching kidnappers. Anyway, what happened at the farm? Is all our gear here?' Davey nodded towards the bar.

'They're talking about it now.' Tommy knocked back his pint and followed Davey to the bar. Rhonda pulled him a fresh pint.

'That's not on the house now,' said Selwyn. Tommy tapped his pockets, not much there. Davey handed a fiver over to Selwyn. 'My round,' he said. Selwyn nodded and Rhonda started to pull fresh pints.

'Private party mind,' he wagged a finger at Sergeant Bradley, who knocked back a large scotch. Someone was tapping on the window. 'That'll be my dad,' said Rhonda. Jack checked the window before unbolting the door. A tired-looking Mr Morrin entered. Rhonda hugged him. Keith stood nearby.

Selwyn drew another large scotch. Handed it over. Mr Morrin knocked it back in one.

'More,' he said. Selwyn fed another scotch into the glass and Mr Morrin knocked it back again. 'Selwyn, hand over the bottle, please. Glasses for all.' He placed two twenty-pound notes on the bar. 'Enough for the stay-over tonight?' Selwyn nodded.

'Usual room upstairs is ready. Blankets here for the lads. No helping yourselves mind!' Mr Morrin nodded. Raised a hand for silence. Selwyn and Rhonda filled the glasses from a bottle of Famous Grouse whisky.

'We are where we are,' he said. 'Pops will be spending the night where he is. Denbigh magistrates in the morning on a charge of manslaughter.' Rhonda gasped.

'Sergeant Bradley—update if you please?'

'My sources tell me there is no suspicion of foul play. Mad-Dog Dylan trespassed where he wasn't invited, intent on causing criminal damage. He was carrying a large jerry can of petrol. Previous form was clear—he had tried to burn out Mr Morrin. He was armed with a cutthroat razor and a loaded air rifle that has been identified as stolen property from the old mill estate.' Tommy looked keenly at Keith, who raised an eyebrow.

'Out near these lads' campsite, preparing a supper, Pops had spotted the trespass and challenged Mad-Dog, who raised and aimed the rifle at him. Luckily, Pops had his own weapon and fired first—a straight and clear case of self-defence. All the lads here have signed statements to the fact that there had been a prior threat issued by said Mad-Dog. Amen.' He knocked back his Scotch. Selwyn refilled glasses and a heady, intoxicated, tiredness—a heavy mood swept across the bar.

'Sit down and quick chat, lads. Rest the legs, been a very long day,' said Mr Morrin.

They congregated at the tables and chairs near the fireplace. 'Appreciate all your help,' said Mr Morrin. 'Horrible business. For anyone who wants it, there's a job on my farm.' Jack raised a hand; Mr Morrin nodded. 'I know, Jack, it's meant more for Tommy and Davey here. I know you and Ken have further education lined up.' The phone rang. Selwyn answered and passed it to Sergeant Bradley.

'Christ, I need to piss,' said Mr Morrin. He indicated Tommy should join him. Davey passed him a look and shrugged. Tommy followed Mr Morrin to the bogs.

Inside, Mr Morrin raised a finger—'shush'—and took out a black marker pen and headed for trap one. He wrote on the wall 'don't beam me up Scottie... I'm taking a shit.' The handwriting was familiar to Tommy as the work of the artist he'd first seen on the day he'd arrived in Wales. Mr Morrin was laughing.

'Me and Keith—we are in competition if you like. Drives Selwyn mad, it does.'

Tommy realised the comment had an even deeper meaning than the implied lightness. Tommy half-laughed, half-yawned. Straightening, he took a piss in the urinal. A thought occurred.

'Mr Morrin, was it you who donated the Dickens' books to the charity shop? To cheer Rhonda up over losing her horse?'

'Ah, you've found me out...'

'Does having money make everything better?'

'Only if it's used in the right way... Tommy, talk to me. Tell me things. I know you took that rifle from the old mill. Temptation too much?'

Tommy felt no guilt. He yawned again. The whole day weighed on him, the lager and whisky turning sour in his stomach.

'You write graffiti on the walls. You killed a man and have it covered up by... by your people around you and...'

'My property, Tommy. I own this place as well.' Mr Morrin waved his arms, encompassing the whole area. 'All mine. Selwyn has the license and I pay him as a normal customer would. We split the profit.' He took a deep breath. 'Give me a cigarette, please?' Tommy lit one in his mouth, taking in a deep pull. Handed it over. 'You are like me, Tommy, when I was younger.' Tommy folded his arms. 'Tempted by everything—afraid of nothing. Thought I was one of God's chosen ones, I did.' *A Master*, thought Tommy. 'But I wasn't. Took Rhonda as my own child. Her mother... had to kill her husband Mathew Irfan...'

Tommy felt chilled. Mr Morrin laid a hand on his shoulder. Looked him in the eyes. 'He needed killing Tommy. He took delight in the slaughterhouse, he did. God help me, but Rhonda's mother turned up in chapel every Sunday with makeup barely concealing her black eyes. The whole village hated him for what he was doing. There were mumblings and murmurings of someone doing something to sort him out, but no one lifted a finger until it was too late. Poor woman died in a terrible accident. Crushed by a tractor Mathew Irfan been driving. Their child Rhonda was walking alongside—saw it all through her innocent eyes. The Inquest was a farce—he got away with it. Whole village knew the real story. I took him out one cold night near Christmas.

'Challenged him to a fight outside the old mill. Walked with him and he pulled a knife on me, but Pops was there—right behind me. Shot him and buried him in a field. He's still there… rotted away. Pops bought the vacant land. I took over the farm and guardianship of Rhonda. She was three years old. I know temptation, Tommy. I know about the rifle you took. You are me when I was a young man. I am lucky. I got away with it… Seeing as how I'm confessing to you, here's another truth, Tommy. This one may be too much for even you.'

Tommy felt unnerved. Mr Morrin spoke almost at a whisper, 'I lured mister Mad-Dog to the farm tonight. Promised him money for him to move far away. Knew he couldn't resist. Appealed to the vanity in his own head. Planted the seed that I was living in fear of him. Five thousand pounds, I offered him. It had to be tonight while you were all out the way—and it couldn't be next week as I wanted you for the statement you gave to the police. He came to the farm, Tommy, hoping to collect a lot of money. Instead, he got a bullet in his head. Temptation can be the end of you—always remember that. Which way will your own temptations take you? The school certificates, bah, trifles for your vanity. Burn them. Go to New Zealand with your family. Start again. You don't need to prove you are better than you are…'

Back in the bar, the lights had been turned down. Jack and Davey had set up blankets on chairs near the fireplace. No one was speaking. Keith had left, and Mr Morrin, Selwyn and Rhonda headed upstairs to their rooms.

Later, much later, Tommy turned in his blanket, half asleep. Davey and Jack were snoring softly. The fire had petered. A hand gently shook him awake. Tommy half expected it to be the ghost in white. It was Rhonda. In the dim light, she beckoned and Tommy rose and followed her outside to a grey dawn. The swelling in his knee had faded away. Rhonda had the keys to the converted stable.

Laying a blanket on the floor, Rhonda gave Tommy all the loving he had ever wanted from Linda.

24
BACK HOME

The long journey home had been silent. Big Eddie had turned up at six in the morning. It was cloudy, like the sun had forgotten how to shine. Rhonda waved goodbye from the upstairs window of the Llindir Inn. Tommy had the phone number safely tucked in his back pocket.

No Moody Blues blasting through the car. Tommy's thoughts focussed on the Inspector's comment, 'Trouble follows you.' After the events of the past week, this was plainly true: scarecrow man on the bridge, ultra-violence in the park, school break-ins, run-in with Mad-Dog in Wales. What if he had stayed in Walsall instead of coming home to see Linda before she went off to Paris? There would have been no meeting with Davey. But, if he hadn't come home, would there have been any future in his relationship with Linda? Looking over the past few days, that thought was not as painful as it had been before Wales. Was she due back today? Tomorrow? He was unsure. It wasn't as important anymore. He'd had a more than pleasant experience with Rhonda to thank for that.

Yet his thoughts turned back to the event of the week. Another man with a link to Tommy had been killed. Mr Morrin had admitted to his part in the deaths of two men, the murder of two men. What had he said to Linda? Thirteen days away, unlucky for someone… Well, that had come true.

Mr Morrin—murderer… Tommy would never have dreamt he could hold the highest regard for a cold-blooded killer. In Mr Morrin's shoes, would he have taken the same action? Emphatically yes—hadn't he done the same? Too much thinking—*stop it.* Hit by a banging headache, Tommy closed his eyes.

The sky was filled with ominous black clouds, but at least the water hammer had been fixed at home and he would soon be there, safe and free.

Outside Jack's house in Sulgrave Close, Davey had his head down. He quietly said to Tommy, 'Look, I'm going to lie low for a few days. I won't be going out anywhere.'

Tommy, stretching stiff legs, considered. 'You fucking me off, Davey?'

'Tommy, I feel sick to my bones, mate. There was a dead body near the tent!'

'A dead dog…'

'Tommy, I don't want to talk about it, okay?'

'Okay, whatever. You walking down towards the Greenhills?'

'No, my dad; he's picking me up. Jack will be letting him know I'm here. You don't have to wait, Tommy…'

'You mean you don't want me to hang around?'

'Look, I'll see you sometime, okay?' Davey held his hand out. Tommy shook it and walked away. For the first time in weeks, it rained heavily.

The downpour chilled Tommy. Dripping, he headed towards Score Lane. Nearing the house, he saw a car parked nearby. Headlights flashed him. Police?

The car door opened and Sean Duncan got out. 'Fucking hell, Tommy. Where have you been hiding? Get in the car.'

Tommy's instinct was to run past and get into his house. The déjà vu was overwhelming—get in the house, get the sword.

'Tommy, come on, mate, it's pissing down,' Sean said unnecessarily. This was no threat. Tommy could see there was only Nobby in the driving seat—no sign of Chris Lawler.

Reluctantly, Tommy got into the back seat.

'Put the heating on, Nobby—can't you see Tommy's freezing,' said Sean. Tommy was shivering—was it fear?

'We knocked at yours earlier, been knocking for days. Your mam wouldn't tell us where you were—said you'd moved to Scotland for a new job.'

'We know you've been to We-we-Welsh… Wales though,' said Nobby.

'All right, Nobby, I'll do the talking,' said Sean. 'We've been patrolling, waiting for you to show.' He took his jacket off. 'Here, throw this around you mate. Catch your death shivering like that.' *Death*, thought Tommy, taking the coat—there was a lot of it about.

'So, what about it? How was Wales? Any decent fanny there?'

'It was good for a few days at least.'

'Well, you're back. We need to take you to Chris's house.' Sean was sat forward. He'd positioned the reverse mirror so he could see Tommy's face. Nobby was watching them.

'To Chris Lawler's, what for?'

'To see him and his mam actually. There's plenty to talk about. Not least, the business over Joey Finn.'

Tommy stopped shivering. The coat helped. Two ears, one mouth he thought. Say nothing until you've heard what was going on. There was a short silence.

'Tommy, have you spoken to the bizzies about what happened?'

'What do you mean?'

'He fucking well has! He's fucked us up—that's why he fucked off to Welsh Wales.' Nobby was worked up. Sean laid a restraining hand on him.

'Tommy, just spit it out, will you? Have you made a statement to the bizzies about what happened the last time we parked up here?'

'In a way.'

'I fucking told you,' shouted Nobby. He had a flick knife in his hand. Sean had opened the glove compartment in front of him. He was reaching in—Tommy had to calm this down.

'I've been sitting in a police cell in Wales for hours before getting a lift back. They pulled me up after a fight in a local church hall. I thought I was getting done for kidnapping Joey…'

'But you fucking told them it was us—get out the car now!'

'They told me there was no charges, but I could make a voluntary statement once I got home.'

'But why did they keep you for hours?'

'Because someone got shot on the farm we were staying at. I had to give them a statement.' There was another long silence. Nobby and Sean looked at each other. Nobby was no longer angry.

'You'd better come with us to Chris's house,' said Sean. Nobby had put the knife away and was starting the car.

'Sean—I'm tired and wet, I'm frigging knackered, mate. Just tell me what I should say if I do make a voluntary statement about Joey Finn?'

'Okay. You'll come to see Chris later?'

'I'd rather not, but I will though. Just give me the gist, hey?'

'Right, let's start again. There is no Joey Finn situation.'

'No one's getting done?'

'There's a couple of charges to do with carrying—you saw Nobby and Chris with the knives, and for no tax and insurance on the car, and no driving licence, and for the little bit of weed we had on us. But nothing serious.'

'Right… nothing serious like,' repeated Tommy.

'We were going to get charged with kidnapping and assault and all kinds of other shit, but Chris's mam sorted it. She went to see Joey's al fella and paid him off. You've been paid as well. Make sure you have a word with you al fella… Turns out we're all a gang of mates having a laugh.'

'And Joey agreed? I thought his al fella was inside?'

'Out a few days ago, working for us now. Joey got himself a nice few quid as well. We're all making money Tommy—bags of it, more money than you could ever earn in a lifetime. You can join us, Tommy. I know Chris would let you in.'

'I've never been keen on drugs.'

'So what? I'm sure you'd welcome the money it brings in.'

'Mmm, more money than soft Joe,' said Nobby

'Really? But what were you saying about Joey Finn?'

'The bizzies called at his house last night. Told them you'd been nicked in Wales and asked him to confirm you were in on the great laugh we'd had with our little cheeky bastard mate. Joey's al fella got in touch with Chris's mam. We've been waiting for you for the past hours.'

Tommy let this sink in. 'But, what about Mad-Mick? Joey's cousin…'

'He's out the way for now. Still banged up for nearly killing one of the St John's bikers crew in the swing park. He's away for a long time. Chris's mam is going to pay someone on the inside to make sure the only way he gets out of nick will be in a wheelchair. I'll tell you more when you come round to Chris's. No rush now, we know you're okay with the bizzies.'

'All right,' said Tommy.

He got out of the car and headed up his path. Opening the front door, he listened to the house and sensed no one was awake; upstairs he found Butch snoring on his bed, wagging his tail. Welcome back to sunny Liverpool indeed.

25
DEAR TOMMY

Tommy woke with a new appreciation for how comfortable a bed could be. No sign of Butch. His mam was staring at him from the door. She looked better. Makeup on her face.

'Cup of tea?'

'I'd love one, thanks.' Downstairs, the radio was tuned into BBC Merseyside. Tea and toast ready at the small kitchen table. Butch was in next-door's garden, sniffing and pissing furiously at a flowerbed.

'Good time?'

'Mostly, yeah,' said Tommy. 'Where's me al fella? Patricia?'

'He's taken her down to the 'Pool' to get the tickets and dates sorted. Been going there nearly every day for the past week. It's come through, Tommy—the job in New Zealand. He's going to be a steward on a cruise liner travelling from Queenstown to Sydney. A job for me—and for you, if you want?' Tommy nodded, wolfing his toast. He dipped a crust into the mug of tea. His mam had an eyebrow lifted quizzically.

'Well?'

'Well, what?'

'You know what, Tommy! Speak to me—yay, nay—what? For Christ's sake, teenagers these days, have you forgotten how to speak?'

'No.'

'Oh, for God's sake! You'd better start thinking; he'll be home soon. But leave that aside for now; what the hell was going on outside here on the day? Sorry, the minute before you left? And who's this Mrs Lawler who knocked here—and I'm sure she's given money to your dad. And why has Steve Duncan and that ginger idiot been hanging around, hey?'

'Alright, Mother—one at a time!'

'And another thing, there's a letter there from Linda, I think.'

'What, where? You think?'

'Well okay, I did open it…'

'Mother!'

'I haven't read it—I was going to burn it…'

'You haven't read it, but you were going to burn it? For fuck sake, mother, where is it?'

The slap was sharp and hard on Tommy's face. 'Don't you… don't you talk to me like that. Don't you ever talk to me like that!' Her makeup was wearing off. Tommy saw the colour drain from her face. She turned from him to cry.

Tommy stood, rocking on the balls of his feet, his cheek smarting from the slap. The deserved slap. He was torn between apologising and tearing the house apart to get that letter. His mother picked up her handbag from the windowsill and took out an envelope. She handed it to Tommy, before walking out of the kitchen.

Tommy stared at the envelope, a heady manifestation of fate held between his fingertips. A great weariness from the weight of events the past week, the past twenty-four hours, yawed him into dizziness. Maybe he should burn this piece of paper? Its contents had already hurt his mother. Surely, there was no good news inside.

This letter… Linda was the past. One way forward was sixth form. Relocation to the farthest place on Earth from Liverpool was another direction. Distance… Tommy fingered the paper as though holding a litmus test. Temptation—or was it aspiration? Could be Linda had enjoyed wet dreams in Gay Paree and was smouldering to get back with him? His fingertips detected otherwise. The letter had been postmarked in Paris. He opened the pre-opened letter. Braced himself…

Dear Tommy,

I hope you and your family are okay. I haven't got much time as we are packing up and ready to leave for the coach. I have loved this place and it has given me the time and space to learn more about who I am and what I want out of life. Tommy, I've strained my mind to find the best way to tell you this. You may think it's cowardly to be saying it in a letter, but I did tell you to your face the last time I saw you, and I can only confirm… I don't want to see you anymore. Maybe after a few months, we could become friends, but for now, I want to find my own space. I'm going to be starting my trainee nurse job as soon as I get home, and that's all I want to concentrate on. I'm sorry, Tommy, but I don't want to strain my mind anymore.

Love and Fondness,

Linda

Also, before you hear any gossip about Danny Clarke and me, we are both starting work at Broadgreen Hospital at the same time. I hope there will be no animosity over this.

Danny *bastard* Clark! The fight or flight syndrome overwhelmed Tommy. He'd known this was coming, it wasn't even deep down—it was right there. The slight guilt he had felt for his liaison with Rhonda could be banished. Right there on paper, he hadn't simply been jibbed, he had lost hands down—the words laughed at him—goodbye Tommy, I'm going out with Danny fucking Clarke! He should have painted the name on his sword. Wasn't it the reason he'd bought it—to kill off rivals? He raised both fists and covered his mouth.

'Bastard, bastard, bastard!' Tommy had an overwhelming need to kick and punch.

‘Tommy, I know how you feel, son, but you will get over it.’ His mother laid a hand gently on his shoulder. ‘Think of the new life we are all going to have in New Zealand. You’ll meet someone there.’ Tommy thought of Rhonda and her travel plans.

As if on cue, the front door opened, and Patricia skipped into the hall, smiling. ‘You’re back, Tommy,’ she said warmly. Behind her, Tommy’s dad closed the door. He was looking happier than Tommy had ever seen.

‘It’s on, the travel date’s confirmed,’ he said. ‘There’s a job for me, for you, sweetheart—and for you if you want it, son.’

At the crossroads… Davey didn’t want to know him. Linda had jibbed him and there was now an opportunity to cross to the other side of the world. Davey wasn’t so bad. Danny Clarke—he had it coming, and boy was he going to get it. His mam and dad were wrapped in each other’s arms, Patricia in the middle.

Tommy scrunched the ‘Dear John’ letter into a ball, taking a calming breath. He believed in the timing of fate. ‘When are we supposed to be leaving?’

‘Ten days. I’ve just been to see our Darren and Michelle. Darren’s moving in. It means we can always come back if things don’t work over there. Christ, it’s taken so long to work out the travel arrangements. We’ll be sailing from here in Liverpool—me and your mother will be working as ship crew.’

‘He hasn’t said if he wants to go,’ said Tommy’s mother.

Patricia smiled at Tommy. She nudged her dad to speak.

‘Of course he’s coming—aren’t you, son?’

Tommy stared at the scrunched paper in his hand. Distance. Danny Clarkes’ head from the swing of his sword. He could do this, then sail away forever. ‘I am, Dad. I’ve got a couple of things to sort out first.’

‘Okay, but Tommy, stay out of any trouble, hey son. Oh, and this is for you.’ He was holding a stack of notes—five, ten-pound notes. ‘Maybe get yourself and Patricia some new gear? It’s winter where we’re going.’

‘That’s off that Lawler woman,’ said Tommy’s mam. ‘I told you to give it back!’

‘I haven’t touched a penny, and they’ll need to get warm clothes. It’s a gift for doing nothing. You haven’t been to the police, have you, son? That business outside before you went camping?’

‘No.’

‘Like I said—money for nothing. If you get the chance, say thanks to her and that’s it.’

‘Okay. But will you take the money, mother? Get us all some new clothes.’ Reluctantly, as if tainted, she reached out to take hold of the money. Tommy’s dad held back a tenner.

‘My share,’ he said. ‘Don’t forget, son—stay out of any trouble.’

26
CHRIS LAWLER'S MAM

Tommy headed down Childwall Valley Road with mixed emotions. Linda's letter soured the wonder of leaving Liverpool.

A convoy of mopeds, six or seven Yamaha FS1s—fizzes — passed by, heading down the valley towards the bridge. He started to run, then sprint and in an instant, he was a mile away—outside the block of flats in Hartsbourne Avenue, the Lawler family residence. A moby was nearby with a large queue waiting to traverse the wooden steps to get served.

Tommy knew the Lawler family ran at least six of these throughout Childwall: a large retail van moving in and out of selected spots, hated by local tax and rate-paying competitors, catering for basic groceries, ciggies, newspapers, sweets, and whatever else the Lawler family sold from beneath the counter. He could see a couple of lads staring from the balcony on the sixth floor of the block of flats above.

On the ground, outside of a graffiti-dashed phone box, he saw two hippies—the weedy twins who had been smoking on the bus—chatting to a group of teenagers sitting on a nearby wall. The twins stared with hostility at Tommy as he approached the door to the flats. Two of the teenagers on the wall were chatting into walkie-talkies.

'What the fuck are you looking at?' asked the taller hippy—his voice several octaves above normal.

'What did you say?' Tommy stared back; he'd picked a poor moment to try intimidation. The lad was about twenty and his long Afghan coat exuded a pungent waft of the joint his mate was smoking.

'I said—who the fuck are you looking at?'

Tommy stepped into the hippy's space and head-butted him hard—knocking him clean over the wall. The teenagers stood and took a step back.

The shorter hippy held up both hands 'No—Nigel, no! What have you done to my beautiful mate!'

Tommy's forehead was throbbing, but it was pleasant like hitting a nail down flat with a hammer in one fell swing.

'Screw you and your beautiful mate—hippy-dippy pair of gobshites, if you two are still here when I come out, I'll knock the shit out of the pair of you.' Tommy looked up and saw the lads on the balcony looking down. One waved, Sean Duncan. The lift to the sixth-floor stank of urine and Tommy was relieved to get out. Chris Lawler opened the door, and his smile was as lopsided as a cat with only two legs.

'Here's the shit-kicking stranger. My mam wants a word with you.'

Tommy nodded and entered the small, opulent flat. Drape wallpaper covered the hall. It was the same style as the lush Blue Room in the Fiveways boozer. There was a small metal frame at the side of the door. Chris picked this up and slotted it between the inside door frame and the nearest wall—blocking the door from getting kicked in. The thick carpet would feel luxurious on bare feet. Three phones were attached three feet apart on the wall in the hall—green, cream and red. A mildly unpleasant aroma was wafting from the kitchen—like an overflowing toilet someone had cleaned out. There were numerous stacked-up crates and goods for the mobies: cigarette cartons, tinned vegetables, Tate and Lyle sugar, soaps, and toilet rolls. All kinds of confectionary: Opal Fruits, Marathons, Mars Bars. Enough stock for a long siege.

In the living room, Mrs Lawler sat at an antique desk. In her forties, she wore little or no makeup to disguise her face. She stared unblinking at Tommy. Her eyes appeared black. This was a cold and dangerous woman. She had her auburn hair tied in a severe bun. There was a long silver hairpin stuck through it. *Tread lightly*, Tommy warned himself. In front of her was a wad of twenty-pound notes a donkey would choke on. Strewn on the desk were more coins and notes, and a copy of the Daily Post.

Tommy had interrupted her counting. Outside, on the open door to the balcony, Sean Duncan sat at a garden patio table with Nobby. They were wearing expensive sunglasses. Both waved hello. Both had binoculars. Both on lookout. Three powerful air rifles were leant against the balcony wall. Near the door was a large hammer, crowbar and spiked baseball bat. The location of the flat appeared ideal for a drug dealer. The view allowed a panoramic early warning system against police or customs officers. No doubt the hippies and the teenagers near the phone box were additional lookouts.

'Sit, Tommy Dwyer.' Tommy took a seat in front of Mrs Lawler. 'Been on a little holiday, I hear?'

'Camping in Wales.' Tommy heard an Irish inflexion in her voice.

'Chris thought you'd done a bunk when you saw the police pulling up over that little business with Joey Finn? Right outside your house.'

'It was the timing—I was going away anyway.'

'But you kept out of it—didn't think of coming forward and help explain it was all a laugh, a prank on a mate?'

'It all happened so quick. I was late for getting the lift to Wales and I thought if I hang around, the bizzies would keep me there all day.'

'That would be true. But you did get a pull in Wales. What did you tell them?'

‘I didn’t tell them anything. The farmer we stayed with, Mr Morrin—he had his solicitor come and see me. He found out that any charges had been dropped.’

‘He paid for and brought in his own solicitor to help you?’

‘Well, he wasn’t just there for me…’

‘Have any involvement with this?’ She picked up the newspaper and showed Tommy the headline: ‘Arsonist killed on farm—Welsh police arrest wealthy landowner.’ Tommy stared at the paper. *Tread lightly…*

‘They’ve got the headline wrong,’ he said. ‘It was the wealthy landowners' dad, Pops, who was arrested.’

‘Go on…’

‘It was on Mr Morrin’s farm where he got shot.’

‘And what was your involvement?’

‘I had a run-in with Mad-Dog…’

‘Mad-Dog! Any relation to Mad-Mick?’ asked Chris.

‘No, he was the bloke who was killed, shot on the farm. He’d just come out of nick for trying to burn the farm down a few years earlier. He came at me with a razor, after I’d had words with some of his cousins.’

‘And he ends up dead? Shotgun?’

‘Body near our tent.’

‘He fails to burn the farm down first time, comes back to finish the job off, and he meets up with you, then ends up dead?’

‘Er, yep, I suppose that’s one way to look at it.’ Mrs Lawler placed the newspaper down. The harshness in her eyes receding. Was that a slight respect Tommy could detect? This was a hard woman to impress.

‘Told you, mam,’ said Chris, ‘told you he was handy. You should have seen the way he twatted Nigel down there.’ Mrs Lawler held up a hand for silence.

‘I know your dad—Robert Dwyer.’

‘Me mam said you’d been around.’

'I've known him since kids. I came from Belfast to Bevington Bush. Know all about the Dwyer's in Eldon Grove. Good people. Do you want a drink? Tea, coffee, milk, lemonade, beer, a short?' Opulence indeed.

'Any brandy?'

'Fucking brandy! State of him,' said Chris. Sean's girlfriend Rita entered from the small kitchen holding a crystal glass and took it over to a large ornate world atlas globe—and pulled the top part open. Tommy had only seen such a bar on the telly—was it Steeds' house in The Avengers? Rita had had more tattoos inked on her arm. The off-odour was coming from her—or whatever she was cooking in the kitchen. She selected a bottle and looked to Mrs Lawler, got a nod back, poured a quadruple measure, and handed the glass to Tommy.

To mask the rising rank odour, Tommy breathed in the fumes and sipped at the brandy. As good, if not better, than Mr Morrin's brand. And yet there was a definite sour aftertaste—Tommy struggled to mask a gag reflex.

The suspicion of a smile crossed Mrs Lawler's features. 'You know your way around a gun?'

Tommy nodded.

She had arrived at a decision. 'You have potential. Are you ambitious, Tommy?' she asked, glancing at the pile of money.

'This is nothing—fuck all, this is peanuts,' said Chris. 'You know we sell the weed—that's been small time up to now. We've set up a deal with a farmer in Kirby.'

'Enough… I asked you a question, Tommy. Are you ambitious?' Steve and Nobby had entered. The expression 'If I tell you too much, I'll have to kill you' crossed Tommy's mind. He stole a glance at the weapons near the balcony door. The balcony oozed danger. Distance—six floors was a long way up and an even longer way down.

Vertigo passed over Tommy. He wiped his forehead. 'I suppose I am… ambitious.'

'I heard you were going on to sixth form college at the Holt?'

'Good market,' said Chris. His mother gave him a nod. 'We're expanding, Tommy. We've got the mobies around Childwall, and we've been looking at other areas—Huyton, Old Swan, Dovecote, Page Moss, Netherly, Halewood.'

'And Wavertree,' said Sean. 'We've put feelers out to all the dealers in other areas—all the hard cases.'

'Fucking plant pots, most of them,' said Chris. 'With Mad-Mick out the way, we're running Childwall. He was always against us selling, the mad fucker. All the mobies have a small gang that live near where they park up. They do the running and we pay them more pocket money than their mams and dads could ever give them.'

'Plus,' said Sean, 'if they get a pull, they're all underage and will only get a telling off by the bizzies. They know what'll happen to them if they grass us up. It's a good thing we've got going here, Tommy…'

'They grass us up and we cut the fuckers,' said Chris. Tommy thought back to the reason he was here. Tidying up the Joey Finn business.

'Is that why you came after Joey?' Tommy doubted Joey had been working for them—he was perpetually skint. Sean and Chris passed a look to each other.

Chris continued, 'The little fucker threatened to grass us up. With Mad-Mick out the way, we gave loads of free samples to kids around here. Giving them a taste so they'd come back for more. That little prick put his nose in too far. But that's sorted now. He's had a warning and we gave his al fella a few quid. He knows the score.'

'Has your dad spoken to you?' asked Mrs Lawler.

'He has—thanks very much, Mrs Lawler. Really appreciate the money.' She nodded—indicated for Sean to continue.

'We've set up a meeting with the main lads,' said Sean, 'in Court Hey Park. All of them, Tommy, it's never been done—a meeting of all the main gangs. It hasn't been organised like this before. We've already talked with crews from the Swan, Lee Park and Dovecote. We're seeing the top lads from Huyton, the St John's Angels and Page Moss next. Eventually, they'll come around.'

Tommy envisaged the scene. Deep in the wooded area—away from the main public side of the park. Away from Davey's back garden and the pleasant and innocent views. Gangs from all over, converging—not for the normal kick-off, but business… No. This was insane. It would never happen. One of the crews—maybe all—would find some spark and it would kick off into a bloodbath.

'Chris, Sean, this won't work—can you see Blue Face Maloney from Wavertree shaking hands with the Netherly Boot Boys or the Page Moss Skinheads? They'll be murdered! And you'll be right in the middle.'

'We're building up on security,' said Mrs Lawler. 'Not only for the meeting, we're looking at this for the long term.'

'Me mam's got visitors coming on the ferry right now,' said Chris. 'These are the men from Belfast, Tommy. If it all goes okay—happy days. If it kicks off, they get us out. Whatever happens, they are going to help us set it up, and we move into the other areas either with or without …'

'Have you got a girlfriend, Tommy?' asked Mrs Lawler. 'I'll bet a good-looking boy like you has a few, hey? Think what you could do for her—nice clothes, jewellery—take her to the best clubs and away on lovely holidays.'

Tommy pictured himself lounging on a golden beach with Rhonda. The image gave Tommy a mental double flip—Linda had not been his choice of companion.

'Think how you could look after your mam and dad—sending them money whenever you felt like.'

'You know they are going to New Zealand?'

'I do, but your dad said he wasn't sure if you'd be going with them. You could fly out there to stay with them—spend Christmases out there in the sunshine. You'd be living like a lord. Wine, women and song.'

I could stay in Liverpool, Darren and Michelle—they could look after me. In fact—I could look after them. It wasn't my idea to move out of Liverpool… Tommy felt a sharp rush—an urge to pick up the wad of notes and feel the heft.

'Go on, see how it feels,' said Mrs Lawler. She passed the pile over to Tommy, whose eyes were transfixed on the money. Chris and Sean moved to each side of Tommy.

'You know you want it,' said Chris.

'Tommy—it's what you've always dreamed about,' said Sean.

'We'll earn more money than footballers—one hundred quid a week!'

'Think about it, Tommy… We would be Masters.'

Tommy was thinking: driving lessons, his own car, expensive suits, champagne, jewellery, exotic holidays, an electric guitar, an antique sword, impressing and winning Linda back, all swelled up in Tommy's mind.

'Masters of the universe, Tommy!' The image expanded like a giant bubble and Tommy was almost giddy with the potential of what such an income would give him.

The Beatles' 'Can't Buy Me Love' entered his mind's ears and, as if sharing the same melody, Mrs Lawler said quietly,

'The only thing money can't buy is poverty,' and the bubble swelled up bigger and rose and then, inevitably, popped…

The now rank smell wrinkled Tommy's nose. Filthy money? He knocked back the rest of the brandy. He looked out beyond the balcony outside and stared at the Childwall Valley and the Greenhills, and the image of his younger sister—standing near Jake's shop, hollow-eyed and lifeless. She's holding out her hands as she begs for money for her next fix. She begins to lift her skirt as a gentleman walks by.

The rank smell ripened. Tommy had to get out. If this was mastery of the universe, Tommy wanted no part. He shifted as though a hidden weight had been removed from his shoulders. He smelt the ripeness for what it was—temptation and corruption. The brandy had soured in his stomach—it rose like a copper bullet into his throat. He stood, hand covering his mouth, and rushed to the bathroom—just about making it. Toilet flushed, he rinsed his face in cold water. There was a heavy knocking on the door—Sean.

'You okay in there, Tommy?'

'Be out in a minute.' He stared at himself in the mirror. Tanned. Eyes bluer than normal. He rinsed his face again. He took a breath, composing himself. Say whatever was needed to get out in one piece. He dried off, painted a smile on his face—toned it down—opened the door. Chris, Sean and Nobby were standing outside, staring at him.

'Sorry about that—just came up. I haven't made a mess.'

'Brandy too much for you?' asked Sean.

'Much too much. My stomach can't handle it.'

Chris and Nobby passed a look before heading back into the living room. Mrs Lawler was wearing a lopsided grin.

'Caught short—too rich for you… Should have told you the brandy was uncut—ninety per cent proof. I wouldn't let it pass my lips without cutting it by two-thirds. You want another to top back up, no? Didn't think you would…'

Well, why the hell didn't you tell me—bitch? Get this over with. Get out. 'I should have made this clear. I am going to New Zealand. I want to be with my family.'

'What?' asked Chris.

'I am, I decided on the way down. But this meeting, it really is madness. All that's going to happen is the hardest gang is going to kick off and…'

'That's why we've got the biggest gang. With Mad-Mick out the way, we've had free rein in Childwall. Even if he does manage to show his face here again, all the bikers from St John's will be waiting to catch up with him after what he did in the swing park…'

'Enough!' Mrs Lawler interrupted. 'He's said he's not with us. You can get out now.' The harshness was back in her voice. She took the pin out of her hair and shook loose. The long auburn locks framed her face like hydras. 'But don't forget before you go,' she picked up the newspaper, 'If a word of what was said is repeated, there are five witnesses who heard you confess a murder.' The newspaper was slammed hard against the desk.

That's good—you hold that thought, bitch—tell the police I confessed to a murder I committed while I was locked up in a prison cell.

Heading for the door, one of the phones started to ring. Chris picked up the cream one—another phone was still ringing. He picked up the green one, 'Ello—ah fuck,' the red telephone was still ringing, he snatched this, 'Ello—yeah, it's Chris…. Out? When? Are you sure? All right, yeah, thanks.' He replaced the handset. 'Fuck-fuck. Bad news…' Mrs Lawler was in the hall, standing taller than Tommy.

'What's wrong?'

'Fucking Mad-Mick—he's out of jail. We owe another fifty quid to our tame bizzie in Belle Vale.'

'Shit,' said Sean. 'Does this change the plans?'

'It changes nothing. I'll assign four of the Irish crew to take care of him. Is he still here?' she said, looking at Tommy.

Chris followed him out of the flat to the doors of the lift, saying, 'You keep that shut. If I find out you've mentioned a word to fucking anyone, I'll drop you from the top of these flats. Wherever you are, I'll come and get you, Dwyer, and your little sister.' Tommy stared hard into Chris's eyes, tempted to lash out with everything he had and obliterate the creature. Standing behind Chris, Sean Duncan was shaking his head, silently warning—'Don't do it, Tommy… not here.'

Both of Tommy's hands were shaking as he tasted the clean air. He was walking back up the Childwall Valley Road. He stared at the railway bridge ahead. Throw me off the top of the flats, will you, Lawler? I don't think so, mate… I'm the shit-kicker who throws people off things…

He paused underneath the bridge, reliving the impact of the scarecrow man with the lorry—he still wasn't sure if the man had hit the truck or the road first. Tommy checked his conscience… yep—all clear. He would give everything for the scarecrow man to have been Chris Lawler. Good riddance to scumbags who needed nothing better than to get wasted. Tommy shivered involuntarily as he remembered the cutting edge on the machete in the red right hand that had been waved at him.

He walked up the hill to Score Lane Gardens park and sat alone on the grass for over two hours, pondering the loss of one ridiculously childish ambition—master of the universe—and the attainment of a more achievable one—do the right thing. He needed to get retired Sergeant Bradley's phone number from Rhonda.

27
LIVERPOOL CALLING

Tommy headed down to the shops and found Joey on his wall. Joey was unusually subdued. He slid off the wall and started to walk away.

'All right, Joey?' Joey stared back warily. He took a good look, checking the passing traffic. A Malaguti moped drove past slowly, the roar too loud for the 50cc engine. The rider and passenger took a good look at Tommy. The Saint John Angels motif was skilfully sprayed onto the plastic windshield, and SJA initials were on both sides of the petrol tank. The driver had the initials JD on the front of his jacket; the passenger had JJ on his. Tommy stared back, avoiding giving them two fingers. You never knew what they were carrying. He turned back to Joey.

'Listen, I had nothing to do with what happened. I thought you knew that?'

'I heard you saying you couldn't stand me. And something about selling you a fake pound note.'

'Joey, I couldn't take them on—not three of them.'

'You could have done something to help, though.'

'I got them to come round to my house so I could pick up my sword and…'

'Yeah, so you say…'

'It's the truth!'

'Yeah, okay… and then you go missing for nearly a week.'

'Look, you tit, I had a camping holiday planned—I had to get away quick—I'd have been in the police station for hours giving statements.'

'And you wouldn't want to do that—not grass them up, give evidence against them. Been paid off, have you?'

This was true. Tommy winced but recovered. 'Okay, I got paid off, but so did you and your newly released al fella—all charges dropped, I heard—so don't come on all high and mighty.'

Joey stared at the ground and said quietly, 'I didn't want to take any money. They're drug dealers, Tommy. Trying to spread it out to all the kids around here.'

'I know, Joey.'

'That's why our Mad-Mick's after them. He's out, you know.'

'I know, Joey. Listen, I've got something to tell you, it's important, but you didn't hear it from me, okay?' Joey made full eye contact. 'Tomorrow, all day, you keep away from Court Hey Park. Keep your mates—anyone you know—and this did not come from me—make sure the park is off limits.'

'What's happening, a big kick-off?'

'Can't say,' Tommy nodded. Joey read the meaning. 'Maybe your kid, your Mad-Mick, might fancy a walk around there, take in the park air. He might bump into Chris Lawler and his crew, along with a couple of other mobs from Huyton and Page Moss.'

'The bikers from St John's estate are after him, like that Malaguti that's just gone past. That was John Davies and John Jones, the leaders of the St John's Angels. They want to do him because of what happened in the swing park. They've been patrolling, looking. I don't know how they found out he's out of jail. Are you staying away from the park, Tommy?'

'What park? I don't know any parks?'

Joey smiled, his shoulders relaxed for the first time since this meeting. He tutted, 'I knew you weren't on their side, Tommy. Your Patricia came around to find me and told me what you'd said on that day.'

'Good. We're okay then?' Tommy offered his hand. Joey clenched a fist and they touched knuckles.

Tommy placed a small pile of five-pence pieces on top of the shelf in the phone box. The Llindir Inn landlord, Selwyn, answered the phone.

'Hi Selwyn, it's Tommy—Tommy from Liverpool.'

'I recognised the voice. I suppose it'll be Rhonda you're looking for, is it? Out with Keith Piperello I'm afraid, you've just missed her. I'll tell her you called though.'

'Actually, you may be able to help, Selwyn. I was after a phone number for Sergeant Bradley.'

'So, it's news of Mr Morrin and Pops…'

'Are they okay?'

'Pops has been released on bail—back home now, where he should be.'

'That's good. I'm glad. But do you have a contact number for Sergeant Bradley?'

'Haven't they heard of phone books in Liverpool? No matter, he's here in the bar, hang on a minute.' Tommy fed more coins into the phone box. He opened the door and had a good look to make sure no one could eavesdrop.

'Now then, Tommy, what can I do for you?' Tommy explained the gist of Lawler's plan and Sergeant Bradley went silent. 'Are you sure they haven't been reading *The Godfather*—Mario Pizza, all this mafia business? They didn't make you an offer you couldn't refuse?'

'They made me an offer… and I did refuse—and it's Mario Puzo, not Pizza. They think they've got a hold over me. They threatened to grass me up saying I'd confessed to shooting Mad-Dog.'

'That's preposterous—you were banged up in a cell.'

'They don't know that. Chris Lawler said he'd throw me off the block of flats if I mentioned any of their plans.'

The Sergeant interrupted several more times—finally making notes. Tommy's money supply was running out, so he asked the sergeant to call back. Waiting, Tommy was startled by a rapping on the glass door. Outside, the old soldier, Jimmy, was making 'get out' gestures. Once again, he was wearing a heavy overcoat, flat cap, scarf and gloves.

Tommy pointed at the phone box. 'I'm getting a call-back.'

The pensioner opened the door. 'Twenty minutes you've been in here son.'

'I know, look, I'm sorry, but this is urgent. Someone's calling me back now. Any second. There's another phone box in the launderette.'

'I know that, son, but it only takes fivepences—not twos, and anyway, you wouldn't find me taking one step in there, not since… I didn't fight in the war to…'

'It's police business…'

'What was that—police?'

'I shouldn't tell you, but I'm working undercover.' Where the hell was the call-back?

'Ah, so finally you're doing something about those types that have been using the launderette?'

Tommy nodded.

'You should have said, son,' the pensioner tapped the side of his nose conspiratorially and took five steps back as though forming a guard.

The phone rang. 'Sorry about the delay, Tommy, I had to practically threaten Selwyn to let me call you back, and I wanted him out of earshot. These are serious allegations. Are you sure of what you've told me?'

'It's known throughout the whole area they're dealers.'

‘That’s not what concerns me most, Tommy. Look, is there any way you can get down here so we can speak in person; take a statement?’

‘No chance! Let’s be clear, this is an anonymous call—a tip-off.’

‘Okay, I understand. I’ll make sure that your name is never mentioned. I’m going to pass this all on to an Inspector I know…’

‘Marlon—Inspector Marlon?’

‘Yes, he’s very efficient.’

‘In that case, you need to promise me right now my name isn’t even hinted at.’ Tommy shuddered recalling the Inspector’s slamming.

‘I’ll make you that promise, Tommy. Now, are you sure there was no mention of any police officers by name?’

‘No, all he said was it’s one of our tame bizzes. Must be from Belle Vale. That’s the local station.’

‘Okay. And you say the Irish connection were on the way over to Liverpool by ferry?’

‘Yeah, on the way over today, tonight. The meeting with the gangs is set for tomorrow in Court Hey Park. Can you get the park closed or something?’

‘That may not be a good idea. At least we know where they intend to meet, and besides, what can we do if several gangs meet up in a public place to have a discussion?’

‘But there’s going to be a blood bath!’

‘And if we raise an alert and these tame bizzies get word back to this Lawler family?’

‘I didn’t think of that…’

‘This plan of theirs, it still sounds a bit, well… over ambitious… A Liverpool mafia!’

‘What are you going to do?’

'I'm going to see Inspector Marlon immediately. These Irish on the way over, it wouldn't look too bad if we collared them straight off the boat, the activities of the IRA would account for it alone.'

'Shit—the IRA!'

'Keep your ears to the ground, Tommy, and call me back if you hear more. Rhonda's here asking to speak to you, but first, take down this number.' Tommy repeated the number. He opened the phone box door.

'Excuse me, Sir—do you have a pen I could use?'

28
THE BIG BATTLE

Waking, Tommy had no clue whether it was day or night, Monday or Tuesday. All he knew was the sun was shining, and Linda was back home in Liverpool.

After his tea and toast, Tommy entered his bedroom and stared at the posters. Carefully, he peeled off the Bruce Lee and Master posters and started to crumple them into a ball, before deciding better. He'd give them to Joey. The gaps they left on the wall were fresh, in contrast to the faded green wall paint.

He took a Beatles album, *Revolver*, out of the sleeve and placed it on the record player. Track eight—'For No One'. He imagined Linda sitting on the floor smiling like an empty ephemeral ghost. He placed the stylus on the album. Hired the volume to maximum; *Your day breaks, your mind aches…*

Butch entered. He had a double take at the missing posters. He sniffed the spot Tommy was staring at on the floor. Tommy switched to track four—'Here There and Everywhere'. The image of Linda faded, replaced by Rhonda. Speaking to her last night made him realise how much she had come to mean, despite their brief and recent acquaintanceship. He was glad she'd agreed to come to Liverpool in the next few days. Tommy let the lyrics of the song wash over him… *Changing my life with a wave of her hand.*

Tommy read the crumpled letter from Linda again. 'It's a goodbye to everything.' He wiped a tear from his eye and opened the window. A heady aroma of violets entered the room—Rhonda's perfume. He shook his head. He knew he could live without Linda.

Downstairs, empty tea chests had arrived, and his mam was busy wrapping ancient ornaments in newspaper and carefully placing them in the chests. She seemed quietly happy.

'Have to get your stuff sorted as well, Tommy?' His dad was looking on with frustration.

'Carol, we can't take crates with us. Just suitcases…' Tommy paused and went back to his room to pick up the bulging bag of felt tip pens, and the separate bag of recorders.

He headed down to the shops in search of Joey, characteristically perched on the wall outside the launderette. On seeing Tommy, Joey jumped down.

'You still shagging that bird, Tommy? I was in Court Hey half an hour ago, telling the lads to stay away, and she was in there with some bloke and another girl who looked like her.'

'Linda? Must have been her sister. I knew she was due back—hang on, what did the bloke look like—was he tall and skinny?'

'Yeah, nearly as tall as our Mad-Mick. He had a perm—a curly perm like Kevin Keegan.'

'Bastard, bastard, bastard—Danny frigging Clarke!'

'So that's what this big kick-off about—you going down there cos he's copped for your bird? Why do you want our Mad-Mick there—is he hard, this Danny Clarke?'

'No, it's for something else… Do you think she's still there?'

'Don't know, I was going to tell them to get off, but the dirty look she gave me!'

'I wonder why? I bet you asked her if she was shagging this new fella…'

'I might have said something along those lines...'

Tommy shook his head, caught in a dilemma. He'd have to warn Linda and her sister to get out of the park, but it would appear confrontational. Maybe it needed to happen anyway. Danny fucking Clarke…

He hefted the bags of felt-tip pens and recorders and handed it over to Joey.

'What's this?' He opened the bags. 'For me? Oh, that's sound, Tommy—thanks, mate. Are you going to the park now—I'll come with you if you want?'

'What the hell, Joey—how many times do I have to say—stay away from the park!' Digging out his coins, Tommy headed to the phone box.

From memory, he dialled Linda's home number. No answer. He redialled, waited five minutes, still no answer. Shit—he was going to have to go to the park to warn her. Every instinct was warning him to stay away.

Davey's phone number was written on the fake prescription ID from his pocket. Tommy dialled and slotted a two-pence coin as the bleeps started. 'Hello, can I speak to Davey, please… Sorry, David, yes… it's his mate Tommy.' Tommy waited a good two minutes and slotted in another coin. 'Davey, it's me Tommy—you okay?'

'Not bad Tommy… what's up?' There was a tangible remoteness in Davey's speech. As if he'd been interrupted while he was doing something more important than speaking to Tommy.

'Davey, I know you meant what you said as we got back to Jack's—and that's okay, but I need a favour, mate.'

'Tommy, I'm not sure…'

'I'm moving from Liverpool, my al fella's job has come good—we've got the dates set, we'll be moving to New Zealand pretty soon.'

'Oh, okay. That's good news; I mean, it's good news for you, Tommy.' Davey's voice had perked up. 'What is it? What do you want, Tommy?'

'I need you to have a quick look in the park. I'm heading there myself, but you've got to find Linda and her sister, and… some other bloke and tell them to get out of the park.'

'But why—what's going on?'

'There's going to be murder there sometime today.'

'In the park? Shit…'

'Have you seen any gangs knocking about there?'

'I have actually. There's been loads of bikers coming and going. My dad kicked off when they were revving outside near our back garden. He threatened to call the police.'

'That would be a good idea… Look, have a quick butchers. I'm on my way now, just got to pick something up from the house first… and Davey, make sure you take a golf club.'

Tommy entered Court Hey Park from the Thingwall Road entrance, near where Davey's back garden bordered the park. No sign of Davey. No sign of bikers. There were five other entry gates, the main one on Bowring Park Road, which had a drive-in roadway.

A mile long and half a mile wide, the park was usually milling with kids playing football, cricket and golf. Splitting the middle of the park was a long, overgrown stream that ran from the park, under Childwall Valley Road and the girl's High School. The ornamental gardens and woodland area were a popular spot for dog and pram walkers. After nightfall, members of the public stayed away as it was notorious for battling gangs. Open land, the ease of retreat and places to hide or ambush attracted them. Also, the park served as a boundary between the districts of Childwall, Huyton, and Page Moss.

Tommy walked along a pathway leading to a woodland area. He was carrying a long wooden box. It was the first time he'd taken the sword outside. Through the trees, he came to a circular ornamental garden that had a bowling green type lawn.

Public benches evenly dotted the circle. Several young mothers were strolling. Tommy lit a cigarette and walked slowly. He pondered—*this is the place I'd setup the meeting—the centre of the park. Have the Irish crew dotted out to cover all of the entrances so they could clock whoever came in. I would have arranged it for after midnight when all the witnesses were gone, not in the middle of the afternoon.*

He stopped near a flower border and traced a square box in the soil with his finger.

'Boo!' Tommy jumped up and twirled to find Davey standing next to him with a big smile. 'Got ya.'

'For god's sake, Davey—nearly gave me a heart attack.'

'Sorry, Tommy—I watched you come into the park and saw you heading this way. I've been trailing you since you came through the trees. There's no sign of Linda. The whole park is a bit deserted. Them bikers probably scared people off. So, what's going on?'

Tommy exhaled, felt his nerves settle. He saw Davey was carrying a nine-iron golf club. For the first time, Tommy decided to tell Davey about the encounter with the scarecrow man and Lawler's plan for the big meeting with the gang leaders.

For five minutes, Davey was speechless.

'This scarecrow bloke—there was nothing on the news, in the papers. I haven't heard anyone mention it.'

'I shut down for two days. Went through two novels. Kept waiting for the police to come around and take me away.'

'That's when I knocked a couple of times; your Patricia, she doesn't lie well. There was something not right when she said you wasn't in.'

'I didn't want to see anyone. I felt guilty.'

'But you didn't start it, you were only looking after yourself.'

'I know, I went through all this with Mr Morrin.'

'He knows what happened?'

'Told him at the police station.' Davey was silenced again. 'I felt better for telling him.'

'So okay, that's the end of it. Maybe they had him down as a suicide, jumping off the bridge, or as a traffic accident—killed crossing the road?'

'I threw him off the bridge.'

'But, surely the police would be looking for witnesses, trying to find out if anyone saw what happen… someone to identify him? Muggings around the Greenhills happens. Pensioners—money and jewellery taken off them.'

'I've no idea. Maybe they did investigate, maybe he had some ID? He was living rough.'

'Just thought, the police must have had a description of who was doing the mugging, maybe they recognised this bloke, put it down to a revenge attack. I'm sure they wouldn't have too much motivation for finding whoever done him in.'

'Could be right there, Davey…'

'But Linda, you mentioned she was here with some fella?'

'Joey Finn told me he'd seen her here in the park earlier, with her sister and Danny bastard Clarke.'

'Is that why you've brought the sword Tommy? Not planning anything stupid, are you?'

'I'm going to chop Danny Clarke's fucking head off.'

'Tommy… you are kidding?'

'Maybe… or maybe it's handy to have on a day like today. Anyway, it's a pressie for you, Davey. I can't take it away with me, and I don't want to sell it.'

'Well… thanks Tommy, but why would I want a sword? Just remembered, new ID form for you.'

'You don't want the sword? Who doesn't want to have a sword like this? Then again, I don't want any more fake IDs.'

‘But you’re not eighteen yet, Tommy.’

‘I know, but I don’t feel much like a young teenager any more…’ Davey contemplated this as he put Tommy’s ID back into his pocket.

‘Who’s this?’ Davey said this as half a dozen lads came through the trees approaching the circular lawn. In the lead was the one-armed teenager, Sparky, hair recently cropped close to his skull like his mates: the Page Moss Skinheads. They were smiling like old friends. All in white shirts, white trousers and black AirWair boots. Each wore a black Derby hat. Most incongruous of all, each had their left eye painted over with dark makeup—A *Clockwork Orange*—Droog style. The facial image elicited a primeval shiver.

‘Caught us some Childwall meat here boys,’ said Sparky. He whipped out a six-inch knife. ‘Let’s cut them up.’ A young mother pushing a double buggy pram screamed.

Davey was set to run towards his back garden, but Tommy paused, looking for the best direction. He’d seen another gang behind them.

‘This way,’ he pointed towards the Childwall Valley Road entrance half a mile away. Davey didn’t need to be told twice. They didn’t look back as they dashed to the safety of the main road.

Approaching the gates, Tommy was dismayed to see their escape route cut off as another gang came piling through the Childwall Valley entrance ahead—*shit, I can’t keep running*. He and Davey were gasping as they came to a dead stop. Tommy looked back and saw the Page Moss Skinheads in a hand-to-hand fight with ten other teenagers from God knew where.

‘We’ll have to head back to my garden,’ gasped Davey. They turned—judging the best angle to run back onto, and then Tommy saw Sean Duncan coming through the gates, along with Chris Lawler and Nobby, running as fast as they could.

More lads continued running up the Childwall Valley road, away from the park. About a hundred yards away, Tommy could see another gang, twelve to fifteen dressed in a military khaki uniform. Unmistakably in the lead was Mad-Mick, sprinting like an Olympic athlete.

'Leg it, Tommy, Mad-Mick's after us,' said Sean, breathlessly, as he dashed past. Chris Lawler and Nobby both looked like they couldn't run much further.

Tommy was hesitant. He had no arguments with Mad-Mick's crew—same with Davey. If anything, he was more on Mad-Mick's side against Chris Lawler's mob. But to stand in the way of a rampaging Mad-Mick—no way—it would be like standing ground against a stampede of buffalo.

'Run with Sean,' said Tommy to Davey. Again, he needed no second prompt. They headed to the right of the raging battle near the circular lawn—the Page Moss Skinheads were getting hammered.

Running alongside Tommy, between gasps Davey said, 'Let's split off—head towards my back garden.' Tommy did a quick check on the angles; the Page Moss crew was down except for one-armed Sparky, who was circled by the unknown assailants. He wasn't going to last.

'We can't, whoever that crew is, they've finished with the Page Moss lads—they'll catch us easily—it's too close.'

About a hundred yards behind, Mad-Mick was coming through the entrance. Tommy saw Mad-Mick and his crew were no longer racing flat out; it was a fast-paced walk—a march with intent—*preserving energy for whatever they intended for us*, thought Tommy, staring at them. He saw Mad-Mick stop and turn to the Childwall Valley Road—maybe checking for police activity? The rest of his crew turned, in discussion with Mad-Mick. Chris Lawler had also seen this slow down, and he took a necessary breather, his face bright red.

'Chris, where's the Irish lads?'

Chris spat out a huge glob of phlegm and mumbled between heavy breaths, 'Got stopped at Customs… all of them.'

'Stopped for what?' Chris just shook his head. *Nice one, Sergeant Bradley*, thought Tommy ruefully, 'So is this the big meeting?'

Sean Duncan said, 'Only for us and the Huyton crew. Wasn't supposed to happen till later. We got a call saying our moby at the Valley site was getting robbed. Headed straight over and chased some kids off… that little prick Joey Finn was with them… but Mad-Mick was waiting for us down the road with his crew. What have you got in that box, Tommy?'

'It's a sword.'

'Maybe best getting it out. Who the hell is that lot—Chris, are they the Huyton mob?' Sean had spotted the unknown gang only fifty yards away. They were staring back, glancing between them and Mad-Mick's crew as though unsure whom to go at next. With only four other lads, Tommy knew whom he'd go for. Sean saw the bodies lying nearby on the grass.

'Oh fuck,' he said, 'The face makeup, Chris—is that the Page Moss Skinheads?'

'The lads on the deck are, or were from Page Moss—had that one-armed lad Sparky with them,' said Tommy.

'That makes sense, the Huyton boys told us they were going to war with Page Moss. Chris, are they on our side?' Chris shook his head again—he was breathing hard, his face an unnatural red. Chris nodded in the Huyton gang's direction. *He's having an asthma attack*, thought Tommy.

'What's their names, Chris?'

'It's C-c-c-col-c-c-c,' stuttered Nobby.

'Fucking say it!' demanded Sean.

'Colin Parry.'

'Let's go to them,' ordered Sean. He took hold of Chris's arm and pulled him along with him, shouting, 'Colin, Colin Parry.' The lads from Huyton moved towards them, one waving. Could easily be a trap.

One of them shouted, 'Chris, Nobby…'

Mad-Mick and his crew had stopped seventy yards away, weighing up the odds. Twelve of them against fifteen? Not an issue with Mad-Mick involved—they marched on.

Tommy whispered to Davey, 'As soon as we get near the lawn, we leg it into the woods towards your garden.' Davey nodded—it was what he had intended. All of the Huyton crew had switchblades in their hands. The Page Moss Skinheads were lying immobile on the grass nearby. Some were groaning, some trying to crawl. Sparky was covered from head to toe in blood. A tall, muscular blonde lad wiped his blade between his lips.

'I'm Colin. He looked better last time we saw him,' he pointed his blade at Chris who was now sitting on the grass next to Sparky and breathing heavily in gasps. 'Who are these other phonies… looks like Mad-Mick—not in our little alliance I take it?'

'No,' said Sean.

'This'll be twice we've saved you today, Tommy Dwyer.' Tommy stared hard trying to place the unfamiliar face—Colin Parry. His brain had almost shut down, his body concerned only with fight or flight. I'll remember later.

'Thanks, Colin,' he said.

Mad-Mick was thirty yards away. He opened his khaki jacket and unrolled a steel chain from his chest. His other lads did the same—stepping ten feet aside from one another as they began to whip their chains around their heads with a blood-curdling whooshing noise. Together, they marched forward.

Tommy closed his eyes, hearing an inner voice, *You've got no fight against Mad-Mick, or this Colin bloke and the lads from Huyton... Speak to them all—stop this madness,* but the whooshing noise got louder and became a great whirl of engine throbbing and revving and exhausts roaring in an eardrum explosion—noise all around them as ten, twelve, fifteen, twenty and counting motorbikes and scooters came racing through the park gates.

'Fuck this,' shouted Colin. 'It's the St John's Angels—fucking run—head for the trees.' As they started to run, half a dozen bikers cut them off from behind, their pillion passengers waving a combination of iron bars and hammers.

A petrol bomb skimmed past Tommy's head, exploding into flames behind him—more and more were airing through the sky, smashing and bursting into life. He ran through the black fog as fast as he had ever run.

In panic, Tommy was almost knocked out as he collided into a tree. Bouncing back up, he could see the bikers had formed a large rolling figure of eight, surrounding Mad-Mick's crew in one hole, with Colin and the Huyton crew in another.

A Malaguti bike blocked the entrance to the park. The rider and passenger made arm gestures as though directing the action.

Tommy could see Sean, Chris and Nobby were on the ground. The bikers were between him and the safety of Davey's—anyone's—back garden. The shallow Brook was on the far side—two hundred yards away was not an option, too much open ground.

Three of the Huyton lads were standing nearby, hiding as best they could behind trees, unsure which direction to run. There was no sign of Davey. Tommy dropped the box to the floor and took out the sword. Seeing this, the Huyton lads moved in closer.

Half the bikers were carrying passengers, all of whom were standing straight, waving and shouting as they circled in the pulsating figure of eight. Two of the bikers had split off from the main group and were scanning the park for stragglers. One of the passengers sat back down to light the rag in a petrol-filled milk bottle.

'Let's climb up the trees,' said one of the Huyton lads and, as though he had heard, the biker changed directions as the passenger pointed to them. Another biker split off and also came racing towards them, performing a stunning wheelie as he approached the trees. The Huyton lads had climbed up a trunk and were limbering higher up the tree like monkeys.

Tommy's legs felt like stone as his mind reeled through escape options. *Climb the tree? Can't outrun them. Stand and fight? Stand and die!*

As the bike raced at him, Tommy jumped aside and swung the sword against the rider's leg, cutting deeply. The bike lurched and somersaulted through the air with the rider flung screaming to one side. Tommy saw a bike's passenger throw his petrol bomb, smashing against a tree—sending flames racing around the trunk.

Wary of the sword, the biker stopped short of Tommy and revved. Tommy saw the passenger had taken another milk bottle filled with petrol—Molotov cocktail, shaken, not stirred—from a box at the back of the bike and was about to light it. Tommy was on him, slashing at his arm with the sword. The petrol spilt over the bike, rider and passenger and burst into flame, sending them both screaming and flailing at the fire.

Tommy looked back to the circling bikers. The figure of eight had broken up. Although dispersing, there was still black fog swirling around the field. Mad-Mick punched, kicked, and chained, crashing bikers to the ground.

Several bikes lay on the floor, their engines still running. The stink of burning grass, petrol and motorbike exhaust fumes was overpowering. Tommy searched desperately for any sign of Davey—feeling guilty that if Davey had been hurt, it would be his fault.

He could taste petrol in his mouth. Something smashed into the back of his head, and the lights went out.

Tommy opened his eyes and found himself in a black-and-white void. He was in woodland, surrounded by black smoke and fires. He tasted earth in his mouth and realised he was lying on the grass. Two fireflies lit up bright orange against the monochrome background and transformed into human shapes above him. To the right stood his Grandma, to the left, his Granddad. Both had departed from the Earth months ago. These were not malevolent spirits come to afflict him. These were loved ones, their passing still heavy in Tommy's heart.

'Doesn't look too good,' said his Granddad.

'He'll be all right,' said his Grandma, looking closely into Tommy's eyes. 'He will be if you shift yourself, you great lump.'

'You hang your horses here, missus. Tommy, you need to stand up.'

'Well, help him, don't just stand there gawping.'

'Tommy, there's a lad behind you, looking down at you. Reach across and pick up the sword. Sweep it across his legs to keep him from you. Help is on the way,' said his Granddad.

'Chop his bloody legs off if you need to,' said his Grandma.

As if moving through molasses, Tommy's arm attempted to pick up the sword in front of him. Touching the blade, Tommy's vision switched to fast-motion Technicolor.

He swung the sword in an arc behind him and heard a frightened yell. The black-and-white image of his grandparents, no, his Godparents, had vanished.

The sound of police sirens raced closer. Several bikers stopped revving and stared at the Childwall Valley Road entrance. Tommy heard police whistles coming from the Bowring Park Road entrance.

The two lads on the Malaguti—the leaders—were waving towards the park gates—action over, retreat.

Knowing that Davey—wherever he was—would at least get help, Tommy ran to the overgrown vegetation near the Brook. Wary of the deep thorn and brambles, he slashed a clear path for him to sit, wait and hide, until he heard and saw police dogs straining against their handlers, sniffing, searching.

Throwing the sword deeper into the brambles, he slipped into the shallow waters of the Brook and waded down until he came to the first house. He climbed over the back garden fence and let himself out through the back onto the street.

Tommy walked numbly, mindlessly to the Broadgreen Hospital. The car park outside of the Casualty entrance was overrun with ambulances and police cars. A television crew arrived, and a camera was pointing at a well-known local news presenter. Tommy could not recall his name.

Entering the casualty ward, he saw chaos as the medical staff worked flat out. Faces, some familiar; Joey Finn was shouting, gesticulating at Linda. Tommy heard him say, 'You fucking bitch.'

He remembered she worked here. A woman and a young girl were staring open-mouthed at him, as if he were a ghost. They looked familiar.

He croaked, 'Mother, Patricia, what are you doing here?'

His mother dropped in a dead faint. 'Can someone help her, please?' he whispered. Joey Finn was walking around him as if to confirm whom he was seeing, which was making Tommy dizzier.

'If you are here, who's in the operating theatre—who is it that's in a coma?'

Tommy lurched, about to feint himself. Who was Joey talking about? Linda stepped over and held him up. Tommy whispered, 'How was he identified?'

'He had something with your name and address in his pocket. He looked like you.'

'Linda, get someone to ring Davey Crocket's mam and dad,' and with that, Tommy slid off Linda and fell to the floor.

29
LEAVING LIVERPOOL

The events in Court Hey Park had made national headline news, with the chaotic scenes at the hospital on repeat—both on television and inside Tommy's mind. He'd stopped eating and had refused to see his GP despite the home visit.

Uncle Darren and Auntie Michelle had practically moved into the house, only going back home to sleep. Butch, as if anticipating a new master, followed Uncle Darren around as keenly as he had Tommy.

Rhonda had arrived unannounced after the third day of Tommy's hibernation in his bedroom. As if in a dream, the quiet request, 'Tommy, please open the door,' reached into his consciousness like a beacon. His appetite for life was restored.

They visited Davey together in the Broadgreen Hospital ward. He'd come face to face with Danny Clarke and Linda, which was no coincidence with them both working in the hospital.

He'd seen Linda appraising Rhonda. For his part, any anger or jealousy had dissipated. He had Rhonda to thank. He knew her arrival helped prevent him from falling into the kind of depression from which his mother was slowly returning.

Their only separation, night and day, had been the few hours Rhonda had travelled back to Henllan to say her goodbyes to Mr Morrin, Pops, Keith Piperello, and Selwyn and to pack her suitcase.

Today would be the last hospital visit as the Dwyer family was due to set sail from Liverpool en route to Abu Dhabi, Sydney, and then Queenstown, New Zealand. That Rhonda would be travelling with them had never been discussed as a family issue. Despite the newness of their relationship, it was clear they fit.

Inside the hospital, apart from parents, the ward had a strict one-visitor rule. As usual, Tommy and Rhonda had waited outside of the ward until Davey's parents left. They had stopped giving Tommy the daggers after the fifth day when Davey had come out of the coma—on the way to full recovery.

Tommy knew that if he weren't leaving Liverpool, they would have insisted on barring him altogether from seeing their son. He didn't blame them.

Leaving Rhonda in the waiting room, Tommy entered the ward. Davey was propped up in bed, reading one of Tommy's Sven Hassel novels. He folded a page over to bookmark where he was up to.

'I've told you not to do that,' said Tommy. 'Use a bus ticket or a piece of paper—you're damaging the book doing that.'

Davey smiled, looking almost fully back to normal, except for the stitched scar across his forehead from a Stanley knife slash. It was this head wound with the copious blood flow, plus the prescription ID in his pocket, that had led to the mistaken identity. The scar would fade. It was the hammer to the back of his head that had done all the damage.

Davey unfolded the bookmark and then turned to Tommy. 'Wait, it's my book anyway; you gave them all to me.' There was a pile of books behind the get-well-soon cards on his bedside cabinet.

'Do you want to talk more about that day?' Davey nodded—they knew it was better to get it in the open.

'The one image that stays with me is when Sparky Lad brought the knife out and the *Clockwork Orange* makeup! I think it was only the fact I had a golf club in my hand that made him hesitate.'

'You and me both, mate. I still don't know that Colin Parry bloke. The St John Angels had been waiting for Mad-Mick to get out of jail after he'd filled them in that day in the swing park. Bad timing for us—they'd been cruising Childwall on the lookout, and their leaders, John Davies and John Jones, got them all organised. That's why Mad-Mick and his crew stopped near the entrance. They could hear the bikes.' Davey nodded, his eyelids appearing heavy.

'Chris Lawler, I think you knew on the day he died from an asthma attack. His mam's moved back to Ireland. That's the end of the Liverpool mafia for now. Three other lads were killed—knife wounds. One of the Huyton lads is still in intensive care with petrol burns. Mad-Mick, along with twenty other lads, are in custody on remand. Rhonda saw that retired copper when she went back home. He wouldn't talk, said it was best if Rhonda kept out of it. I'm still not sure if it was him who got the Irish crew pulled when they got off the ferry…'

'That's good news,' said Davey. He had clearly stopped listening to it a short time ago.

'There's better news. All charges have been dropped against Pops, but I'll let Rhonda fill you in on that.' Davey was starting to nod off as a walking tonic entered the ward—her Violetta Penhaligon perfume preceding her entrance as usual.

For the next ten minutes, Rhonda made small talk; Tommy himself was soothed. They could see the tiredness washing over Davey, and the fussy matron had noticed her one-visitor per patient rule had been broken. Davey quietly slipped into a deep sleep; Tommy gently took the book out of his hand and whispered, 'I've applied to go on a writing course in Queenstown in September. You'll be reading novels written by me in a few years, Davey lad…'

The whimpering dog dragged Darren closer to the departing ocean liner. Tommy and Rhonda waved goodbye until they were almost out of sight. 'Tommy, any regrets?' Rhonda followed his gaze to the coastline and Tommy's best friend, Butch.

'Some …'

'I was waiting for the right moment to tell you what my dad offered me.'

'So, he's your Dad now, no more Mr Morrin?'

Rhonda smiled. 'He offered me the farm and the land.'

Tommy shook his head. 'Was the deal dependent on you leaving me behind?'

'No strings, Tommy – with or without you. The offer remains. Let's have our adventure in New Zealand and see how we feel in a year, hey?'

Tommy nodded as Liverpool and Butch faded into the distance. A new life awaited him, and as long as there were no rabid dogs involved, Tommy was ready.

At seventeen, a master of the universe, Tommy knew everything; he could handle every situation and had the hairy arse to prove it.

Morality—well, that was just an opinion. And whatever may happen now, whatever the green hills of New Zealand had in store…

He, Tommy *fucking* Dwyer, had survived the wildest two weeks in the hottest summer on record.

Printed in Great Britain
by Amazon

50123076R00148